PRAISE FOR *FROM THE NECK UP*

"When I read Whiteley's short stories I think of Japanese netsuke – magnificent miniatures, perfect in every detail. But netsuke don't keep me awake at night."   M. R. CAREY

"Readers of Jeff Vandermeer, Meg Ellison, and Jeffrey Ford will love this complex, grotesque, and brilliantly humanistic collection."
PUBLISHERS WEEKLY STARRED REVIEW

"Strange, playful, or downright heartbreaking, each of these tales is a storytelling masterclass. Aliya Whitely's endlessly inventive fiction is clearly in a league of its own."   MARIAN WOMACK

"Aliya Whiteley is one of this generation's most exciting science fiction authors. I adore everything she writes."   HELEN MARSHALL

"Equal parts Shirley Jackson and John Wyndham, these tales are consistently unsettling, yet despite wild concepts they remain warm and humane, populated with recognisable people and their recognisable fears and compulsions. In short, this collection is an absolute triumph."
TIM MAJOR

"A masterful collection from one of the most talented and original speculative fiction writers working today. Strange, unsettling, quietly beautiful and utterly unique. "   STARK HOLBORN

"Aliya's stories are gloriously inventive, wide-ranging and beautifully written. A vibrant collection."   ALISON MOORE

"Darkly delicious and strange, Whiteley uses the future to show us where we are, horror to unbury what we think about love, ageing and loss. I was never quite comfortable reading these stories, which is how it should be. They seize you from the neck up."
ANGELA READMAN

ALSO AVAILABLE FROM
ALIYA WHITELEY AND TITAN BOOKS

The Beauty
The Arrival of Missives
Skein Island
The Loosening Skin

FROM THE
NECK
UP

ALIYA WHITELEY

TITAN BOOKS

From the Neck Up
Print edition ISBN: 9781789094756
E-book edition ISBN: 9781789094763

Published by Titan Books
A division of Titan Publishing Group Ltd.
144 Southwark Street, London SE1 0UP.
www.titanbooks.com

First Titan edition September 2021
10 9 8 7 6 5 4 3 2 1

A CIP catalogue record for this title is available from the British Library.

Printed and bound in the United States

For the Big Bad G

CONTENTS

BRUSHWORK

PART ONE

My real name is gone. I have left it so far in the past that I can pretend it is forgotten. Age, however, I cannot leave behind. It stalks me, and pounces, again and again, shaking me between its teeth until my skin sags and my gums flap.

I have decided not to dwell on the things that have happened and the marks they have left. It is enough to have my place in the biodomes. I am now a product of my situation; that is, the forcing of life into forms and shapes it would never assume if left to its own devices. But it must be made to fit the space assigned to it, and the truth is there's not much space left.

We are squeezed together, the melons and I.

"Mel," says Mr Cecil. I should be paying attention, but instead I'm chewing over the fact that he, too, started off as a worker and now I must call him Mister while he uses a nickname for me. "How's impregnation going?"

"Areas twelve to twenty-two are done."

"Good, good. Anything you need?"

1

A fresh life, Mr Cecil, I should say. "No, thank you."

"I'm off to Courgettes, then. Shout if there's a problem." Off he goes in his little motorised buggy. I watch it recede along the rows and then the calm of the melons reasserts itself. No sound. No sound at all.

Home-grown, the labels will say. Organic home-grown cantaloupe melons, low carbon emissions, no pesticides, one hundred per cent UK workers, and they will cost more than an entire synthetic pig, but that's fine. Some people are rich and they spend their money on the strangest things without ever once finding a space in which they fit.

Today is impregnation day in twenty areas. The paintbrush must be dipped into the male flowers to collect a dab of pollen. This is an orange powder, so bright, so fine. I use a sable brush so I can see the pollen clearly. I like to know exactly how much I have collected; I would hate to waste this precious stuff. It has the most important job in the world to do. Here it goes – I take it to the female flower, and stroke it inside her opening.

Do you know how you tell it's a female flower? At the base of the petals she bulges into a ball: a perfect sphere, a promise of intention. If she receives the pollen, she will continue to swell to giant proportions long after the pretty little flower dies and drops away. Instead, there nestles a monster and the stem thickens to support it. A melon grows to the size of my head, larger. I will put it inside a net that hangs from the pole structure to which the plants cling. Inside each melon lurk so many new seeds, to start the process all over again.

This is my favourite part of the job.

* * *

Communal dinner hour is five to six o'clock. Some complain about the earliness of the hour for the final meal of the day, but it suits me; I'll be asleep by nine, after spending a little time on my slides. I don't know why everyone enjoys complaining so, or how they have the energy for it. None of us are spring chickens anymore. Chickens in spring, scratching and pecking and laying their eggs. Apparently, they still do this in the Livestock part of Blossom Farm. Imagine – spring chickens. Their tender drumsticks must fetch a fortune.

I'm eating a cheese-flavoured sandwich when Lonnie and Jim carry their trays to my table at the back of the dining room. They take the seats opposite and continue a loud conversation. I get the feeling I'm meant to overhear it.

"It's always the same in Strawberries," says Jim. "Too much temptation for us old 'uns. That sweetness takes years off you."

He smacks his lips together under his white moustache. I don't believe he's tasted a strawberry for a moment. How is it possible to have that much hair on your mouth and none on your head? The shiny, greasy expanse of skin hanging loose on his skull is too much reality for me. I put down my sandwich and sip my water instead.

"Mmmm," says Lonnie, shaking her head. Her cumbersome earrings jangle. The lobes have been stretched to incredible proportions over years of abuse in the name of decoration, and now she must always wear big earrings or leave her ears flapping in the simulated weather of the Satsuma section.

I'm cruel, I know, I know. I am a cruel old lady and I am no less ugly than they are. My distaste is centred on them only because there is no mirror here with which to catch my own reflection.

"Out in the cold," says Jim, mournfully. "Straight out, with nothing but a coat and that collection of teddy bears stuffed into two bin bags."

So now I know who they're talking about. It's Daisy. Daisy has been caught stuffing her face with strawberries and has been kicked out of Blossom Farm.

This is why Jim and Lonnie chose to sit here. They know about Daisy and me. She had such fresh blue eyes, even though she was older than many here. And a laugh! A laugh I loved.

But that was a long time ago.

I wonder what made her eat those strawberries.

"You knew Daisy, didn't you?" asks Jim.

Why does he want a response from me? What possible entertainment could it give him?

"No," I say. "Not really."

Another little part of what is left of my emotions shrivels up and crumbles to dust. Jim and Lonnie exchange glances, then change the subject to that old favourite, the weather.

"Minus ten out there today," says Jim. "Not bad for the time of year. Wind chill will take it down, though. Northerly, isn't it? I checked the board first thing."

Lonnie huffs.

We have all become expert meteorologists and our habit is fed by the board, updated daily, with information on what blows and falls outside the biodomes.

They talk on. My thoughts turn to those teddy bears. Daisy loved them so, making them from scraps of clothing that you would have thought unsalvageable. If you had a shirt you thought beyond stitching she would bother you for it, offering to fetch you a replacement from stores, and the next thing you know it would have been turned into a cheeky little fellow, fuzzy and friendly and determined to make you smile. She kept them all in her room and gave them names at least three syllables long, sounding like they belonged in a world of stately homes and tea parties. Peregrine. Terpsichory. Sir Xavier Hugsalot the Third.

Enough. I get up. I leave behind my sandwich and ignore Jim when he calls, "Aren't you going to eat that?" to my back. I walk through the dining area with its bright white lights shining down on the stained tabletops, and then I walk through the communal area where mismatched armchairs and sofas jostle – each one bearing knitted covers courtesy of the workers – and down the corridors that lead to my room.

We all take up our spare time with these silly obsessions. Making antimacassars or putting boats in bottles. Teddy bears from scraps of material. And the scraps of my memory lead to my obsession: the slides.

* * *

I paint a moment of my life on each glass pane. The good moments stay in my room where I can see them often. The bad ones go elsewhere.

The glass comes from the very beginnings of Blossom Farm when tomatoes were grown in greenhouses rather than the biodomes. I remember a greenhouse. It belonged to my grandmother. I can see it standing at the bottom of an orderly garden behind the tall, tied sticks around which pea shoots twirled. The strange thing was that the little building did not seem to be made of glass. It was so full of grapevines, cuttings and plants just starting their growth that the whole space within appeared green to my eyes, green to the point of bursting forth and overrunning the structure.

I used to be a little afraid of it, and of the bottom of the garden.

My grandmother. I have never remembered her as clearly as the greenhouse. I would like to make an image of her face but we don't choose what we remember, do we? And I only have space in my head for emotions, not people. It's the fear I paint.

My room is small and safe. I work for a while, on my painting of the greenhouse. I have only black paint left over in metal pots from when the farm had a Welcome sign out front, but that is good enough; why are so many people unhappy with what they have? It must be made to suit, and that is all. Mr Taylor, the forerunner of Mr Cecil, gave me the code to the old storeroom where all obsolete things lurk. He was very kind to me, in many ways.

Enough. Bedtime.

I pack away my paintbrush, stolen from the task of melon impregnation, and evaluate the black lines that make my greenhouse on glass.

* * *

Slide 117

"It's nothing to be scared of," said Nane.

But Flori resisted. She didn't want to go inside, no matter what her grandmother said. The earth, the smell, the brush of damp leaves, the touch of tendrils.

"Come help me with the plants," said Nane, and pushed her inside.

It was a different, denser world in there and hardly had room for the little girl. And what was that sound? She crouched as the low thrum of a wasp manoeuvred around her head – driven dizzy by the sweetness of the grapes – and then it was in her face, zipping and dipping, and prickling her ear.

Nane said, "Stay still. Stay very still."

* * *

I don't remember what happened next, and I'm too tired to care. My little bed calls to me. I stack the latest glass pane under the bed, with the others, and then turn out the light.

I can't hear the wind but I imagine it's blowing. I can't see the snow but I can picture it piling high, drifting and blizzarding, blanketing the biodomes throughout the night.

Somewhere out there are two bin bags filled with teddy bears. Goodbye, Sir Xavier Hugsalot the Third. You were, once upon a time, my favourite.

* * *

Mr Cecil likes to talk about yield. He manages a team of five and insists on making a presentation for our weekly meetings. It was his big innovation upon taking over from Mr Taylor two years ago. How much will each section yield? He doesn't seem to remember that it is not a matter of the plants yielding to us at all. One of these days they will grow so fast and so free that they will dominate once more – and that is how it should be.

He provides his estimates in brightly coloured bar charts that he prints out on paper and hands around the meeting room. What a waste. Well, not entirely a waste; we save up the sheets for Brian from Peppers, who creates very amusing wordsearches on the reverse. Brian has a knack for resurrecting the past in bite-sized, bittersweet chunks that don't choke us. The wordsearches hide within them different makes of chocolate bar; names of English counties; types of car. It's amazing how much we remember about things that are gone and how little we want to retain about our here and now.

Mr Cecil has reached the topic of melon yield, and I don't care. Just let me be among them, warm and safe. Just let me be. Still, I make my polite face and the others are doing the same. Melons. Peppers. Chillies. Courgettes. Butternut squash. We're an odd group, I'll give you, lacking the obvious coherence of Berry Fruits, say, but we rub along. Mainly through the mutual bond of Brian's wordsearches.

Suroopa – Courgettes – looks tired this morning. Usually her clothes are clean and pressed, her short black hair brushed well, but today she yawns and her face is as crumpled as her shirt.

"Are you not feeling well?" Mr Cecil asks her after a particularly large yawn. "You look all at sea today, Suroopa."

She reassures him that all is well. What an expression. All at sea. It reminds me of old rhymes, sailing away to the Land of Nod, owls and pussycats and beautiful pea green boats. They sailed and took the fairy tales with them. They sailed on one of the last ferries; I watched them go from the bus.

"Mel," says Mr Cecil, and his voice cuts through my dreams and brings me back to the here and now. "Don't tell me you're busy woolgathering as well today?"

"No, Mr Cecil," I tell him. "Sorry."

He carries on.

Where does he get these ancient expressions from? He must have a thesaurus tucked away in his room somewhere. He probably reads it in bed every night looking for another obscure thing to say, thinking – *that's an interesting one, oh yes, I must use that.*

Today, in sections five to fifteen, I must take soil temperature readings. It can be hell on the back, all that stooping, so my first thought when the alarm bell rings is of annoyance. Not another drill, not today. I really can't be bothered to hang around for hours pretending to care.

I look at Mr Cecil's face and that tells me something I don't want to believe. This is not a drill.

He doesn't know what's happening.

The alarm whoops, a long wail that climbs up and falls down, over and over.

I stand up.

"No," says Mr Cecil, putting up his hands. "It will stop, it will stop, it's just a… a problem with the—"

"A malfunction?" says Gregor, who is small and well-muscled for his age and looks like the sort of man who has learned the hard way not to trust anyone when alarms are ringing. He stands up and then so do Suroopa, and Brian, and Zena. Mr Cecil, in the face of overwhelming odds, changes his tune.

"Adopt lockdown procedures," he calls, and leads the way from the meeting room out into the curved corridor where the alarm is louder still and others are scurrying to their own positions, their faces scrunched up with surprise and fear.

Mr Cecil sets a fast pace and we move as a group, single file. My body aches, but it's a pain I'm used to. I'm still better off than Brian, with his chest complaints. I can hear him wheezing behind me as we make it back to Sector K.

At the entrance to Sector K, Mr Cecil turns and waves us all through. We know what happens now. We will all be locked inside with the plants. Something in me thinks this is a really good idea. You don't live as long as I have without getting a gut instinct for things.

I wait until the others are through and then call back to Mr Cecil, who looks up from fumbling with his utility belt.

"Mr Cecil," I say. I can tell what he's thinking. He means to stand outside, to break protocol, and I have to shake that thought from his head. I know why this system was set up. I've seen the reason why.

"No, I think, today, I should…"

"No," I tell him. "No."

But he says, "Stop fussing, please, Mel," and closes the door. Through the safety glass panels of the door I see him type in the special code to shut down the door. Then he disappears from view.

Brian wheezes on. Suroopa gets him seated at the orange plastic table and chairs next to the water dispenser. The others stand around staring at him.

Reception Area K reminds me of a hand. There are five walkways leading off, like fingers, from the square palm of the main room. Beyond lie the segmented parts of our dome. I want to go into mine and work, alone and safe.

"Breathe," Suroopa tells Brian. "Breathe." The others watch, spectators to a private battle. Is he losing? No – he nods, nods, and there, he is controlling his lungs, mastering his body.

"Well done," says Suroopa, patting his arm.

The alarm winds down, slowly falling in pitch until it cuts out and leaves an eerie silence. It has never done that before.

"Right," whispers Zena. I don't know why she's whispering. "Someone page Cecil and get him to let us out."

"Not yet," I say, and am surprised to find it comes out as a whisper too.

"I don't think we should wait," says Suroopa. "Brian needs to see the doctor." She straightens up and pushes the button on her pager. We all listen. There it is, the tinny sound of his pager from the other side of the door. Then it stops. He must have turned it off.

Someone walks past.

"Who was that?" says Gregor, and then says something in his own language. He moves to the door and puts his face to the glass, then retreats behind Brian's chair.

"I think it was Jack from, ah…" says Suroopa.

"No," I say. "It wasn't."

There are voices outside, voices I don't recognise. This is a secure compound; there are guards, automated systems, nobody gets in without permission. But I don't recognise those voices.

Mr Cecil replies. I can't make out the words but his voice is high. He has been trained for this sort of situation. He has a weapon that he carries on his utility belt. I've seen it. A taser. Has he drawn it? Does he have it ready, in his hand?

Shouting. It builds, it is loud.

Then everything goes quiet.

They will make him open the door. They will force him to and I would not blame him, not when I think of all the things they could do to him. I know the things pain can make you do. I would open the door too.

No. I wouldn't. I wouldn't open the door. I would protect my safe place, my growing plants, because there is nothing else left.

The silence stretches on. It is long enough and deep enough for doubts to form. Is this an elaborate part of the drill just to check we won't open the door under any circumstances? The relief I feel at that idea is crazy. I want to cling on to it. All we have to do is hold on for a few more minutes and then Mr Cecil will appear with a wink and tell us we did well, as if we are children who have been left unattended in a school room.

I'm lost in this concept when a face appears at the safety glass.

It's a man. A very young man with a beard tinged with ice, bluish lips buried deep, and red-rimmed eyes. The chill of ice is stuck fast to his skin. I had forgotten how beautiful young men could be.

Suroopa wails behind me. He looks at each of us in turn. His eyes linger on Brian, who is still slumped over in his chair but breathing regularly. The man can't hear that, of course; as far as he's concerned, Brian might be dead. His eyes don't register any emotion. He points downwards, I'm guessing at the keypad for the door.

I shake my head.

He doesn't seem bothered by my refusal. He points again, but none of us move.

He walks away.

If he can't get in, if he's relying on us to input the code, then it can only mean one thing – Mr Cecil is incapable of giving him what he wants.

"Don't let him in," says Gregor, and Zena says, "What does he want? What does he want?"

Brian sits up and wheezes out the thought that has invaded my mind. "Agro-terrorist."

Please, no. They'll destroy the melons. They deal in the destruction of the good things to eat, that only the rich can afford, in the name of fairness, for the idea of making this a natural world once more. "Look," I say. "No matter what happens, we can't let him in. The guards will sort this out, but we need to be strong. We've got water and food. It's an emergency – they'll understand if we eat a bit of the fruit. We can stay here for days keeping the plants, and ourselves, safe."

"Days?" says Suroopa.

"It won't take that long," I say. "This place is top security. They'll get it under control in no time."

"Where's Mr Cecil?" says Zena. "Should I page him again?"

Gregor and I exchange looks. If I've thought about Mr Cecil's chances out there, then Gregor has done the same and come to the same conclusion. That's how his mind works.

"No," says Gregor. "Do not page him."

"He'll be busy," I say. "Negotiating." It sounds official. It's the right word. The others visibly relax.

"Sit tight," wheezes Brian. He manages a smile.

I look at them. Four old, scared people. And I make five. How quickly things change. Ten minutes ago, I was thinking about my soil samples and my problems were molehills. I thought I would have my melons to care for, and my slides to paint, and that those things would be enough for the tail end of a beast of a life. But although I was done with difficult times, it seems they are not done with me.

I can wait this out. I can survive. And so can my plants.

"We'll take it in turns to see to our areas," I say. "There's no reason to let the plants suffer, and it will keep our minds off—"

A new face appears at the glass. Not a new face. An old face. Daisy.

Her eyes are blue, bluer than ever before. Then I realise they only look that way because of the blood on her face. It's so red against her white skin, and her eyes are translucent but they see me clearly. They focus on me and hold me close.

The blood is a smear that stretches from her forehead to her cheek, daubed on, like warpaint. She puts the back of her hand to her face, and wipes it, and that's when I realise it's her own blood. She's daubing herself in the blood that is coming from her heavily bandaged fingers. Ripped material has been wrapped around and around, and it has soaked through, turned bright red.

Not good enough for a teddy bear, Daisy, I want to say. Not even you could salvage that old rag.

She looks so tired. No, that's not it: she looks destroyed. Worn down to pieces that are somehow still managing to move around. Her mouth is forming shapes.

Open the door, her lips are saying without sound.

Mel. Open the door.

I don't move.

Please open the door.

Gregor comes to stand behind me, so light on his feet. He says, "Don't open the door," and I feel his hand on my back, just a slight pressure. But he's too much of a coward to do anything to stop me. I've seen him cover his face when one of the supervisors shouts; he's trapped in some past that will keep him forever fearful.

Please.

She looks as if she'll die, right there. She died once already to me, only a few days ago. This time around I have a choice. I don't have to let her die alone.

I move forward, to the door, and put in the key code. The lock releases. I step out into the corridor and take Daisy in my arms.

* * *

"Everything will continue as normal," says the man. This is another new face among many, but this one is definitely in charge. He carries it on his shoulders.

I look around the refectory and find the face that first appeared at the Sector K door. He is eating a plate of beans not far from me. I take care not to stare but observe him from the corner of my eye. He shovels the beans in with a spoon as if hot food has not passed his lips in years. Maybe it hasn't.

"There is no need to worry. All we need is your cooperation," says the man in charge. He stands in the centre of the room, on a table, so we can all look up at him. He is a little older, but still so many years away from becoming like us shrivelled wrecks of workers. There are about thirty young people among us now, and they are joined in some purpose that is about to be passed down to us like divine wisdom. We've seen it all before.

"The food you are producing will be given to those who need it, not only to those who can afford it."

Ah, I see. This is a zealous enterprise. They are fighting the good fight. No doubt they, above all others, are deserving of my melons.

"Keep fulfilling your duties and you will be fed and watered as usual. Nothing has changed for you, that's all you need to remember."

Jim, sitting next to me, raises his hand. Is he asking permission to speak? I can't help but despise him.

"Go ahead," says the man in charge.

"Where are all the supervisors? And the guards?"

"That's not something you need to feel concerned about."

"Blossom Farm won't let you get away with this, you know," Jim says, quickly, then sits down and crosses his arms.

The man in charge ignores him.

"My name is Stephan," he says. "If you want to talk to me in an equal and open way then I am here. But I'm not here to answer stupid questions. Try to remember that we are all in this together now. Enjoy your lunch."

All in this together – he's as bad as Mr Cecil. What a fatuous phrase. If we're all in it together, why did the newcomers, his merry band of men, get fed before us workers? People always say what they think will bring them an easy life and others believe it for the same reason. But not me. Not this time.

We queue up for our beans. I take an extra plate for Daisy, ignoring the stares of those around me. There is no guard to stop me now. I carefully manoeuvre around all the extra people who fill up my space and carry both plates back to my room.

Daisy lies still in my bed. I stand for a while, beans in hand, and watch her. It's years since I've seen her this way in sleep. Safe. But here's the thing. Her skin is waxy and her breathing is fast. As I look down on her I can see that she is not safe, not really.

I put the plates down on my small table and carefully lift the blanket to look down at her body still bundled up tight in her clothes. If I was to remove them, I think I might find patches of black. Black toes, black fingers. If there are any fingers and toes left. The bandage around her hand is useless now and the blood is seeping through to my mattress, but I can't unravel it. I can't face what is underneath.

She coughs, a weak rumbling at the back of her throat. "Be up soon," she says. "Strawberries. Doctor?"

I tuck the blanket back around her and sit on the side of the bed. I put my hand to her forehead like a professional. "No doctor, I'm afraid. Nobody's seen her since your friends arrived. But you'll be up and around in no time."

She seems to come back to herself, blinking, as if clearing her eyes from sleep. "Oh, it's you," she says, in her usual voice. "I thought we were all done."

"Apparently not."

"Apparently not," she mimics. How cruel she can be. "Still better than the rest of us, aren't you?"

I wish I'd never told her a thing about me, not one real fact that she could use as a weapon. I should have told her I was once a farmer's wife, or a baker, or unemployed, in a council flat; some simple thing she couldn't find fault with. Not a schoolteacher to the privileged elite, somebody who came to this place through having connections. I had never suffered the right kind of suffering for her.

"Why did you help them?" I ask. "They'll destroy the domes."

She rolls her eyes. "No, they won't. They want a better world, Mel. They deserve their chance to fight for it. Don't you remember what it was like to want to fight?"

"I never wanted to fight."

"No." She coughs again, a softer sound. "I believe that."

How do you say to someone – I think we should make up now because you're very probably about to die? I sit quietly, my hand on her head, and try to think of a way to work that particular sentiment into the conversation. How very controlled I am.

"I'm so, so sorry," I tell her. "For everything."

"It's like that, is it?" She nods her head on the pillow, seeing right through me, as always. "Thought so. They found me too late, I suppose. I had the bears with me and I lay down with them in the snow, that was all I wanted, and I could still taste the strawberries. But then there was this young face in front of my eyes and all the bears were gone. I don't know where they went. All gone. The young man said, *Help me, help us, help us get in and take what should belong to everyone*, and it just seemed so sensible, Mel. Not that it should belong to everyone. But it should belong to them, to the young. To the kids who grew up without ever tasting a strawberry. That's not right, is it? That's not how it's meant to be."

She stops talking. All her energy has been sucked up by that speech. I get the feeling she's been saying it to herself, over and over, in her head. Her reasons for getting them in.

I lie down beside her, and she doesn't have the strength to tell me to go away.

"I loved you," I tell her.

"I'm not going right this minute," she slurs, but she turns over towards me and puts her good hand – in its thick mitten – on the old, loose curve of my breast. How could she have given up on me, on this? How could she have told me that she wanted to sit at a different table for every single meal and never hear my voice again?

I lie there, trying not to breathe, until she falls back into sleep. Then I peel her hand away and stand up. The two plates of beans have congealed, but I don't care. I am passionate for their flavour, their scent, their taste. I'm alive and I eat for both of us.

* * *

It comes to me, as I work through the afternoon under the guise of normality, that I'm not just alive, not in the same way I was before. I'm more alive. Every breath sings in my chest. Every time I stoop to take a soil sample the pain in my back is an epiphany – a promise that I hurt, I hate, I love, I live.

The feelings swell as the hours pass. I don't care whether the others are working or what happens outside my area. The feelings swell to the point of bursting open.

I hear the approach of Mr Cecil's buggy.

I feel hope like the sharpness of citrus in my mouth, a long-forgotten taste, but when I turn around I make out, behind the wheel, the face of the man who stared at me through the glass panel in the door to Sector K and I remember that Mr Cecil is probably dead, and that I never liked him much anyway.

The buggy comes to a juddering halt a few yards away – he needs some driving practice – and he climbs out, a smile set in place, as if we're about to be introduced at a garden party.

"Mel?" he says.

I don't answer.

His lovely face has lost all signs of the cold, and his beard is brown and dishevelled, a sturdy, thriving mess of hair. How tall he stands. And he has left his thick coats elsewhere to reveal strong arms the colour of milk. No softness to his body at all. He must be boiling in this sudden change of temperature.

"I'm Lucas," he says. "Has Daisy talked about me?"

"No."

"I found her, out in the snow. She's in your room, right? The others said she'd be with you. How is she?"

21

It surprises me that what felt like a lifetime for me was obviously just a blip to the other workers. Mel and Daisy – still a couple in the eyes of the biodomes, intertwined like the roots of the plants that surround us. That's how it appears, even if you're outside the experience.

When I still don't respond he changes tack and his smile drops away. "I'm going to be looking after Sector K," he says. He has a strange accent. "We'll be working together."

"Good for you, young man," I tell him, trying to remember my schoolteacher tones. "Now let me get on with my job."

"Daisy said you could be difficult."

"So, you know all about me, do you?" I don't care if he's in charge or if he killed Mr Cecil himself, or even if he kills me, just so long as he goes away.

"No. And you don't know me."

"No, I don't."

He looks around at the high, curved dome of white and the orange globes amid the tall, curling tendrils. Can he recognise paradise when he sees it, or is it just an asset to be jotted down on the plus column of what he feels he is owed?

"Listen," he says. "I need to see Daisy."

"Why?"

He swipes at his forehead with his palm. "You should stop asking so many questions."

"Actually, I don't care for what I should or shouldn't do." I turn and pretend to be absorbed in the plant growth behind me. But he moves around to stand in my eyeline once more, and now he's wearing a deep frown as if he's only just realised that this place is unfamiliar to him.

"She's dead," I tell him.

This piece of news doesn't change his expression.

"Come on, then," I say. "Let's go and see her. Since you don't believe me." I march past the buggy towards the sliding door that seals up tight to keep in the moisture. A moment later I hear him reversing the buggy, then following along behind me.

"You can ride with me," he says.

"That's for management."

"I'm not management."

"I thought you said you were in charge of Sector K?"

He doesn't respond. I walk the entire way. At some point, in the corridors, he abandons the buggy.

* * *

I don't like the way Lucas holds Daisy's bandaged hand, as if he has a right to touch her and she would not have minded. The fact that she is dead does not change my feelings about this in the least: to touch someone, you should definitely have their permission.

He stays very still, sitting on the side of the bed, just as I did a few hours earlier. The empty plates, stained orange with bean juice, have a strong smell that fills the room. I wish I had returned them to the refectory.

"At least she didn't die alone," he says.

"We all die alone."

"I've seen a lot of deaths and some of them were better than others."

"Then you weren't seeing them properly," I say. "Are you trying to thank me for staying with her? Or blame me for going back to work afterwards?"

"I'm not saying either of those things," he says.

How incredibly easy it is for him to make me feel angry. What makes a good death, and what makes a bad death? Who is he to decide?

"I think you should go now," I say. He looks up at me as if he might refuse, but then he puts down Daisy's hand and stands up.

"I'll get a crew to come by and take her – the body – away."

"No hurry." I step back as he passes, folding my arms over my chest. I'm determined not to look at his face, but I can't help myself – I need to see what's there. The rough surfaces of his cheeks, the plain of his forehead, and more: there is something I recognise in his eyes and in an uncontrollable instant I feel my expression change to mirror his. It's a great task, then, to hold on to my emotions until he's gone, but I manage it. And then I'm alone.

The sound spills out of me and uncurls to fill all corners of the room. It's a deep, low growl – the equal and opposite of the alarm that led to this moment, but it means the same thing. Danger is here. It is breaking down the doors, ripping its way through my warm, safe places, bringing an icy wind.

God. Now there's a name that has not graced my lips for many years, but the concept comes back to me easily and I curse it. God, fate, everlasting life, whatever: I curse it all, in my head, while the sound coming from my open mouth winds down to nothing.

I get up. I pull the blanket over Daisy's head, taking care not to look at the mouth that I am not allowed to kiss.

How long will it take Lucas to come back, with others in tow, for disposal duty? I'm not sure. I have the feeling that time isn't running right anyway. Outside the bedroom it is sprinting in circles, hands around the face of an ancient and unstoppable clock. But not in here.

I kneel down and reach under the bed for my stacked glass slides, carefully searching through them until I find the one I want. Four black lines topped with a curve for a handle. A paint pot. And underneath, one word: Eurydice.

* * *

Slide 32

The arrival of new workers always upset her.

They had been given fresh clothes, but they still wore the outside world in their expressions and what Mel saw there was pinched, and cold, and desperate. But those expressions never lasted long. They all sank into the stupor of the warm and well fed. The mind was always so keen to forget.

The new ones were dotted between the familiar faces in the common room: Miriam and Barry doing a jigsaw puzzle; Gareth strumming something cheery using big open *chords on his battered guitar. He had attracted a crowd, who mumbled through the familiar lines of the few songs he was able to play. They all sang along, and all angst disappeared and soon everyone would go off to bed with a smile.*

Mel sat alone, digging the dirt out from under her fingernails, and considered what to paint next. She painted many aspects of her past, capturing a range of experiences, trapping them on glass so that she did not have to feel them anymore. She never wanted life to feel fresh and newly opened; she didn't want anything else to happen that might take her attention away from the past.

She thought about being left with only melons to paint and the idea made her smile. To paint a melon – yes, she should do one, at least. A big, round, juicy one, for posterity. She got up and left the noise of the common room behind, taking her time down the dimly lit corridors, the floor level solar lamps glowing so yellow that they reminded her of candle flame. A real fire – that was another thing she should paint. A fire like her father used to make. How easily subjects were coming to her tonight.

The corridors were empty. They curved around the domes to link everything together in loops and twirls that had once made her dizzy. It had taken her months to learn the patterns of the pathways, but now she did not need to think about the route to the storeroom. She could have found it with her eyes closed.

Mel reached the door and entered the code on the keypad. It clicked open and the drop in temperature hit her as she stepped over the threshold, into the darkness, where the metal shelves ran in high rows, holding crates and containers that were once essential to the running of Blossom Farm. Signposts, stacked in the far corner, back when the place had wanted to be found. But the only thing that interested Mel was the paint. The tins filled up the shelf on the back wall and she was always relieved to see so many of them: like a promise. And in this place, where only a wall separated her from the outside, she could hear the wind. It howled with lonely pleasure. She felt she understood it.

* * *

Outside, a woman was waiting for her. She was round and creamy and gave the impression of being filled with something heavy. None of the shock of the new sat upon her, although Mel had never seen her before. She felt certain she would have remembered somebody who seemed so much more real than the rest of the place.

"You're from up north, right?" the woman said.

"No," said Mel.

"I saw you in York. That meeting. You spoke about fuel prices, and then it all kicked off. Twenty years ago."

"No," said Mel again. "I'm from Portsmouth. I was. From Portsmouth."

"That's only down the road." The woman looked at the paint tin, and Mel decided to answer no more questions.

"Excuse me," she said, as the woman said, at the same time, "I followed you."

"What?"

"From the main room. The jigsaws, the guitar. You slipped out. You looked like you were going someplace better. You should cover your tracks if you're not meant to be in there."

"I am allowed to be in there. I have permission."

"Great! Good for you. Privileges." The woman reached into the pocket of her knitted cardigan – no doubt made by the endlessly creating brigade of Sue, Poppy, Alicia and Geoff – and produced a small stuffed bear. "This is Eurydice." She made four syllables of the name.

It was the mixture of accusation and charm that befuddled Mel to the point of actually smiling. "Hello Eurydice," she said, taking herself by surprise.

The woman leaned forward conspiratorially. "She can't actually speak," she said. "Nobody gave her a mouth. I made her when I was a little girl and I didn't think she needed one back then."

"You could make one for her now."

"Oh no. I don't think she's actually that bothered. There's nothing that facilitates the abdication of responsibility so much as not having a mouth in the first place." She said this long sentence in one breath like a well-rehearsed speech, and Mel felt a sudden bond, as if she had more in common with this person than with anybody else she had met in such a long time, even from before coming to the farm. If those words were a test, Mel felt certain that she wanted to pass it.

"Have you been allocated an area yet?"

"Me, or Eurydice?"

"I'm assuming your beautiful lost soul of a bear will get to be a lotus-eater."

"Yes, you're probably right. The Winery, they said. But no room allocations yet. We're meant to bunk down in the big room tonight."

"The common room," Mel said. "You won't get any sleep in there. Come on. You can stay with me."

"Will you tell me what that tin is for?"

"No," said Mel, and the smile she received in return was an affirmation. Yes, she passed the test. She passed the test on that day, at least.

*　*　*

Three of them come for the body. Two men and a woman. Lucas is not among them. They have a dirty trolley that usually takes seedlings from the nursery to the sectors and they lay her on that, keeping my blanket over her. It's fine. I don't want it anymore, anyway.

When people die here—

When people die here there's a process, but that seems to have been overturned. I didn't give it much thought before, except that the process made sense. Everything worked in a certain way. But these new young people know nothing of it and don't care to ask. They set off down the corridor with Daisy, and I follow along behind until one of them turns around and says, "Get back to work. There are mouths to feed."

He's a tall man, bone thin. The other man and the woman both stop walking and stare at him. Something tells me this is the first time he's assumed such a level of command, and he's enjoying the sensation. They look at his enjoyment and say nothing.

The only replies that come to mind are pathetic variations of, 'You're not the boss of me,' and experience has taught me nobody emerges from such statements with any dignity. In fact, there's no dignity to be salvaged here at all, no matter what I say or do. There are words that this man would be happy to throw at me, labels that would define me as less than him. I need to keep myself free from such words, but I also have to know what they're going to do with Daisy.

I choose my words so very carefully. "I just need to see her laid to rest, please."

"Want to sing a hymn or two, do you?" He laughs, and the woman lays a hand on his shoulder from behind, so gently. Ahhhhh, I see what this is: he has had such a hard life, she is telling herself as she touches him. He's only known the toughest way to be, to survive, and he can't express himself any other way, but he means well. She's determined to back up his pain as the most important in the room. Oh, the difficulties of being such a strong young man in charge.

"Fine," he says, and the woman smiles at me as if she's done me a favour. She's hardly more than a teenager, and she's already well practised in feminine idiocy.

We start moving again. The woman checks a piece of paper, perhaps a map, as she pushes the trolley along. We cross through the sectors, working our way out to the grapevines and the Winery beyond, which would be a perfect place for Daisy. The corridors are mainly empty – it's still working hours – and everything looks normal, apart from one buggy that has been overturned, onto its roof, like a practical joke without explanation. The men and the woman steer the trolley around it without comment.

We pass through the Winery where the large wooden vats stand, and the smell is sharp and sour. Green bottles sit on a long trestle table, each one bearing a label that says *Blossom Farm's Finest Table Wine* in curly letters with a picture of a bunch of beautiful grapes. The workers take care not to look straight at us; the way they know to avoid their eyes tells me that more trolleys have passed this way.

Beyond the Winery there is a place I've never visited before: a corridor, crates of bottles piled against the walls, ending at a door. The lock has been prised free and dangles loose on two electrical wires. This must be how these agro-terrorists got in here, away from the cameras and the guards. An emergency exit, of all things, forgotten about. Except that Daisy found it, once upon a time. She did always love to explore.

"Stay," the tall man says to me.

"Let her say goodbye?" says the woman.

I think he won't mind if I touch Daisy one last time. But here's the thing: I don't want to touch her, not here, not in front of them. Besides, I tell myself over and over, she's dead, she's dead. What does flesh on a trolley mean? It means nothing at all. Whatever happens next, it doesn't matter.

"No, it's fine," I say.

"Let's do this quick," says the other man.

The woman pushes the door, and when it doesn't give the men join in, all three straining until it moves. A drift of snow tumbles into the corridor along with the freezing cold. Outside, I can see only white.

The men take either end of the body and carry it out.

"Why out there?" I say to the woman who stays behind, wrapping her arms around herself.

"The snow will cover them," she says. "I'm sorry, the ground's too hard for a proper burial."

"So they'll just leave her?" I stand beside her and look out at the afternoon, the sun already low in the sky. It's not snowing right now; the drifts stretch away, so beautiful, and the cold is a hammer to my chest. I gasp and look around and see the men not far away. They are already coming back, leaving my blanket, the body wrapped within it, lying in a dip between two mounds of snow. In fact, it's a field of regularly spaced mounds. Bodies, covered in white. Many bodies, making hillocks. The guards, the supervisors, and now Daisy.

The woman grabs my arm and pulls me back.

"Why?" I ask her, knowing I have only moments before the men return and she will no longer speak to me.

"Why what? I told you."

"No. No. Don't you understand? We're not important. It's the plants. You die and you go under the ground in your sector. To feed the plants. Out there—" I point at the broken door, the way outside that is swallowing our heat so greedily, "—is no good to anyone. The plants need the nutrients."

"You bury people under the plants?"

"Of course. The nutrients. That's where Daisy should be. In Strawberries. She worked Strawberries, in the end."

The men return and slam the door shut, then kick their boots against the corridor walls, flinging around snow. "It's strange how quickly you get used to the warm," reflects the tall one, and then he remembers me and assumes the tone of command once more. "Off you go, then," he says. "Work."

And off I go.

* * *

There is an hour left to the day. I return to Sector K and find Lucas there, standing on my soil. He touches the fruit with his fingertips.

The rage that comes over me can't be contained, even though it is dangerous. I walk towards him with the plan to slap his face for something I can't define. He sidesteps me, and then I'm deep in the tangle of the plants and my leg is caught. I fall to the earth. It's easier to hit the soil than to hit him, anyway. It gives under my weight. It understands me.

Lucas stands over me, hovering on tiptoes.

"Go away," I tell him, when I have enough control of myself.

"Are you all right?"

"What do you think?"

"Can I help you up?"

I don't take his hand but after a while he squats down next to me. Here, in the green, it's harder to hate him.

"They put Daisy outside," I say, to his knees. "It's a waste. Tell them. Bodies go in the ground. Here." I pat the soil and then meet his eyes. His youth, his newness, is so alien, like the wings of an insect or the bright yellow beak of a bird. "Here's where I want to end up. Right here."

"You'd give everything to Blossom Farm."

"Not the farm." Don't they see it? They all act as if there are only institutions in this world and nothing else worth talking about, nothing else worth saving.

"They don't care about you," he says, and I know he hasn't understood.

"Neither do your lot."

"No," he says. "You're probably right."

He sits down next to me. After a while he says, "This place is too beautiful to survive."

"It's the beautiful things that live on."

"Not anymore. Not out there."

"We're not out there."

He shakes his head. "Daisy said you came in here before it got bad. That you were working in a private school and there was a special arrangement, friends in high places…"

"Daisy said an awful lot to you considering she hadn't said a word to me in three years."

He laughs. The sound is clear and strong. "Maybe she'd been saving it all up. Her need to talk about you."

Think clearly, I remind myself; this is no time to fall back in love with youth. "Please leave me alone," I tell him. "I'll take care of the melons. You can have the fruit, eat it, give it to orphaned children, dance round it in your underwear, I don't care. But please leave me alone, and don't come back into this area again."

"What are you afraid of?" he asks, and that undoes me. I put my dirty hands, fresh from the soil, over my face and whisper, "It's not always about being afraid."

"Isn't it?" he says, reflectively. When I take my hands away, I see in his eyes a lifetime of being afraid, more than any fair share, more than I have felt. Fear as a default setting – not just in waking hours but creeping into dreams, even the good ones. I have had moments of safety, of love, of comfort, and they have kept me going. I'm not sure Lucas has.

"Did you really care about her?" I ask him. "Why?"

"I don't know. She seemed... real to me."

"Don't tell me. She reminded you of your mother."

"She wasn't anybody's mother. Not like you."

"I never had children," I tell him.

"That doesn't mean you weren't a mother. She told me. You loved those kids. You fought for them. To get them away."

Yes, I did, I fought for them, and even though it sounds clichéd I can't deny that I was all those children had in their difficult moments, and I did my very best by them.

"It's a good thing," says Lucas, "to be a mother. But Daisy wasn't one. I could see that as soon as I found her. People think I'm a follower. Lucas, who does what he's told. When she got better, she started to talk to me as if I could make my own decisions. I've not felt that before. It's a different way for people to be."

"What kind of way?"

"Friends," he says, simply. "We were friends."

I feel something open within me. It is pride, flowering. I'm proud of this man, this stranger, who would call a prickly old lady a friend. A description of equal terms.

"Help me up," I say.

He stands and holds out his hands once more, and this time I let him pull me up. We emerge from the plants and stand on the walkway, side by side. The dome looks different. Perhaps the lights have started to dim as part of the cycle. Soon the sprinklers will kick in.

"The storeroom," I say. "Why did you want to get in there?"

"Daisy said there were materials." He wets his lips. "Paint."

"You want paint?"

"Not a lot. Just a little."

The way he says it tells me that Daisy has told him about this side of my personality too.

"Right. Right."

He knows that I have the code to the storeroom and he didn't pressure me for it. Is that decency or manipulation on his part?

Either way, it helps me to make a decision. "I'll let you in. But I won't give you the code. You only come in and out with me, understood?"

"Certainly. It's your space, after all."

Does he really believe that? He's wily enough to keep any streak of sarcasm out of his voice.

Either way, the deal is done. We walk along together and talk of what life is like for a child on the outside. I wonder if Blossom Farm should have given their jobs to the very young, rather than the very old. But it makes perfect sense. I'm ashamed to realise that the old are so much easier to control.

PART TWO

I no longer have a blanket.

But this doesn't matter, because I no longer have a room.

"It's a reallocation to make sure everyone gets a place to sleep," says the woman standing in my doorway. Behind her, another woman is sitting at my small table polishing a long knife with a cloth, taking care not to look at me. "Go to the common room and they'll set you up."

"But this is my room," I say. All I want is to get inside it. Coming back down the corridor from the storeroom, I was thinking only about the fact that I had no blanket. What was I going to do? No warm blanket anymore. It's strange how quickly priorities can change.

"We all have to make sacrifices," says the woman in the doorway. "It's not that you don't have a place to sleep. It's just this is a big room and we thought the original workers might want to stick together, so you'll have been allocated a place with your own kind." She nibbles her cracked bottom lip; the change in temperature must be playing havoc with her skin.

"So off you trot," says the woman with the knife, who

looks as clean and brutal as a teenager. She doesn't even bother to make eye contact with me. She is a parody of a threat, like she's practised it for hours and is now happy to seize her chance.

"Keep your knickers on," I tell her. I've had a bad enough day to no longer care. Besides, she's obviously all bark and no bite. Who seriously polishes a knife just to scare an old lady?

"We could throw you out in the cold instead," she says. Something in her voice suggests this isn't the first time she's thought of this idea, or voiced it.

The other woman, the one at my door, says, "I put your stuff in here." She reaches around the door and brings out a white plastic sack, half full. I take it and look inside: my clothes, books, hairbrush and cream for my legs when they ache. Not my slides. They must still be under the bed. I can't leave them behind. But carrying them would be a job for more than one person, and where would I put them? How would I explain them? The one with the knife – she would smash them if she suspected they were important to me. I'm beginning to recognise this look some of them have, as if the things they've experienced outside will justify the things they do in here.

"Thanks," I say, to the one at the door. I set off for the common room. It's nearly dinner time and my body is hurting. It will only get worse tomorrow. I want my bed. I want my slides, my happy places. I want. I want my blanket.

I want to see Daisy. I want her to ignore me over dinner, sitting at a different table, feeling hatred, feeling disgust, just feeling something personal and real and Daisyish at me.

Earlier, in the storeroom, Lucas said, "Look at all the stuff in here. People get killed for this outside. Petrol. Look. Batteries. Torches. Inflatable tents. Solar warmers." He spoke softly, in awe, as if entering a cathedral.

"I thought you wanted paint," I said, watching him from the door. "It's against the far wall."

"Thanks." But he didn't move quickly. He examined each shelf in turn: top, middle, bottom, as he walked down the rows. "How come they gave you access to this place? They must really trust you."

"I was friends with the supervisor before Mr Cecil," I said.

"I thought you were… friends with Daisy?"

"I thought you of all people would understand there's more than one kind of friend in the world."

Mr Taylor, I had called him, once I worked for him. Once upon a time, in a classroom not too far away, he had called me Miss Baris. He was a good boy, although he didn't believe it, and he turned into a better man. When it all went wrong he came for me.

"What are these?" asked Lucas. He touched my slides, the ones that I painted and left behind in the storeroom; the ones that I didn't want to be reminded of so often, unless a dark mood took me.

"Nothing."

He picked one at random and held it up. It was a painting of a day I never want to think about. Another day of goodbyes, years ago.

* * *

Slide 58

She counted them getting onto the bus, and she counted them leaving it, even though they could not have gone anywhere during the journey. Old habits. There were only five of them left. They didn't even sit together on the thirty-minute trip to the port but spaced themselves evenly throughout the bus, leaving a pattern of empty seats. Miss Baris wished there was some way she could tell them they needed each other but she had been a teacher long enough to know that children never, ever believed such sentiments. They thought themselves invincible, and maybe that would be enough to get them through.

They gathered in front of the doors to Departures, the kids shivering even in their expensive coats. A light sleet was falling. It looked like snow if you stared up into it, but on the skin and on the concrete it was grey, and wet, and dull.

"Let's run through it again," said Miss Baris, and they all groaned as one. At least they were united in some things. "Natalya, start us off."

"Number one: stay together at all times," said the smallest girl, so small. So eager to please with her prompt reply and her smart manners.

"Omar?"

"Number two: board the ferry and don't speak to anyone except the people in charge." He was a pain in class, big and

bullish, but if any of them had grasped the seriousness of the situation it was him, and she saw a determination in his eyes that gave her hope for them all.

"Quentin, number three."

The boy gaped at her. He wasn't the brightest, but he had a soft heart and loved all animals, choosing to spend most of his time in the school stables. He had told her once that he wanted to study to become a vet, and she had told him to work hard. That was what teachers said in the face of unrealistic dreams.

"Disembark at..." she prompted him.

"Disembark at Bilbao and use the Euros to pay for a taxi to the train station. From there get tickets to Madrid."

"Well done," she said. "Number four. Lupita."

"Once we arrive in Madrid, get to the Russian Embassy. Ask for our parents to be contacted," said Lupita, in a bored voice. She wanted so much to be the ideal woman and ended up looking more like a child than any of them with her hitched-up skirt and her practised, sulky attitude. She was the weakest link. If she felt the urge to wander off, she would, and the rest would fall apart in her absence.

"I'm relying on you, Lupita," Miss Baris said, knowing it wouldn't help but unable to stop herself. "Five, Dimitri."

"Five. Stay together at all times," recited Dimitri, the cheeky one, working on becoming tall and handsome and trouble to the world in general. "Miss, why is rule five the same as rule one?"

Lupita nudged him. "Because it's the most important, you moron."

"We don't call each other morons, Lupita," said Miss Baris.

"And our parents will pick us up there?" asked Natalya.

"That's right." Lies came so easily to teachers. She had long since learned to ignore any twinge of conscience. She was the last teacher left in the school and these were the last pupils. There would soon be no more food, no more light, no more heating. After the extortionate cost of bribing the official to secure five places on the ferry, there was simply no more money.

And at the other end, what happens then? She had contacted so many people, trying to get hold of the parents who hadn't bothered to come for their own children when the Gulf Stream began to fail. Powerful people. Dignitaries, celebrities, billionaires. She had to hope that her failure to reach them could be put right by the Embassy. Two of the children had that nationality, at least, and she had sent them an email informing them that any attempt to split up these children would result in the press being contacted. She had an inkling the kids could also make bargaining chips against other countries, but knew next to nothing about politics.

Stop, she told herself, stop. You've done the best that you could do.

"Aren't you coming, Miss?" said Omar, managing to look vulnerable.

"No, I'm needed here," she said. "But you are all capable of doing this. I have great faith in you all. Just make sure you stay together."

They groaned.

"Right," she said. "Off you go."

They did. They walked through the doors without looking back, because this was an adventure and she was only a teacher.

Back at the bus, she sat behind the wheel until the ferry had swung away from the dock. Then she took the printed email and the map from her coat pocket and read the words through again.

I hope you remember me. Billy Taylor; I was in your biology class fifteen years ago at Portsdown. You taught me about plants. I was fascinated. You made it all seem so important. I went on to study Agriculture at college and I work for Blossom Farm now. Have you heard of them? They have a series of bio-farms not far from the school. They're employing older people, dependable people, to look after the plants, and I thought of you. You inspired me.

Would you consider coming here? I don't know what's happening to this country, but I heard the school was closing as everyone with enough money to get away was leaving, like rats on a sinking ship, I suppose. I don't know if you remember that English never was my strongest subject. But if you are staying in the UK and you need a place to go then you are welcome here. I've enclosed a map. When you arrive ask the guards at the gate to page me. It's warm and safe, and I can get you a good room of your own.

Miss Baris started the engine, and drove away, hoping the roads were still clear enough to make it through.

* * *

"Is it a bus?" said Lucas.

"Can't you tell?" I said.

He frowned at it, then put it back on the pile. He carried on looking around the treasures of the storeroom, and said quietly, "I won't tell anyone about this place, okay?"

"Why don't I believe you?"

He said, "Something tells me you're a scientist at heart. Don't believe anything until it's proved, that's what you think. So just wait and I'll prove it to you. You don't have much choice, anyway."

"That's true," I said.

He picked up a paint tin, then reached for the signs. "Can I take these too? I like to paint. I'm no good at it either. Well, I wasn't. Back when I was little. I can remember it: a warm room, some paper, a painting kit. Colours. I'd like to get good at it, some day. Maybe we should both get some practice in."

"I don't do it to be good at it."

"No. I can understand that." He was so very reasonable that it hurt.

He came back to me, at the door, loaded up with his spoils, and said, "I think us painters should stick together."

And even though I knew he was saying it only for his own reasons, I heard myself saying, "Yes." Yes, with the memory of another time, another instruction to stick together, in my mind. Rules one and five are still with me, even if I don't look at the black lines on the glass that make up that bus journey. "Yes," I said. "Stick together."

I reach the common room and find it filled with confused old people to whom I don't want to belong. It turns out the room allocations are not going smoothly after all.

* * *

It's not that anybody is obviously angry. Maybe you get too old to show anger, visibly, even if you're never too old to feel it. But there are so many people in the common room who are unhappy, crying, standing around with white plastic sacks in hand, and I join them, push my way through the groups, looking for somebody in charge.

By the archway to the refectory is a cluster of young people, all women; I recognise one of them. She took Daisy away earlier. She holds a clipboard and the others are gathered around it, frowning. Some of them are wearing pagers and utility belts that must have once belonged to the supervisors.

Lucas isn't here, and neither is the leader – Stephan, he called himself. Room allocation is obviously not an important topic to those in charge. I'm thinking they must already be ensconced in the supervisors' old rooms. No question of double bunking in those.

I watch them squabble over the clipboard for a while. This could take all night, and I'm not brave enough to approach them.

"Mel."

Jim is behind me with Lonnie in tow.

"Have they taken your room?" He gives me a sympathetic smile. "I suppose that would be the first one they'd want. It is the biggest of the workers' rooms."

He's not holding a white plastic sack, I notice. "At least you're okay," I say, trying to sound friendly.

"Well, since we're a two sharing already I expect it makes more sense to let us keep the space. But we were thinking – if you need a place to sleep, come bunk with us. We have spare blankets and a pillow. It's still sleeping on the floor, but I don't think anybody is going to find a bed of their own tonight."

His generosity shames me. Of course, he wants something. Everybody does. But even so, it's no small thing to give up your personal space. And it's the best offer I'm going to get.

"Thank you," I say. "Thanks Lonnie."

Her smile is a little more lopsided than Jim's. I'm guessing she's not quite so keen on the idea as he is. Still, she doesn't complain as we leave the common room behind.

Their room is smaller than mine and there are more personal touches evident, from a stack of books to photographs of young people – people from the past, I should say – stuck to the walls and looking straight at me. The bed has a stack of crocheted blankets upon it. That's Lonnie's hobby. I don't know how she got hold of so much wool over the years. What does she trade to indulge her hobby? I'm starting to see that my knowledge of Blossom Farm only scratches the surface. I know it geographically; socially, now that's a different matter.

"You'll be okay," Jim says, as he lays things on the floor: the blankets, the pillow. We take it in turns to use the adjoining bathroom and I hate the smell of it. The smell of them, scrunched up together in their own sweat, neither of them able to tell their scents apart. Lonnie removes her enormous earrings and leaves them by the bed, ready for the morning.

Then we're three old people in standard green flannel pyjamas, so laughable, being polite to each other. *Am I ready for lights out?* Jim asks me, courteously. I tell him yes. It's only once the dim light is out and everyone is tucked up in bed that Jim begins to speak and say real things. This is why I'm here. So that I can't just walk away.

"It's us and them," he says, softly, into the dark. "Us and them, Mel, and they want us to think it's not, but we're not stupid. They say Blossom Farm has been using us, cheap compliant labour, practically slaves, but they're no different. They're worse, with their pretence of equality and their big statements: food for all, freedom. They'll just run this place into the ground because they know nothing about plants, do they? Nothing."

"No," I whisper. They know a lot about being cold and frozen inside, and about hating us. But we're catching up fast.

"Blossom Farm won't stand for it. I talked to this Stephan, man to man. I said I was the representative for the workers, somebody has to be. Stephan said all the supervisors and guards were escorted away, but we can stay and keep working – that's part of the deal. He says there's going to be a profit-sharing agreement for a peaceful solution. But Blossom Farm would never agree to that, would they?"

"No."

Stephan said the guards and Mr Cecil left. But I saw the mounds in the snow. I could start a war here with just a few words. If I just describe those mounds, Jim will start to mobilise us all with the righteous ire of the fed and warm and unimaginative.

Jim talks and talks and talks.

I feel a new sense of sympathy for Lonnie by the time my eyes start to close, regardless of the endless sound of Jim's voice. He's busy talking himself into importance. Has he done this every night since the terrorists came? No wonder she looks so tired.

* * *

The sound jolts me from sleep.

At first I think something heavy has been thrown against the door but then it comes again, shaking me all the way into wakefulness, and I realise it's so much bigger than that. Something has been thrown against the domes.

It's so dark. There's another bang, and voices in the corridor, panicked, and running feet, and I feel fear like I never have before, so sharp, like pain.

The melons.

Not the melons, not when everything else has gone, but someone shouts, "Winery!" and the relief is so keen, like ice on a burn; I go numb and the aches of my body don't matter as I get up, get dressed, and head towards the noise.

I don't think. I just move, in the flow with the others. Is Jim behind me? I hear a man shouting my name but I ignore it. I'm caught up in the crowd, young and old moving together, and I can't tell them apart anymore.

The heat hits me when we reach the entrance to the Winery and the crowd panics, parts, and disperses into smaller groups as I press on past the shelves. There are flakes of snow whirling in the orange glow up ahead, hot and cold, fire and frost, mixing, mingling, making crazy patterns. The back wall of the Winery is gone. The barrels are alight, and the puddles, puddles all around, burn. The hole in the wall, like a ragged mouth, is terrifying. The fire runs and roars; it is a monster.

I can't make out faces, or understand what is being shouted, but I see the concerted movements around me. Some people are attempting to control the blaze. The young ones use blankets, handfuls of snow, even their feet as they stamp and stamp in the fiery liquid. Stephan is there, a central point, standing tall against the blaze and facing it down with the confidence of one who is used to getting his own way. The fire will lose the battle. It begins to obey.

Someone catches at my arm. It's Jim. I'm beginning to grow sick of his face.

"Come on," he says, "come away. They've got it." He pushes at me and I nearly lose my balance, but he's right: we should go. When the fire goes out there will only be the hole, and the cold pouring through it, and this section will be closed off as well as the terrorists can manage to stop the endless winter from touching our plants. And to hide the sight of those mounds.

"Where's Lonnie?" I say, as we push past the milling crowds, their mouths open, their eyes glassy. Rubberneckers, that's what they used to be called. The desire to stare at a car crash, when somebody else's world has gone wrong. Except this is our world – don't we have the right to stare?

"I told her to stay in bed," Jim says. "You took off so fast. I was worried about you." He holds onto my arm, so tightly.

"I needed to know what's happening."

"What was always going to happen." The corridor is quieter; all attention is focused behind us, on the blaze. Jim slows a little and loosens his grip. He speaks more quietly, and with well-chosen words. I get the feeling he's been rehearsing this in his mind. "They'll never hold this place. They'll tell us all sorts of lies to keep us working, but they have to know they have a few days more at best. This was a message Blossom Farm was always going to send."

"You think Blossom Farm deliberately blew up the Winery?"

"It's the easiest and cheapest area to replace," he says. "It's just equipment, not even under the domes. Not organic. But it shows they'd rather destroy it than share it."

I can't accept it, I can't; destroy the melons, the strawberries, the oranges, the sugar snap peas, because if they don't own it, they think nobody should.

"Lonnie is getting more confused," Jim says. "It's all this uncertainty. You know what happens when one of us gets confused. They put us outside. There's no reason to keep someone who can't work. But if I make myself indispensable, they'll want to keep me happy, and then she's got a chance. We have to outlast this band of idiots and then, once they're gone, the farm will need new supervisors, ones who understand the situation here and do their best to help the rightful owners."

He stops walking and pulls me to a halt beside him.

"Listen," he says. "You've been here so long, you've had privileges, you know how this works. You've got access to stuff, and you know every inch of the place. We can keep the workers together, unite them, keep them strong so they don't help the enemy. Days, that's all it will take until the cavalry arrives. Days."

"You want to form an underground movement?" I ask him. Is he picturing us striking some valiant blow for a business that doesn't care about us one way or another? His desperation is repulsive, but I've been in love. I know what it's like to think you'll do anything to keep someone close. Still, I'm too old for this nonsense.

"Listen," I say. I step in close to him and hold his gaze so he can be in no doubt that I mean this. "I can't help you. I'm done with getting involved. I came here for an easy life and I just care about the melons. That's it."

"You don't get to have an easy life now, you silly old woman," he says. "You silly, silly old woman. This is going to be hard, and you're part of it whether you like it or not. In the morning they'll call a meeting, wait and see. They'll say that Blossom Farm never cared about us, and they'll try to split us up. They don't get it. We know we never mattered to anybody but ourselves, but there comes a point when you have to stand up. For meaning something, if only to yourself. And you do care, Mel. We're approaching the moment when you won't be able to pretend otherwise anymore. When it arrives, remember my offer, and remember what you need to do to survive." He steps back and puts his hand on the door handle. "And don't mention any of this to Lonnie. She doesn't need to get upset."

I follow him into the room and in the warm darkness it's possible to believe that Lonnie is sleeping, escaping into good dreams. I crawl back into my nest on the floor and Jim returns to his place beside her.

Us and them. Everything is us and them. Even if there were just us three – Jim and Lonnie and me – there would be the divide that splits the heart of all humanity. And if it came to it, they would both turn on me.

Did Lucas mean it? That we painters should stick together? I wish I had seen him at the fire, just to see his face. But it's so dangerous to trust anyone. Even Daisy, Daisy who had me in her hand, could not be trusted in the end.

No, I won't trust anyone. That's the only way to be. If it must be us and them, I'll stand alone and take no sides, no matter what happens.

Jim's breathing slows and I know he's found sleep. How lucky he is to believe in his own importance. He protects Lonnie as if he is a superhero.

Super Jim. The thought makes me smile.

Yes, he's ridiculous, but as I lie there, feeling the inevitable creep towards morning, I loose the reins of my imagination and picture myself as a young woman, running away over the snow, flanked by the people who make me super too. We are so young and pretty and free, Daisy and Lucas and me.

* * *

It's eggs on toast in the morning, with the strange metallic taste of artificial eggs sticking to the back of my throat. I don't know how they make them, but I always picture robot chickens sitting above a giant conveyor belt, their necks stretching as they pop out egg after egg.

Damn these stupid thoughts, and my old, sore bones, and sleeping on the floor. And damn Stephan, who looks like a proper leader as he stands on the table at the front of the room and shouts, having started softly before working himself up into a frenzy worthy of a politician. I think he's missed his calling.

"We offered them a good deal!" he shouts. "A fair deal! Half the produce for the starving and half for them and their fat shareholders, as long as they left us alone to form a new collective, a place where young and old could work together towards a future for us all!" He holds out his hands and knits his fingers together. I finish off the last mouthful of eggs.

"And this is their answer," says Stephan. He drops his hands and his voice. "They destroy. They don't care who gets hurt. They don't care about you, and they don't care about the future. They would rather blow this place to hell than simply take a little less for themselves! This is the kind of thinking that got us all into this mess in the first place. No care for each other, no care for the natural world, no care for the planet. Nothing but greed. We need to show them that they're wrong. We won't be scared by their tactics. We won't give in to fear. We'll stand strong, and take care of the plants and of each other, until they see sense."

Does he really think this will work? He flicks his eyes over us all and I see calculations taking place. He thinks he has us where he wants us.

From my position in the far corner, I look around the refectory and see the young ones are spread out, sitting in twos and threes, alert, none of them eating. Stephan is a very dangerous man.

"Now, I know that you must be feeling a lot of things about what happened last night. But now is not the time to give in to negativity. Let's all stay strong, and together we can prove to Blossom Farm that although they enslaved you, they never managed to brainwash you. You will always be, in your hearts, free men and women."

Across from me, Jim coughs, and catches my eye. *You see?* his expression says, as clear as day. *I told you so.*

In my expression I try to put the thought, *Don't start trouble, Jim. Don't start trouble, they're ready for you.*

"Any questions?" says Stephan, pleasantly.

Jim raises his hand. He turns in his chair to face Stephan, and all I can see is the back of his head where the hairs are combed so carefully. He was in the bathroom for ages this morning.

"Yes?"

"It's not so much a question as an observation," says Jim.

"Please," Stephan says, waving a hand. "Go ahead."

He stands up. "We're a pretty old bunch of folks, sir. And we've all heard this kind of nonsense before. You want to fight a war, you go right ahead. Don't let us stop you. But I think I speak for all of us when I say we're not about to fight it for you. Not for all the tea in China."

"I'm disappointed to hear you feel that way," says Stephan, looking disappointed and righteous. "I'm afraid the time has come to choose where you stand, and everybody has to make their own choice. I see that you are choosing to stand with Blossom Farm."

"Oh, really?" says Jim. "If I'm not with you I'm against you, is that it? I've heard that before, son. And we're for ourselves, by the way. You lot can be for yourselves and we'll be for ourselves. End of story." He sits down. I'm so glad I can't see his face. I get the feeling he looks pleased with himself.

"Ah, I'm sad that life has been so difficult for you that you can't tell when a good offer comes along," says Stephan. "I think we should get together, man to man, and discuss this personally."

If Jim thought this was how he would keep Lonnie alive, he's an idiot. I wonder if he's beginning to realise that.

"But no matter how you feel about us," says Stephan, addressing the entire room once more, "I hope we can all agree that the plants come first. Let's work hard for them, if not yet for each other."

He climbs down from the table and people begin to move, taking their trays bearing empty plates and cups to the stacking holders, setting off for their sectors with dull, tired expressions. Do I care for them? Will I stand with them? No, I won't.

The man who took away Daisy's body comes to our table, and says to Jim, "Wait here."

Jim says nothing. He shrinks down in his seat and Lonnie, beside him, looks up and around as if waking from a dream.

"What is it?" she says, and I say, "Work. Come on." She follows me, thank God, looking back once or twice at Jim, but she still has the sense to come away.

I drop Lonnie off at Satsumas and then lose myself among my melons. Some areas are ripening, and I check for colour, size and shape, and write yield estimates just as Mr Cecil would have liked. The fruits are good and heavy but I won't pick them, not yet.

Today the desire to taste one is so very strong. If I split it open it would reveal the perfect colour of sunrise. My mouth moistens. I'm salivating all morning with the thought of the taste. It hasn't bothered me this way for years, but right now my body is on fire with sensation. The aches and pains, the tiredness, only prove that I'm still alive, and I'm grateful for it. I haven't felt this way for so long. I can remember exactly when I last felt so glad to still have these old arms and legs, this tired and struggling heart.

I remember it, and I want to put it on glass.

When the lunchtime bell goes, I pocket my paintbrush and head to the storeroom. The paint awaits me. It slides thick and easy over the surface of the pane.

* * *

Slide 118

The reception area of Sector K was a mockery of an earlier time when there might have been guests to this state-of-the-art biodome complex, but the doors had been shut and the gates erected before Mel's arrival. The orange seats, the potted palm and the water dispenser were used only by the workers, and had become invisible, beyond comment. But the stranger looked hard at them and Mel saw them again, as if for the first time. The orange seats were lurid and the potted palm lopsided. How ridiculous it all looked.

The man's face was slick with sweat. He wore a padded coat that was so bulky he had barely squeezed through the door. But his shoes, and his beard, were still white with snow. He sneered at them both.

Mr Taylor said, "Can I help you?" His voice was very mild.

The man opened his coat. Inside was a bundle, strapped to his chest by a length of sacking material, brown and coarse, looping over his shoulders and around his waist. He unveiled himself, as if something meaningful had been revealed.

Mel thought – a bomb. A bomb. She didn't move.

She had heard stories. New workers, arriving from the

changed world outside, had told tales of separatism, agro-terrorism, people demanding to live under their own rules to make a fairer world. She had eavesdropped on these conversations with vague interest, as if it was happening in another country, far away. Outside – the foreign country. Now the outside was here.

"Don't do anything," said Mr Taylor. "Okay? Nobody needs to do anything."

The bundle on the man's chest squirmed. A small arm emerged through a gap in the sacking. It had folds of fat, chubby creases and a fist that clenched and unclenched.

The man stroked the fist and put it back inside the material, using only one hand. In the other hand was a knife.

No, not a knife. It was a trowel. One of the small steel trowels they used for planting. He must have come here through the nurseries, Mel thought.

"Put the knife down, okay?" said Mr Taylor, who had stretched out his own hands in that classic gesture of placation.

The man mumbled.

"What? I'm sorry. I didn't hear."

"I need milk."

"You need the Meat section. You're in Fruit. Fruit's no good for a baby." Mr Taylor pointed. "Here. I'll show you the way."

"Real milk. From a real cow."

"Yes, that's what we do here. Real cows. I promise you. This way."

The man watched Mr Taylor edge around so he stood beside him, by the entrance. How strange that only a moment ago they *had been discussing the weather. Another cold one, Mr Taylor had said, do you remember what summer used to be like? I was on the football team and we played out there in shorts.*

"How far?" said the man.

"Not far." Mr Taylor flicked his eyes to Mel. It was an instruction, so obviously; no, a plea. To do something. What did he want her to do? The man saw it, and read it quickly and completely. He raised the trowel and brought it down, that steel point digging into the space between Mr Taylor's neck and his chest, right where the collar of his white shirt sat.

Mel looked away. She simply looked away: not there, not there, not there, she heard in her head.

When she came back to herself, she was kneeling by the entrance to her melon area and Mr Taylor was on the ground, not far away. His blood had formed a lake around him, so red, reaching the feet of the orange chairs, the colours clashing.

She crawled over to him. His mouth opening and shutting. His eyes were on her. He looked very much younger.

"Billy," she said.

* * *

There's a cheery knock at the storeroom door, a young person's knock, and I just know it's Lucas. I hate myself for feeling pleased at the thought.

I put down the paintbrush and open the door. He is standing there with a big smile. I let him enter, check the corridor is empty, and then close the door. We are alone in the only space left to me. Why don't I mind him being here? I should mind it.

"What are you painting?" he says. "Is that a melon?"

"It's not finished yet. And it's not a melon. It doesn't look anything like a melon."

We stand side by side and stare at the black curves on the glass.

"It looks exactly like a melon," he says.

I nudge him in the ribs.

"Well, what is it, then?"

"It's a baby. Look, there's the head, there's an eye, that's a little hand."

"Is that a hand, then? Not a flower? I can't believe I didn't see it immediately. You're a painting genius. Look at that brushwork."

"Shut up," I tell him.

He smiles and smiles, and looks so comfortable with me, like we share something deep. I wish he wouldn't smile. I have to make him stop.

"A man got in here. Into Sector K, I mean. Two years ago. He had a baby strapped to his chest. I can still picture it. That baby. I only saw its hand, though." I shrug. "The mind's a funny thing."

At last, he's stopped smiling. But this sudden feeling of intimacy is worse. The room is so quiet. "What happened?"

"I don't know. Guards caught him eventually, I heard. He would have been dealt with. I heard rumours afterwards, that people outside carry babies around to fatten them up, to... eat them, later."

"Like a packed lunch?" Lucas says, and snorts. "You don't believe that, do you?"

"No," I tell him. "No, I don't believe that." I can see, once more, that man holding that baby's hand, tucking it safely away.

Lucas touches the drying paint with one finger. "Of course, you've never been out there since it all went wrong, so you don't know. And you're right: the mind is a funny thing. But, trust me, we don't eat babies."

"All right."

"Not my lot, anyway." He turns away from the picture and scans the shelves.

"What are you looking for?"

"Nothing," he says. "Listen. This whole thing. You and I both know it's not going to work."

For a moment I think he's talking about us – him and me – but he continues, "There won't be an agreement. Stephan was wrong, and he's beginning to realise it. He's given the order to collect as much produce as we can and then get out of here before Blossom Farm get tired of pretending to negotiate and send in their army."

"They have an army?"

"You really don't get who you're dealing with, do you? Blossom Farm have these domes all over the world. They're rich enough to buy people, governments, whole countries. Raising an army is not going to be a problem. All it will take is a little time, and they really don't care if they lose this entire place and everyone in it, so long as they send the message that they don't negotiate with terrorists."

He spits the word out, and I finally see that it's become a meaningless word, describing nobody in this situation accurately.

"But they picked the Winery as a target," I say. "They knew it would be empty and that it's the easiest part to rebuild. It shows they're not totally—"

Lucas shakes his head. He lowers his voice even though there's nobody to overhear. "They didn't blow up the Winery. We did."

"What?"

"We blew it up. To show Blossom Farm that we're serious. Stephan thought it might make them negotiate, if they understood we have the capacity to destroy this place. And still they won't talk to us. I've been out there, holding up signs, trying to get a response. It was the final bluff, and it didn't work. So now it's time. Starting tomorrow, everyone will be asked to pick their areas clean. And then we're going to try to escape."

"You'll take all the fruit? Every bit?"

He touches my arm. "Not the plants, Mel, not the plants. It can all grow again. You'll be left in peace. Stephan can see it now – that it's not worth the effort to try to reason with these people."

"You talked him round?"

"He trusts me. And not everyone is intent on bloodshed."

"Don't say any more," I beg. He puts his hand to my old face and I'm ashamed of my tears and my wrinkles. My pouched eyes, no doubt, contain emotions it would be easy to mock.

"Are you afraid?" he says.

Yes, I'm afraid. Of what will come next, and of what I have to do.

"Don't worry," says Lucas. "One day, one harvest, and I'll be gone. Things will go back to normal."

I'm afraid of that too.

* * *

Knowing that everything will end makes time move in a different way. I go to bed and Jim isn't there. Lonnie says he's at some sort of important meeting and goes about her business in a daze, climbing into her pyjamas and settling down into their bed. She doesn't seem to miss him. In the silence, in the dark, we sleep.

In the morning, Lonnie and I go to the refectory, and Stephan explains that everything will be harvested today and moved to a safe location to protect the fruit in case of further attacks by Blossom Farm. The workers nod. I see one with a bruised face, another holding his arm in an awkward position, and the intruders are no longer sitting down. They stand against the walls, alert. The illusion of working together is so thin you could blow it away with a single exhalation. Maybe that is why we all seem to be holding our breath.

After breakfast I take Lonnie to her section and then go to mine. Gregor is at the water cooler. His hands tremble as he raises a cup to his lips. Crates on trolleys have appeared next to the plastic chairs. I steer one to Melons and look around me.

I pick everything, no matter how small or green. I pick the swollen and the shrivelled, ripening or with the promise of much growing to do. The first crate fills. The plants surround me, brushing my face as I work, tickling my neck. Just before midday, I reach the area where Mr Taylor was buried. I put my hands to the soil and tell him what I've been thinking of since my last painting.

"I think you really wanted to help that man. I think you were trying to tell me not to call security, that day, with that flick of your eyes. I think you wanted to save that baby. I don't know what happened to it."

But I do know. They did the things we don't talk about here.

They killed it. And then I'm guessing they put it under the soil too. We are workers, and assets, and finally we are fertilizer. We are stupid enough to do it all for the sake of a hot meal and a bed because we think that matters more than being a person.

I pick the nearest melon. It's a good one: large, and round, and warm. I scrabble at it with my fingers, but my nails are too short to penetrate it. It won't open for me. I take my paintbrush from behind my ear and stab the end without bristles into the melon.

The smell is divine. The juice drips down over my hand; I lick it off, and breathe in and out, in and out, in great gasps. Memories of my grandmother's garden are so strong, so vibrant. I hear the drone of bees, the weight of warm, real sunshine on the back of my neck. The things I have painted on glass are only shadows of these tastes and touches. I haven't remembered a thing correctly.

I stab the melon again and again until it makes a sucking sound and splits into ragged pieces. My hands are drenched; the liquid soaks into my sleeves. The seeds are wet and glistening in its gash. I scoop up flesh, and eat, and eat, feeling moisture in my mouth and on my cheeks. It will stain me orange and I don't care. I eat.

The dome shudders.

I put the seeds in my dungaree pockets, even though they try to slide through my fingers to find the soil. I go back to picking my melons, and I fill the crates, and listen to the strange noises that mean we have reached the end.

* * *

I work hard and fill five crates. When I'm halfway through the sixth, Lucas finds me. He looks so calm.

I walk to meet him, and he says, "You need to wipe your face."

I feel my mouth turning up at the corners, and I grin, grin like only a girl should.

He lifts his hand and smoothes his sleeve over my mouth, not gently, rubbing at the corners. "There," he says. "That will have to do."

The dome shudders again, as if it is being picked up and shaken. I hear shouts, from what seems like very far away, but I don't care.

"Are you ready?" he says.

"For what?"

"To leave with me."

I never expected this. Never. Even when I dreamed of something like this, I knew it made no sense. I can't think of what to say, what to do. When words do come they are ridiculous ones.

"I'm so old," I tell him, even though I don't feel it at that moment.

"I told you. We're going to stick together. I know how to survive out there and you know how to make things grow."

"I don't. I can't make anything grow. Apart from melons."

"You're picking one hell of a time to argue about this."

The shouts are louder. There's a new sound, too, like someone tapping out a rhythm, fast, with a high drum. Is that gunfire? I've never heard it before.

"Come to the Winery," he says. "We can get out that way. Bring some melons. I'll fetch some supplies and meet you there. We have a chance, since they're attacking from the main gate. I've come up with a way to move fast."

"You've been planning this for days."

"Since Stephan suggested this whole thing. He said to wait for someone who could get us in, and then we found Daisy. It was my responsibility to get her to trust us. But she made me trust her instead. And she told me that the only real difference between people is whether they're willing to hurt others, or try to help them." His calmness is a mask. Underneath it I glimpse – what? Pain. Fury. And then it's gone. "Listen. Stephan has ordered us to burn the place down. He wants to make some great statement to the world.

If it's not for anybody, then it's for nobody. I don't want to be part of his statement. Do you?"

"No. No, I don't."

"Great. Then I'll meet you at the Winery. Say you'll be there." He pulls me into his arms. I'm so lucky, I think, so lucky, when the world I knew is about to end and so many will die, and here I am just being lucky with my boy wrapping his arms tight around me for no reason I can understand.

"I'll be there," I say.

He steps back. "We need to get going. Give me the code."

"What?"

"The code. For the storeroom door. There's no time for us both to go. I can move more quickly alone."

I've been such an idiot. Such an idiot.

To think he could be a friend, a real friend, someone who sees past the way I got into this place, the life I've lived, and the wrinkles on my face.

This was all about the code. All of it.

I should hate him.

But he has been so kind to pretend this way, and make me believe it. We might both be painters but he has a lightness of hand that I have never possessed. One can only admire the brushwork.

"9200," I say. I repeat it, to make sure he's got it.

"Right," he says. "See you at the Winery." He takes my hand, and squeezes it. "Thank you."

Once he's gone, I feel very tired. Tired enough to sleep.

To shrivel up and be done. I lie down for a while among my melons. For a while, I think nothing will ever make me move again.

But then a woman walks into my area. The woman who sharpened her knife at my table and took my room away from me.

She's holding a petrol can; it's heavy, and bumps against her leg as she approaches my plants. That's what makes me stand. Not that it's her, but that she's brought so much petrol along to do the job.

She sees me but doesn't stop. She chooses a spot near the areas I have only just impregnated recently, delicately placing pollen on my brush and easing it inside the flowers. She unscrews the petrol can and begins to pour. The clear fluid drips from the leaves.

"Stop," I say.

"Go to the common room," she tells me, without even bothering to look at me. "That's where all your lot are meant to go. Didn't your supervisor tell you?"

"Stop." She ignores me. I try to think of anything I might say that would change her mind. "If you keep killing everything there'll be no plants left in the world."

"That's rich," she says, "coming from your lot."

I move closer to her. The smell of the petrol is strong and sharp in my nostrils. "What lot?"

"You all fucked it up and now you get to act like the keepers of the flame for some imaginary future where we're not knee deep in fucking snow." She shakes her head and then stares at me, and I see that hatred again. The unique way that the young despise the old for the things we did or didn't do frightens me like nothing else I've seen.

"So just let it all burn?" I ask her.

She frowns and puts the can down near the door. She hasn't doused many of the plants. I get it now: she'll only use a small amount in each area. Once a few plants are alight, the rest will catch easily enough. That one can of petrol could burn the entire farm. Who knows how many she's already done?

"I don't get it," she says. "Why you lot would agree to this, this hoarding, rather than try to save us all. But that's it, isn't it? Choices. You made yours."

"Did I?" I ask. I don't remember making them, exactly, so much as following the paths that were presented. And nothing ever quite seemed like my personal responsibility. Not in the way that these melons are my responsibility. Not in a way that I would bleed for.

"Look at what you left us with," she says. She reaches into her jacket pocket and pulls out a box of matches. I'm too slow and I can't think of anything more to say. She moves back from the soaked plants, strikes a match, and throws it.

They catch so quickly that the air makes a popping sound and within moments the flames are high and orange and flickering through my plants, touching them and making them twist and writhe and shrivel. Black smoke gushes upwards. My stomach does the same and my mind, oh my mind hurts so much I can't think anymore, I can't bear any more. I walk to the door and pick up the can of petrol. I was right. It is heavy. Then I go to her: this woman who thinks I should have solved all her problems before she was born.

She doesn't think me capable of such a thing, so I surprise her when I throw petrol over her. I don't know exactly what I'm expecting to happen. I'm not sure how it does, really. She turns to get away from me, and although she is not very close to the flames they jump through the air to her face and her arms and then she writhes and wriggles, just like my plants. She screams and screams and crashes through the area, and I feel my thoughts turning away from the horror of her. I put down the can and collect my trolley, making sure the door shuts behind me when I leave.

I trundle out to the reception area. Her screaming is so loud, even out here. Gregor crouches behind the water cooler. He peers out at me.

"You need to start again," I tell him. I suspect it's a thought he never quite grasped. I have to raise my voice to be heard over the screams.

Onwards, down the corridor. People run, and their terror is bothersome. I swat at them, shoo them from my path. The taste of the melon lingers.

Goodbye, corridor. Goodbye, everyone. I've done my best but now it's time to move on.

I pass the living quarters, past my old room where the glass plates lie under the bed, undiscovered. I don't stop.

Around the corner there are two men in Blossom Farm uniforms carrying guns, and they point them at me, but I put my head down and mumble to myself and keep moving.

The pretence of being a mad old lady seems to work. Who am I fooling? I am a mad old lady. I could do no harm to anyone, surely. They lower their guns. I crab along.

Behind me, I hear a burst of running feet and then the air is hot and prickly. I smell burning meat, but I don't turn around.

A man yells, "Stop!" and still I don't turn around.

Nothing hits me.

I keep going.

I keep going.

There's a dead body just before the common room. It's one of the terrorists. A woman. Why do people always look so young when they've just died? Perhaps it's in the way her face has relaxed, just as Daisy's did, and Billy's. No more cares. An expression of emptiness only the young would wear.

She leaks blood in all directions from the large tear in her abdomen, through the clothes and skin, so that tubes and coils have rushed, squeezed, and bubbled up. How did it all fit inside her to begin with?

I can't get around all the blood; I push the trolley through it and the wheels leave two red lines. Between the tracks I leave footprints of my clear red intent. I keep looking over my shoulder at them as I go on.

The noise is growing again as I approach the common room. I keep moving, promising myself I won't look up, but the flashes and the screams are impossible to ignore. I freeze, framed in the archway like an actress on a stage, and watch a war. The sofas and chairs are overturned, and the smell of burning is so strong. Drifting black smoke reveals and obscures the two sides in this war. I can't tell them apart. There are only dead bodies and glimpses of people running and crouching; how can they tell if they're trying to kill the right people? Of course, the uniform. Only the uniform makes a difference.

I see Stephan, standing tall among his followers, wearing power like a warm cloak. But it's not enough this time, it won't stop the bullets, and he crumples up like a fallen hero from a painting. Is he dead? I don't know. His magnificent control is gone, the fight begins to scatter, and spread, and turn my way.

Someone grabs my arm and pulls hard. It's Suroopa.

"Come on," she says, and tugs at me with a strength I never suspected she possessed.

"Come on, wake up wake up," she screams over another burst of gunfire, and I give in to her. But I won't leave my melons. The trolley comes too.

She takes me to the refectory, behind the serving area, where we find a huddle of familiar workers on the floor leaning against the stainless-steel cabinets. I know them all, which surprises me, as I've never thought of them much before and haven't even had a short conversation with many. But I know them, just the same.

Suroopa crouches and moves among them. I drop my trolley handle and do the same. They stare at the trolley and the melons.

"I couldn't leave them," I explain. I don't expect them to understand.

But then I see them reach into their pockets, or into the white sacks they carry. Sue has raspberries and Zena has chillies. Geoff is there cuddling a cucumber and Barry has lychees. Plums, persimmons, pomegranates, a spiky-topped pineapple. There, at the end, pressing herself into the corner is Lonnie, holding out a luminous, waxy satsuma in each hand. We had satsumas at Christmas when I was little; why has that not come to me before? I should have painted it.

The gunfire intensifies and there is shouting again. The smoke is thickening; why has the alarm system not gone off? It must not be working. Maybe the sprinklers are pouring down on our plants, keeping them safe from the flames.

When it goes quiet Suroopa says, "They burned my courgettes."

The others nod. Someone wails for a moment. I have things I could say but I don't.

"Blossom Farm will soon deal with them," Suroopa says. "Then we'll grow it all again. Things will go back to normal."

I shake my head. "No, no, it will all burn. It will cost too much to rebuild."

"No, they wouldn't—"

I move away from her. I'm not expecting her to believe me, but there seems no point in pretending we can simply wait here for everything to pass us by.

It's difficult to think in the presence of so much wealth. The leathery, crowned perfection of the pomegranates in Miriam's lap, and the warm smiles of the bunch of bright green bananas beside Poppy. It comes to me that we can't give up. And our best chance is not here, trapped in the centre of the burning biodomes.

Lonnie says, "Jim. Jim. Where's Jim?"

I think I know the answer to that question. And it gives me some sort of answer as to where we can go. If a place has already been destroyed, why would they fight over it?

"I can take you to him," I tell her. "Would you like that?"

"Jim," she says. For a moment I think she's too far gone to understand, but then she stands up and looks at me expectantly.

I say to the others, "We need to get the produce to a safe place."

"Where?" says Suroopa. She gets up too and that's enough to get them all moving.

I pick up the handle to my trolley once more and turn away from the bloody track I've left, leading them away from the common room. They trail after me. We move away from the noise of the fighting. In my mind I hold a map of these domes and how they link. If the plants are burning, the doors might have automatically shut and locked, which will give us a little time. Still, I can't risk a direct route. I wind around the edges, using the less frequented corridors, where you can almost feel the cold through the walls.

Whenever I look behind me, I'm surprised by the way they all walk, in an orderly fashion, pairs holding hands in some cases. When I was a teacher, I would have thought nothing of it. Form a crocodile, I would have said, and they would have obeyed. Another image I have failed to capture on glass, and perhaps by now my slides have melted together as the fire sweeps through the living quarters. All of it will burn: the woollen antimacassars, the cuddly toys and the jigsaws, the board games with the plastic pieces squirming in the heat.

I lead the crocodile. "One," I say. "Stick together."

We're not far from the Winery when the alarm bell finally starts to ring. It gives long blasts. I suppose Blossom Farm must have reconnected it and taken control in areas. We all know what it means. *Return to your sections. Adopt lockdown procedures.* But my section is burning.

I carry on walking and the others follow. The cold intensifies. The solar lights flicker. It must be late afternoon by now. The sun will soon set.

The Winery walls are black. The barrels are warped and charred, the green glass on the shelves has produced a smooth, melted mess of strange shapes. The smell of smoke is older here, greasier, and the snow has started claiming the ground through the hole in the outside wall, where once there was an emergency exit, forgotten by everyone but Daisy. I was right: it's getting dark already. Or maybe it's just that the sun can't shine through those huge black clouds. They block the sky, and suddenly the fear comes back to me again. Fear of the dark sky, the endless snow, and that huge expanse of freezing, dirty air, flowing over those mounds where the dead live.

Lucas will be long gone by now, miles away with the emergency kit, the tent, the solar heater, all the things he needs to survive, and I am glad.

I stop walking, and the others stop too. They look at me with such expectation, waiting to be told what happens next. All I have to do is assume that tone of voice once more, and they will obey.

But that voice doesn't come so easily anymore. I hear the crack and whine in the words when I say, "We need to wait outside."

Nobody speaks.

I set off again with my trolley, but I can hear they haven't moved.

"Outside?" calls Suroopa.

I turn back to her. "Where else is there?"

"Why outside? Why not just here?"

The answer to that won't come to me. All I say is that it seems important to stand in the snow and be outside of the domes. Perhaps I want to be near Daisy again.

"The fruits will freeze," says Sue.

"They'll be all right for a short while."

"No," says Suroopa, in sudden decision. "Let's wait here."

"Jim?" Lonnie's loud voice surprises me, from the back of the group. She pushes her way forwards. "Where's Jim?"

I point through the hole in the wall. "Out there."

She doesn't hesitate. She sets off, still clutching her two satsumas, and I go with her. We walk through that hole in the wall, as if it's the easiest thing in the world to be outside once more. My lungs constrict. It's like being clutched in a freezing fist, and squeezed, and it hurts, it hurts, but Lonnie keeps going, getting snow on her plain brown shoes, holding her satsumas before her. In only a few steps I'm shivering.

My eyes adapt to the dusk slowly. I make out the hills beyond the complex, the lines of the fence, and I look for the mounds. But they are no longer there. The snow has covered the bodies, and made a smooth, level field of them. No trace of them remains.

"Jim!" calls Lonnie. She keeps walking. Out of the shelter of the building the weather grows in confidence. It can claim us. The wheels of the trolley seize in the snow and they will no longer turn. I have to leave it behind as I chase after her.

I grab her and lead her to where I think Jim's body must be. "Here," I shout. The wind is strong, and it steals my voice.

"Jim!" she calls. She shakes free of me and strides away. It occurs to me that maybe Jim isn't here at all. Maybe he's in the biodomes somewhere, safe and warm and hoping someone is looking after his Lonnie. I go after her, but she is quick with new-found purpose and it's so very cold here; a cold that numbs, paralyses.

What am I doing? What the hell am I doing?

I sink down into the snow and close my eyes. Is this it? This final burst of guilt and pain, is that all I've been waiting for?

I want to let go. Maybe now I can let go.

I feel a light touch upon my face.

Lucas. Lucas is here, with me, and he takes his hand from my cheek and helps me to stand. We retreat back to the shelter of the building, by the hole. He shows me how he has made skis from the signs he took from my storeroom, straps them to my feet and wraps me in extra layers of material. Peering out through the hole are the others, watching these preparations.

"Why?" I ask him.

"Why what?"

"We won't survive."

"Nobody will," he agrees, and the way he says it makes me think it's not such a bad thing anymore. "The trick is in how you try."

The night is falling fast, and the crackle and roar of the domes on fire is fighting the wind for dominance. "You ready?" says Lucas, and I nod.

Suroopa calls my name: "Mel!"

She holds out one of the white plastic bags. She doesn't step through the hole, and her hand trembles as it emerges into the cold. I take the bag, and look in it.

A pomegranate. A banana. Raspberries, chillies, persimmons, plums, a cucumber, a courgette. A handful of lychees. It's like one of those old still life portraits, with the fruits filling up my eyes, belonging together in a way I haven't seen before.

"Keep them safe," she says.

It's a promise I can't make, but I understand why she asks it of me. I hold the bag tight and abandon my own melons, still in the useless trolley, to the cold. The seeds sit in my pockets, anyway.

I will have to find a new name.

Lucas and I head out through the snow, away from Blossom Farm, in a direction that leads to places I don't yet know. Our tracks will leave thin lines in the white canvas of the landscape; between us, we are making delicate brushwork.

MANY-EYED MONSTERS

When the first one emerged from my mouth it interrupted one of the rare luxurious moments of my life. I was indulging in a bit of pampering, in the textbook fashion; the kind that was meant to make other women jealous. A deep bubble bath. White wine, condensation forming on the slippery curve of the glass. Candles swaying to mood music, and the rise and fall of my breasts as I breathed in the steam. It was meant to be the perfect example of luxurious relaxation, and yet I could see clearly the valley of wrinkles, that criss-cross of aging skin between those shining globes of mine. No amount of white wine was going to take away the persistent thought that I really needed to moisturise more often, and I was getting old. Not as old as dear Aggie next door – surely I'd never be that old? – but certainly on the downward slope.

It started as a feeling of fullness. Cold wine in a hot stomach, I thought, but then the feeling moved. It became a tug, an ache, and it climbed inside me, higher, higher, until my throat was tight and sore. I sat up and put my hand to my neck, leaning over the side of the bath, caught in that fight between the desire and the disgust of sickness. And then I opened my mouth, heaved my chest, and out it popped.

A small, wrinkled bag of skin. A bag of skin with eyes.

It watched me. There were so many eyes, each with its own lid and lashes. Brown, green, hazel, grey, and one very blue one right at the top of its fleshy, circular body that resembled my own skin, although it was slick with mucus. Did the slime come from my stomach, or was it creating its own sticky substance? I don't know.

I do know it didn't repulse me. It was much like anything that the body produces. It's difficult to be really appalled by the smell of your own faeces or the chunkiness of your vomit; these things come from inside you. And so I felt – not much, actually. I poked it with my foot and then tried to scoop it up with the aim of flushing it down the toilet. The skin pouched under my fingers, and the thing shuddered. That was when I realised it had feelings.

I crouched down and made eye contact with it. I chose a pair of brown ones that happened to be close to each other.

"Hello," I said.

It rolled forward, closing each eyelid in turn as it travelled over them, and pushed itself against my right ankle.

Magnetism – that's the only way I can describe it. A force sucked it in and held it tight against me. It was warm and wet, attached to the hollow underneath my ankle bone. A hum passed through my foot and spread upwards, until a tingling sensation reached my head and left me dizzy.

The eyes that were turned in my direction all held the same expression. Love. I felt that it loved me. It was my many-eyed monster.

"You can't stay," I told it. I tried to pull it free, as gently as possible, but it wouldn't budge. I thought about taking nail scissors to it, just to trim around the edges until it let go. I even took the scissors from the medicine cabinet. What would be underneath that thick layer of skin? Blood, muscle, folds of fat. Or something else. Something not human at all.

I put the scissors back, and my eyes fell on the can of instant freezing solution that Alan used on his verrucas. It seemed like a kinder option. The applicator was a rubber tube over the nozzle; I put it as close as I could to the spot where the monster's skin met mine. Already I could feel our flesh melting together, although there was no pain. It was as if it was burrowing into me. The thought shocked me into action. I pressed the trigger.

It hurt me as much as it hurt the monster, I think – a jet of pure pain, but I held it for as long as I could. The place where our skin joined turned white, but my monster clung on, even as its eyes filled with tears.

I wiped them away with my hand.

"I'm so sorry," I said to it, and it blinked and looked at me with forgiveness.

"I just… I can't go around with you permanently attached," I told it. "I won't be able to get my shoes on. And you'll freak out Alan. Personally, I sort of like you, and I don't want to hurt you, but this isn't going to work."

It regarded me. I had the feeling I had communicated with it.

"Come on," I said, in my softest voice. "Be reasonable."

There was a faint sucking sound and the monster came free and rolled backwards on the bathroom mat.

"Thanks," I said. "I'll show you a safe place to stay."

It followed me to the bedroom, rolling along behind, and I cleared a space in the chest of drawers. It trundled into place among my winter jumpers, apparently not affected by the laws of gravity.

"Be good," I told it. It looked a little disappointed as I closed the drawer, but it did as it was told. Then I sat on the bed and looked at my ankle.

The patch I had tried to freeze throbbed, and there was a growth of thick black hair springing up from it in a circle. I ran a finger along it. It was coarse, like Alan's beard when he didn't shave for a few days over a bank holiday. It prickled when I rubbed it. It wasn't an unpleasant sensation.

I removed the towel, stood up and looked at myself naked in front of the bedroom mirror. The patch of hair was very obvious. I went back to the bathroom and shaved it as closely as I could, but it still left a dark patch. A bit of tinted moisturiser soothed the skin and covered it up nicely.

By the time Alan got back from football I felt almost back to normal. It was hard to believe there was a many-eyed monster hiding in the bedroom. Of course, I didn't say a word about it. It wasn't that I thought he would make a fuss, or think it morally repellent, or anything. I just thought it really wasn't anybody else's business. Even his. He was never interested in women's stuff anyway.

A few days later – in a cubicle in the ladies' bathroom at work – I coughed up the second one.

* * *

This one had all brown eyes, little ones, spaced quite far apart. I watched it roll up my leg and attach itself to my thigh. I wiped, pulled up my knickers, and asked it gently to come free. It was as open to persuasion as the first monster. I popped it into my handbag and examined the immediate growth of hair it had caused. At least it would be covered by my skirt for the rest of the day. I could shave the spot later, along with my ankle, which needed daily depilation. I went back to my seat and carried on with my administrative tasks, not feeling anything much. If anything, I felt calmer than before. It was as if I had expelled some unwanted feelings and now my mind was clear. I had quite a productive day, I would say.

I coughed up another one every now and again. I could feel a monster coming on, and even learned to control it until I could get to a private place. Once we went out to a pizza restaurant and I managed to eat an entire American Hot before we got home and I could expel it in the bedroom. That one was covered in half-digested orange pepperoni pieces, and didn't look amused. It insisted on attaching itself to my neck, which was a real pain to shave later.

I had twenty patches of circular hair growth – one for each monster – when I first saw another person cough one up.

It happened at the supermarket. An elderly man was pushing one of the smaller trolleys down the baked goods aisle, taking his time on his swollen legs, and as I waited for him to go past the bagels he stopped, leaned over to the side and coughed up a slimy, wrinkly little many-eyed monster.

I'd never looked at one objectively before. It was beyond disgusting. Just being near it turned my stomach. It rolled towards him and made its way up his trouser leg, and I thought of it joining with his old, mottled skin. He didn't even look down. He started walking once more, and then I realised this wasn't the first time for him. His legs weren't swollen underneath his brown corduroy trousers. The monsters were attaching themselves to him, and he was doing nothing about it.

I watched this shambling figure make its way into the refrigerated section with the sudden certainty that there was something very wrong about the monsters. It was a horrible, evil thing, this vomiting up of little bags of skin with questing eyes. The fact that I was doing it too was beyond shameful. I wanted to scrub my insides with bleach. I was determined to never, ever bring another many-eyed monster into the world.

When I got home, I went upstairs and stood in front of the chest of drawers where they all lurked. I couldn't bring myself to open it. I knew I should get rid of them all, kill them, smash them into bloody pieces of gore and goo. The only problem was the eyes. Why did they have to have eyes? Perhaps it was a defence mechanism. It made it impossible to hurt them.

I wanted to cry, but tears wouldn't come. Instead, the familiar sensation came over me: another monster was on its way. It built up and up, and would not be controlled or denied. My chest heaved, once, twice – and there it was. Number twenty-one emerged and attached itself to my left arm. It had only three eyes, all green, and long blond lashes that made it look very feminine. It was adorable.

* * *

Alan never noticed anything was wrong. I felt separate from him. I wasn't angry or annoyed with him, I just couldn't say for sure that I loved him. I don't think I loved anyone or anything anymore. The feeling was, somehow, beyond me.

"Have you seen Aggie?" he said, when we reached the first commercial break for the home makeover programme we liked to watch on Wednesday evenings. "I put her bins out for her this morning, but she hasn't wheeled them back yet."

"No," I said. "She's probably just busy." I didn't speculate on what an eighty-three-year-old widow might be busy doing. I had a lot of other things on my mind.

That was when the first advertisement for Smoothcare appeared.

Hairier than you can bear?
Soothe your woes with Smoothcare!

The screen showed your usual semi-naked perfect teenager who looked like she didn't know anything about the concept of unwanted hair. She held the device, which looked a bit like a mini vacuum cleaner, and smiled with delight. Then she placed the perfectly circular nozzle over the perfectly circular patch of black hair just below her exposed collarbone and held it there.

When she removed it the patch of hair was gone.

I looked at Alan. He was watching the screen with interest.

Patches here and patches there?
Smooth away with Smoothcare!

A suspicion began to form in my mind.

"I'm just going to the loo," I said. I tried to act casual, making myself take the stairs slowly. In the bedroom, I ignored the drawer that held my monsters and opened Alan's sock drawer instead. There they were. They all trained their eyes upon me, blinking fast in the light. There were too many to count; in fact, there weren't any socks in the drawer at all.

I heard Alan come into the bedroom behind me.

"How did you know?" he said.

I knelt down and opened my drawer. He knelt next to me. "Wow," he said. "Yours are really… cute."

My many-eyed monsters looked at him with adoration. I realised that I did still love him, but in a very different way. It wasn't a love created from boring human concepts of sex and beauty and mutual attraction – to be honest, that side of our relationship hadn't been great for years anyway. It was a love that came from looking at each other's monsters and being able to accept them.

We hugged for a long time, and laughed together. Then he broke away, and said, "Oh God. Aggie. I hope she's okay. If she's got the monsters too, she won't have a clue what to do about it."

We ran downstairs and across the road. Her living-room light was on, but when Alan rang the doorbell, nobody answered. He tried the handle; it wasn't locked. The door swung back, and he called her name. She didn't answer.

We crept into the living room.

There, by the light of the television screen, Aggie was only recognisable by her small pink mouth in a sea of long black hair. It came out of her in waves and fell around her on the armchair and over the carpet, and it climbed upwards from her head, twirling together to create a thick beanstalk-like base that stretched to the ceiling and splayed out against the roof. A particularly long, luxurious tress had snaked off to the kitchen; we didn't look at what it was doing in there. It was overwhelming, too difficult to comprehend. It was Aggie, but it was not.

"Aggie," whispered Alan.

The hair trembled, then parted in many different places on her body to reveal the many-eyed monsters. They peeked out at us with fearful, guilty stares, as if they had been caught in the act of committing a crime.

But Aggie's mouth moved, and said, "It's fine, it's fine..."

"Aggie? Hold on, we'll get them off you," I told her, having no idea how to even begin that task.

"No, no, it's fine, it's fine." The mouth smiled.

I turned to Alan.

"She seems quite... happy," he said.

It was true. She did seem happy. The smile was gentle, and soft and very believable. It was untroubled.

"Okay then," I said. "Bye, Aggie."

"It's fine," said the mouth. The hair fell back over the many-eyed monsters and lay still.

So, we went home. We sat side by side on the sofa, holding hands, and had a really good talk about what we wanted out of life. The choice seemed clear. Either buy a Smoothcare and spend more and more time depilating so that we could pass for normal, whatever that was, or face the fact that our many-eyed monsters were here to stay.

It wasn't that difficult a decision to make. We went upstairs, stripped, opened the drawers, and lay down on the bed. I didn't see the monsters roll across the carpet; I only closed my eyes and felt them come to me. They put themselves on my skin and the pull was intense, and so good. After that, there was only the feeling of being part of something so much bigger and better than I could ever be.

It came to me at some point during the transformation that I was no longer experiencing any kind of fear. Because, of course, there had been fear. Fear of where that beanstalk hair would lead me. But the monsters had eaten all my fear; in fact, they had sucked up every bad feeling I had ever felt.

I think I reached a state of what some people might call enlightenment.

Far below, Alan's body still rests next to mine, in that little house we used to call home. We grew together, our hair wrapping around us to make us a thick, springy nest from which we climbed into the sky. The roof of the old house didn't last long against our tendrils. And far up, up in the clouds, we found other tendrils. The strength we created in numbers was incredible. We built a platform up there, where the many-eyed monsters can have a roll around and a play if they feel they need to detach for a while. It's such a special place.

I don't know what will happen when we reach right up out of the sky. I don't think our monsters do either. This is a learning experience for us all. I don't really have a concept of good or bad anymore, but I think it might be safe to say I'm having a good time.

I wonder if there are still people out there using Smoothcares, trying to hide their little many-eyed monsters. I wish I could tell them that there's really nothing to worry about. It's only a little body hair, after all.

THREE LOVE LETTERS FROM
AN UNREPEATABLE GARDEN

You asked me in your last letter, my darling, to name my favourite bloom in the garden. I think it is the only flower that produces a scent I am not permitted to smell.

It is kept in a glass house, specially built for the purpose, you see. Those lucky few of us who tend to it daily must wear masks. There is a very good reason for this precaution, but it does mean that we all imagine the wondrous and famous perfume it exudes. We take turns, late at night in the communal sitting room for the gardeners employed here, offering opinions as to whether it would be more like a rose or a lily, or perhaps unlike any flower yet created.

Sometimes the urge to assuage my curiosity is strong. Even to think of the flower, growing alone in that arched construction of glass, brings on my desire. But never fear, my darling, my mind is stronger than my heart in this respect. No, not my heart – the demands of my body. It is akin to the need to taste strawberries simply because I am near them. These animalistic impulses of self-gratification must be mastered. We are not creatures of the garden, but its guardians. We must stand above it, and for it, at all times.

Imagine if the hordes descended. If the fence was battered down by the sheer weight of numbers, and they screamed and stamped across the perfect lawns, churning them to mud and picking clean the fruit trees in the orchard, ripping up the roses, all in the name of their own pleasure. They would pluck the flowers to make posies in the name of something good. *For love*, they might claim. For loftier emotions.

Except there are so many of them, of us all, and there is only one garden. It is worth more than humanity. Every emotion we feel has been replicated so many times in so many ways, that they have become meaningless.

But fear not. The fence holds them at bay, and we maintain the fences and the flowers within, and it is good.

My darling, I read back what I have written and must stress that I do not think our love (yours and mine) is cheap, or less than unique; I can imagine your face reading my foolish lines, your perfect face falling as you think I do not care. Let me explain. I am the mind and the man; I am both, but that does not mean the two get along together. I can despise love as the swamp of sensation it has become en masse, and the way many claim to be mired within it. *For love*: it means, *because I am unable to rise above its sticky, fetid depths.* Or do not wish to, more like.

But our love is not sticky, and it does not drag me down – it elevates me. It gives me wings to rise above the slime. How can this be? I do not know. I only know that just as there are many kinds of flowers in this garden, so there are many kinds of love. And our love resembles that wondrous flower under glass. I will forever keep it safe. I protect it as I protect the thought of you, cossetted and much cherished in my mind because some things are beyond precious. I cannot explain further, and do not think I have to. I have your understanding about my complexities, just as you have my devotion.

* * *

My darling,

In your reply you asked me to elucidate further on the flower kept in the glasshouse, and so I will tell you the story of how it came to be, because although I am weary I cannot sleep. The night is long and dark with only the snores of the other gardeners in the dormitory for company, but writing to you by soft candlelight makes me feel that you are close, and listening, and so I might do such a story justice with the time and care I lavish upon it, as I imagine your enjoyment of the result.

This is only a story, of course. A story of origins, which are always filled with lies. But I like to think all stories either spring from truth or lead us to truth at their end. I leave you to decide which is the case with this particular tale and, after I have written it down, I will tell you the very sad news that is keeping me from sleep tonight.

Here is the story:

There was a great sportsman. He was a boxer and he had won many belts knocking each opponent down. He was fast on his feet and with his tongue; he would taunt those he fought, for he said battles were won with words long before the fighting began. He knew this because he had survived a long and vicious war of words with the one person who should have said only kindnesses – his mother. She had repeatedly played the trick, throughout his childhood, of making herself bigger by reminding him of how small he was, and how she could make him even smaller.

He had overcome her words to grow large, and strong. He was a warrior, and a survivor – rich and whole and beloved around the world. But after each victorious fight he felt a wave of shame for the things he had said and the blows he had landed, and he sent every defeated opponent generous gifts and heartfelt apologies to try to salve his smarting conscience.

A conscience is no easy thing to placate. It would not be quiet. Eventually, the thought came to the boxer that he must be enjoying the act of destruction in some way and that he was turning into his mother. He caught glimpses of her small hands when he examined his own meaty paws as he forced them into his padded gloves. It seemed to him that when he struck out at his opponents, he did damage to them through the part of her – the mean, cruel part – that he must have inherited. The fear began to grow in him that he would one day wake as his mother, shrivelled in hate, and all the experts in the world could not persuade him otherwise.

He stopped fighting. He sat in the grand mansion he had paid for with his winnings, and he walked through his vast garden. People came to his gate, hoping to see him, to cheer him, because he was much loved by the public. But nobody entered apart from the staff, who were loyal to him and who refused to speak to anyone about his sadness, for they loved him too.

Their loyalty was such that they had a meeting in which they mooted many ideas to make the boxer happy again. The gardening staff persuaded the others that their best hope lay in the mysterious and vaunted Mrs Tea, and so they all agreed to pool their generous wages in order to employ her and bring her to the garden.

Mrs Tea was talked about reverently by gardeners, because of her gifts with flora. She could breed such beautiful flowers, strange wonders that could lighten a despondent mood or gladden a sad heart, but her flowers could not propagate. Each one was a unique yet doomed experiment. For this reason, her gift was not celebrated in a world beyond gardens, where resources were running out; duplication was demanded by big business in an age of profit and production. But gardeners know that the sweetest moment is unrepeatable. Gardeners live for each bloom and grieve each winter, never taking the rebirth of spring for granted.

So they paid for Mrs Tea to come to the boxer's garden and create the most wondrous flower of all.

It was pretty to look at – like a daisy with blueish petals and a scarlet heart – but it was the scent that made it so special, and spectacular. The scent was perfection.

Each person who sniffed it described it differently, but nevertheless found a peace they had never known before, and that peace lingered for days, months, even years. Some talked of toffee apples at the fair, and others of exotic breezes from far-off islands. Another might remember the newly washed hair of their babies, who had long since grown to adulthood.

The boxer did not describe what he smelled. He took a deep breath in, and then smiled at Mrs Tea and his gardeners, who had formed a line in front of him and the wondrous flower. They were all hoping, hoping, that he would feel succour in his soul.

And he did.

He realised instantly that he was not his mother and he was not not his mother, and either way his life was a distinct and separate organism. He realised that we are all enclosed within our own thoughts: thoughts that others can touch, but never penetrate. Our mistakes are always our own, and we can either punish or cherish ourselves with them as we see fit. All this was, for him, a revelation wrapped in something like lavender.

He thanked Mrs Tea and offered her a full-time position to transform his entire garden. She accepted and created many transient wonders, but none that equalled that first flower, which the boxer surrounded with a small arched glass pavilion in its honour.

The garden became as famous as the boxer, and he returned to the ring and pulverised many more opponents with his words and deeds. Each defeated enemy received an invitation to sniff the healing flower, and all wrongs were righted.

The boxer was happy.

But then he noticed how each sniff of the wondrous flower took its toll upon its petals. Was it his imagination? No – after a particularly nasty match his beaten opponent breathed in the scent deeply, gratefully, and the boxer watched the flower quiver and droop. A lone petal came free and floated gently down to the ground.

The boxer panicked.

Now, gardeners know that flowers cannot last forever. Boxers do not. He was not ready to let that flower go. He gave up fighting once more and passed an order that nobody would ever sniff that flower again. He scoured the world for Mrs Tea, but she could not be found. Instead, he turned to experts who could prolong its life, and under their care the flower survived for years, as did the garden. But it was thought that one sniff more would kill that wondrous yet unbreedable flower; just one sniff and its beauty would be lost from the world forever.

This is where I come in, my darling, as you know, bringing my green fingers to bear upon this marvellous place. To work here, to tend upon that flower, was an invitation I could not refuse, even though it has parted us.

I have been here for – well, how long is it? I ask you as I consider you to be the keeper of the time that has passed between us, and the holder of our mutual memories, while I fill my minutes and my mind with floral thoughts. Anyhow, in that time the boxer sickened for the scent of the flower. But even as he withered, he refused to take one more sniff. I asked him why, once, and he replied:

I would rather die before becoming responsible for removing its beauty from the world.

And that is what he did.

He died.

But now to my sad news.

Our talents have been exhausted. The most wondrous flower is also near death.

It has one petal left, and that petal droops so low. We are all agreed that it is beyond our care. Outside the fence the sick and desperate clamour to be admitted in the hope of healing. What will they do when they find out it is lost? Will they break down the gates and rampage through the place I have protected and nurtured? We are all afraid for our lives, and sick at the thought of the death of the flower.

What should I do? I wish I did not have to wait for you to reply. If only I could see that dear face and hear your wisdom. You would know what to say. Write back instantly, my darling, and impart your thoughts.

Should I come home and abandon the flower in its last moments? Should I leave the other gardeners in danger as I sneak away in the name of the love I feel for you? Or shall I die here, too, in defence of the failing flower?

* * *

Time is short; I will be brief.

In the absence of your guidance I made a decision, my darling. Why could you not write back with good speed? Perhaps the letter is en route. If so, I will never read it because I am leaving here tonight before my actions are discovered.

The mind and the man are not the same. My love for you wished to defend the flower to the last, to make you proud of me. My mind spoke, in the long nights spent awake, of other things.

There are so many people outside the fence, all in need. One final petal on the flower. Only one person could ever benefit from its miraculous scent again.

Let me tell you of that scent. I can elucidate now.

It is the faint salty tang of the calm sea at sunrise, and it is caramel poured on chocolate cake, and so many more smells mixed up together into one. It is not a single thought, or memory, or even an individual hope. It is the understanding of the complexity that makes up the simplest of beings. When we celebrate one being alone, we celebrate them all, because there is no way to encompass or explain more than the smallest moments of life. It is beyond us, as a species.

It does not matter that the wondrous flower is now dead, or that the hordes will break down the fence, and trample the garden and the gardeners to destruction. And love! I was right about love. That it is meaningless, and commonplace. There are too many of us for love to be celebrated, or even taken into account when making decisions.

And so, my darling, goodbye. I am happy, if that means anything. It means something to me, and that is all that matters. I can picture your face, your plain and trusting countenance projecting pain as you read these words. So, let me put it simply. I do not resemble that famous boxer in any way at all. I do not shy away from causing pain if I must. In fact, I find I can almost enjoy the act. As an example, I have left you twice now, haven't I?

The boxer said he would rather die than kill the flower, and he did. I would rather live, for what good is the most beautiful scent in the world if nobody can smell it?

I must go. To steal away before the others wake and venture forth with the sole purpose of maintaining my personal contentment. I will be the one person on this earth who manages that difficult feat. But this is my new mantra: the happiness of one is better than the happiness of none. And if there can be just one happy man, why should it not be me?

CORWICK GROWS

There were a number of old wooden signs that pointed the way. They could be found at crossroads, jutting from the grass verges, listing the local towns and villages on their pointing fingers. At the bottom, in small letters, one would invariably find:

CORWICK – 4 MILES

I soon realised that it was always four miles away in any given direction, and I became curious. If I followed a sign along a rural road, the adjoining high hedges and hawthorn trees soon blurred together obscuring any view of the land itself, and eventually the next crossroads would appear, with another sign leaning at a rakish angle proclaiming Corwick could be found back the other way. Four miles away, of course.

But then I found it.

* * *

Teri brings me tea in a bowl.

"Are you comfortable?" she asks me, as she checks my tubes. She is only one of the many carriers, but perhaps she is my favourite because she will talk to me, although we have little to discuss. I am as comfortable today as I was yesterday and for the years that preceded it – that is to say, comfort is not a quality that applies to my situation.

"Yes, thank you," I say. "And how are you? How are your children?"

"Oh, growing." She tips the bowl so I can drain the last drops and then moves it to between my legs. I urinate until the bowl is full once more and she takes it away. I lie still, on my cushions. There is no need to move.

Walking was once my pastime, my hobby, my joy. I loved to stamp over the South Downs, following ancient tracks and finding rare flowers – looking up to the sky and spying a freewheeling buzzard, or placing a hand on a yew tree as old as the county itself.

Yew survives for thousands of years. It is the hardiest of woods, as strong as iron, and it makes for a dense black forest. It was used by the archers at Agincourt; they shaped it to make their longbows. My father told me that. He approved of my wanderings, and stories of past deeds, of identity and English courage. He was a historian, widely read, planting his ideas in his long, heavy books. For him, history and the land were the same thing. *We come from the earth and we return to it, my boy*, he said to me, towards the end. He meant Sussex earth, of course. He specified it, in his will.

The walk from the graveyard to our house on the edge of the Downs was not a long one, but I found more steps to add to it every Sunday. I pored over local maps to identify ancient public paths that would take me on circuitous routes. When I ran out of those I took to climbing over barbed wire and blockades laid by farmers, and trampling their crops if they planted to the very edges of the fields. I once heard shouting behind me – *This is private! Private land!* And I ran, ran fast, into a nearby copse where I found metal feeders for pheasants dotted here and there, and I kicked them all over and took great pleasure in doing so. There was the raucous cackling of those brainless birds, and the swift shushing of their wings as they flew away from me. I did not see them. There are so many things in the shades of trees grown close that one does not see.

Corwick, for instance: I was blind to it until I was upon it. I was striding through a valley, the trees twisted, offering dark but welcome protection from the threatening rain. The plan was to skirt Chichester, but then I came across a sign telling me Corwick was ahead. One of the old wooden ones, of course, the letters carved upon it, standing nowhere near any path that I could see. There was no mention of miles and I soon discovered that was because it was simply around the next bend, laid out before me, waiting.

It was the remains of a farm, back then. The stone barns and outbuildings had collapsed roofs and the thatch of the main house was threadbare, pulled askew in chunks by nesting birds. The windows were dark, and the lower part of the front wall bulged outwards. I had the immediate impression that the house itself had slumped, given up. The lack of movement or animal life only confirmed it; this smallholding had long stood dormant.

I would simply have walked past and tried to find my way back to a familiar path, if a young man had not opened an upstairs window and called down to me.

"Friend or foe?" he said, cheerfully.

I had never been asked such a question before. I must admit my previous encounter with that shouting voice – *private land!* – was in my mind. I was a trespasser; only the smile of the man suggested I would be treated otherwise.

"I must have taken a wrong turn somewhere," I replied. "Could you tell me, am I near Kingley Vale?"

"You're in Corwick, and welcome. Hold there." He withdrew from the window, and I waited.

Time spent waiting is a strange time, insular, when the very functions of the body are at their most noticeable. My skin prickled in the light rain; my calf muscles ached from my long ramble; my heart was beating hard, and fast. Was I anxious? I was. I swallowed. I shifted my weight from foot to foot and rubbed my palms together.

The oak door of the farmhouse eased back with a squeak and the young man stood there dressed in white – a long apron, I realised, over unremarkable shirt and trousers. He was wiry and had long, muscular arms. "You've walked far, I'll venture," he said. "The weather's turning, too."

"It was fine when I set out this morning," I told him. The sun and the rain: safe topics for any Englishman.

"Well, it's good to see someone still roaming the old paths. We don't get visitors."

"No. It's strange," I said, "how often I've not found this place, only to come across it now by chance."

"You have been looking for it, before?"

"No. Well, no. The signs would point it out, is all."

"You saw signs?" He did not wait for me to reply; his gaze moved upwards, to the sky, and he said, "I think it's about to pour. Come in for a while and wait for it to pass, if you like."

He was right. The quality of the light had changed, casting the old farmhouse in a darker hue. A sudden squall of wind snatched at the front door but the man held it steady. "I could make tea," he said.

I took up his offer, not knowing what a rarity it was. I stepped over the threshold, and stood within Corwick for the first time.

* * *

Nature makes many rules that we all must follow. It commands us to its bidding. But, like all who control others, it may yet grow an empire that is too vast for it to oversee, and then there may be gaps, holes, secret places, through which one can escape. I believe that. I will continue to look for my own escape. One must have something to look forward to.

Corwick is a city now.

The view from the window is not one of forests and country fields anymore. Instead, there is the tight jumble of many buildings of varying heights, and I look down over all of them. The window will not open, but even through its thick glass I can hear the hum of ceaseless traffic, far below, on the streets that weave through the city like thread. Bright signs for goods give colour here and there. *You are above a shopping centre,* Teri once told me. *The farmhouse has become a skyscraper, and this is now a penthouse.* The words were unfamiliar to me. I did not ask her to explain them, or how she came to know them.

Further out I can see the shining glass and sharp angles of a business district, and further still, the curving rows of house upon house, delineated by strips of grass and the occasional tailored green patch of a park. This stretches away for as far as I can see: house after house after house. Corwick has become a monster.

I have never cared much for cities.

I visited Bristol, once, when I was young. My father was addressing a conference at the university there and took me along. It was soon after mother's death, I remember, and I was a nervous, unsettled boy, ill at home in the sounds and smells outside Temple Meads. We passed a bakery and, thinking to cheer me up I suppose, my father took me inside and bought me a concoction of cream and custard spread between fine layers of flaky pastry, cut into a rectangle, dusted with sugar.

This is the benefit of the urban life, he said. *There can be so many more choices.*

I devoured the treat. But, afterwards, on the long train journey home, it occurred to me that it had only tasted as good and lasted as long as the buns that could be bought from our local bakery. I said as much to my father, and he smiled, and shrugged, and said – *So you would choose the smaller life, my boy? But change will not be stopped and so you must find things to like about it, or be unhappy. It is an inevitability.*

I did not believe his words, then. It strikes me, now, as faintly ridiculous that I did not see how everything must grow, then shrink. My long walks in the woods should have taught me how leaves proliferate and then die back with the seasons, over and over.

Many who inhabit Corwick choose to eat cream and sugar and pastries every day, I'll wager. They grow, and the city grows. I wonder what comes next, when there is nothing left to be swallowed?

* * *

The river runs under it and through everything. Pipes transport it to homes and businesses alike in vast quantities. It flows, it gushes, even into me.

I have thought of taking out the tubes that connect my body to the river and throwing myself from the window, if only I could open it. This could be my escape, if only there was enough time to act before the arrival of the guards and carriers to stop me.

There was a time, long ago it seems, when Corwick was not yet a town, I found the courage to wrench one of the slippery tubes from my arm. I have never felt such pain as when it popped free, and I clamped my hand to the spot on my forearm where it had been fed into my skin. But blood did not flow from me. Instead, the brown liquid of the river gushed from the writhing tube, rhythmically spurting onto the floor. A great sense of ugliness overcame me. The tube heaved and bucked; it took me many tries to catch it, hold it. I put my thumb over the end and ceased the flow, and at that moment the guards arrived in great number – I had not realised how many there were! So many bodies employed in my defence. They searched my room for threats, and I was amazed at the commotion I had caused. Then the carriers came and soothed me, and reinserted the tube with gentle hands. I realised I was not alone, even though I spent nearly all of my time in solitude. I took comfort in their ministrations. I even felt gratitude. I began to understand that I was essential.

I feel less moved by that thought, nowadays.

* * *

It is evening.

Teri returns to see to my care. She proffers my drink, then collects my flow. She looks tired, older, but she serves me without hesitation.

I look down at my own body and it strikes me that I am older too. My skin has become dusky, grey, like the sky before rain (*I think it's about to pour. Come in for a while, and wait for it to pass, if you like,* said the guard, and I stepped inside. Why did I step inside? It was my role, was it not? I would have answers, and there are none, none, none) and when I shift my weight upon my cushion I feel a deep, slow ache building inside me.

"I am ageing," I tell her. "One day soon you will be done with me."

"You are my heart," she says, as if that is all the reply I should need.

"Help me to the window?" I ask. "Please?"

"Of course." She helps me up and I cross to the view, taking care not to knock my tubes.

Corwick is bright, and busy. The streets are jammed with cars and I hear impatient hoots. They want to be about their business; they are part of a mechanism they do not understand. All is well. Impatience is a sign of a thriving multiplication, and they will reach their destinations eventually.

But then I see how the limits of the city have changed. The furthest estates are shrouded in darkness where street lights should keep them aglow. And the houses there are not lit from the inside. There is no orange stream of warmth from each window, or even the blue glow of the devices they watch.

They are empty. And there is new growth approaching. The forest presses closer.

Corwick is shrinking.

I tremble. I turn to escape the sight too quickly, and Teri is there beside me, supporting me. Then others arrive, including the guards, and there is the usual commotion to return me to the cushions and check for danger. The room seems less busy than I would expect. Are there fewer guards and carriers? Are they responding with less urgency than I am used to?

"I'm fine," I tell them, as they settle me back in place. I see them exchange glances when they think I am not looking.

I know what thoughts are running through their minds, and I know what they do when they are not wrapped up in my needs. For myself, my thoughts are only of the beginning. I suppose that is to be expected.

* * *

I heard a groan as I sat in the small, rustic parlour of the old farmhouse, waiting for the man in the white apron to bring tea. Outside, the rain had turned to sleet and then to thick snowfall, which surprised me greatly; it was only the beginning of autumn and yet the flakes were congregating fast on the windowpanes and the room had turned very cold.

I did not react to that first sound, which came from directly above. I assumed an elderly relative lay in bed there. It was not my place, surely, to go to see to their needs or to interfere with the running of the house.

A second moan, louder, brought me to my feet. I heard pain within it, and so did others it seemed, for suddenly there was a parade of people in white running past the doorway and then the drumming of their boots upon the stairs.

I did not know what to do. I considered letting myself out of the house and setting off in any direction, hoping to find familiar ground once more. But it seemed impolite, and so I crossed to the bottom of the stairs and looked up to the landing.

The moaning had stopped.

"Can I be of assistance?" I called.

"Come up," I heard. "Come up." I thought it was the voice of the man who had welcomed me, so I started up the stairs, looking at the plainness of the walls, and the tall, high beams of the ceiling. Each step creaked; what a weary sound. I felt the entire structure would be happy to collapse around me.

On the landing, I caught a glimpse of white and followed it through a doorway to a room in which ten, or maybe twelve, people stood in a circle. They parted as I approached, and I found myself looking down upon a naked elderly man sprawled on a large tasselled cushion of deep red velvet. Thick tubes had been inserted into his spindly limbs. They snaked across the wooden floor to disappear into the walls. I thought they were part of his treatment, and that these people were doctors and nurses. They had a serious yet capable demeanour.

He said something, quietly. He did not seem to have the breath to make more noise, so I knelt down beside him.

"You're here," he said.

I suspected he had mistaken me for someone else, and I was reminded of my own father's death when, at the end, he had not called me his son but said, *My dear sir, my dear sir,* over and over again to me as if I was a stranger. The hospital nurse had urged me to accept it as a part of the process, and so I had replied in a similar manner, as one gentleman to another, to save him embarrassment. Now it felt kind to assume an intimacy that did not exist for the sake of one who thought otherwise.

"Yes," I said. "I'm here."

"I'm so glad. You're late, surely? I've been waiting so very long."

"I'm sorry to have taken my time."

"Oh no," he said, suddenly gaining a moment of startling vivacity. "No, you are not sorry. Not yet." Then he slumped backwards, his eyes closing, and I reached out to him – seeing my father there – to take his hand.

As one, the tubes released him, coming free with a soft, sucking sound, and a moment later I felt them plunge into my own arms and legs. I was captivated by the way they penetrated me; the sensation was strong, but not painful. I fought, I think, although I do not remember it; I hope I did. Yet my attention was fully focused on the act of integration that was taking place, and the figures in white were visible in my peripheral vision as they tidied away the remains of the old man, cut me free of my clothes, and lowered me onto the cushion.

Some time later, I became aware of Teri. She was holding my hand. I heard movement outside the window; horses and carts, perhaps. The room looked bigger and the sunlight stronger. I felt ensconced within the farm. I felt its energy and it felt mine.

"Corwick grows," she said.

LOVES OF THE LONG DEAD

There was a once a magnificent palace on the west bank of the Nile. It was known as the House of the Dazzling Sun, a fitting title for its hardened, baked-brick majesty. It belonged to a ruler of unprecedented artistic sensibility in a time of serendipitous prosperity: Amenhotep III.

To the east of the palace lay a large ceremonial lake connected to a series of canals that led back to the city of Thebes, and the demands of rulership. So it was not surprising that Amenhotep preferred his frequent visits to the House of the Dazzling Sun, where his beloved wife, concubines, and his many sons and daughters lived. He would walk in the courtyard, surrounded by the guards and gardeners, or lie back on his royal bed and enjoy the paintings of the goddess Nekhbet on his royal ceiling. Occasionally he would arrange for a feast, and call his sons and daughters to him so he could listen to their chatter. He knew the eldest ones well, particularly Akhenaten, who would one day become the new pharaoh, but the names of the younger ones often escaped him. He wouldn't have been able to name his fourteenth daughter if he walked past her in the courtyard, but their paths rarely crossed, so their lack of acquaintance worried neither of them.

It was enough to the fourteenth daughter to know that she was a princess, and that her fate was to marry the most handsome man in Egypt.

He was the son of the overseer of the northern section of the palace and she was delighted with the thought of belonging to him. Her life had always been told to her as a story, in which a little girl becomes a flower of a woman, then a rare jewel of a princess. And then, the final transformation of the tale – a wife. The next stage, in which a wife becomes one of many wives and then a mother, and then eventually an old woman, did not interest her so much. She had plans for everlasting perfection, and prayed regularly to Nekhbet for help in this department.

On the day of her wedding it seemed that Nekhbet had heeded her prayers, for the Princess woke up in a sublime state of bliss, and her favourite bodyslave told her, with tears in her Nubian eyes, that she was everything a bride should be. The day was the culmination of all her dreams, right up until the moment when she was alone with her husband for the first time and he decided to saw a knife across her throat until her blood, and her life, had spurted away to nothing.

The wrongness of this death, the inexplicability of it, aroused an intensity of feeling she had never experienced before. Rage swelled and swelled; it outgrew her body, flowed from her eyes and fingers in red hot streaks. It was stronger than death.

She grasped her rage with her stiffening fingers and it kept her tethered to the earth, even as her murderous husband dropped her body onto the bed and rubbed his hands as if to touch her had disgusted him. It was the last she saw of him.

She had been everything a princess should be and many made the mistake of thinking the gods must have blessed her, right up until her murder, which was blamed on a random beggar. But, of course, there are no such things as gods. There are only the ghosts of the displeased departed, who choose not to depart after all. These ghosts float around, eyeing the living with the severe expressions of those that have not been chosen for a team event, and then their eternal depression takes its toll, and they sink. They sink lower and lower into the ground and get caught up in the deep streams that lead to rivers, seas, and then out into the ocean. There they give themselves over to the coldest of the currents that lead to the Pit of Xenophyophores – a spiked congregation of giant unicellular creatures characterised by poisoned thought and prickly sentiment.

An amount of time later, in the darkest of darks, the Princess's ghost settled down within one xenophyophore of so many. She might have stayed there until the time for all stories had passed, if it wasn't for Doctor Chin and her giant deep-sea grabbing machine.

* * *

The xenophyophore was kept within a pressurised environment, simulating 15,750 psi, and it was the star attraction in Doctor Chin's attempt to raise funding for a further trip to the Pit of Xenophyophores, otherwise known as the Mariana Trench.

The Princess awoke. The collective sadness of the other ghosts no longer rubbed against her and at first this new emotion of loneliness permeated her torpor, rather like how music sinks into the dreams of the sleeping. Then it became insistent, and she woke, and became watchful once more. Where was her husband, her murderer? His face as he took the knife to her was as fresh as the memory of her young and beautiful body, and yet everything was intangible, unreadable. She hated. How she hated. The spikes of the xenophyophore she inhabited trembled with her righteous anger.

Through the transparent container the Princess made out a white room and a distorted face. An old woman was watching her. It was the first face she had seen in such a very long time, and there was no beauty in it. She had awoken to a world without beauty, and her time in the deep ocean had not soothed her spirit.

So, when the old woman pushed a long stick through the clear wall of her prison and into the body of her xenophyophore, she felt it as the mother of all outrages – how dare she? How DARE she? She pushed herself up through the stick, out of the tank, and into the arms of the woman. From there it was a short trip to the brain. The Princess found the frontal cortex and curled herself up like a smug parasitic worm making itself comfortable for the long haul.

Dr Chin dropped the probe, stood up straight, and looked around her laboratory with fresh eyes. It had been her home from home for the past four years and it bore the marks of her success. She was one of the stars of the Second Renaissance; her paintings of the deepest places on Earth cycled through the top left corners of the slick screens she had opened around her. She closed them all with a pinching gesture, then returned her gaze to the creature she had found. She saw it as if through fresh eyes. It was not a creature at all. It was everlasting hate.

She found she didn't want to look at it anymore.

She left a voice note on the system for her assistants before leaving the laboratory, taking a slow walk through the campus, avoiding clusters of students. The solar rail transported her to her apartment in the village. There, she took herself to bed and stayed there for hours, while the Princess took out the thoughts she found boring and replaced them with the enduring image of the face of a murderer.

* * *

"It must be the menopause," Doctor Chin said to the image of her son. He looked vibrantly well, as only the young can. He had recently moved to Karachi to be close to his new partner and he said the city was a revelation of colour. Doctor Chin suspected these were the words of his partner, who designed batik clothing adorned with mathematical puzzles, rather than his own. But she had the good sense not to say so. One does not raise a child single-handedly without becoming both a tyrant and a diplomat.

"Can't you get pills for that?" said her son.

"I'm already on pills for that," she reminded him.

"Have you had the dosage checked?"

"I don't think it's that."

"You just said it was."

"I know," she said. She felt like such a stupid child in his newly adult presence.

"Mother," he said, "are you having a thing? Do I need to come over there?"

"No, it's fine." But she was gratified he had asked, even if he didn't really mean it. "It's just this face. I keep seeing him. A man. I feel so angry towards him."

"Is it Dad's face?"

She shook her head. She could understand the question; Tan's father was the only man she did really despise, and such feelings are difficult to keep hidden from those you live with. But all her anger towards him had gone. And her love for Tan was also ebbing. The night before she had looked through her image archive and found no joy in any of those captured smiles from the past. That had been the catalyst for this call. Even with Tan's face before her she could not quite remember how she loved him. That was a terrifying feeling, and she did not want to speak of it.

* * *

The Princess worked fast. She put her ghostly fingers to the brain of Doctor Chin and worked at the definitions stuck there, one at a time. Adventurer. Biologist. Lover of traditional Shadow Play. Atheist. Vegetarian. All of these came loose and fluttered away. New definitions were put in place, taken from a personality long dead.

Royal. Beautiful. Special. A girl, a flower, a jewel, a wife. With each new word she injected her unique contempt. Why had her story ended in such a way? Should she not have been the ultimate bride?

Thoughts of Egypt also pervaded, and it wasn't long before Doctor Chin began to formalise these thoughts into images. She felt she knew the House of the Dazzling Sun better than her own apartment, its scenes of reeds and crocodiles painted on the walls, and geometric designs adorned the ceilings. The lake sparkled bright blue through the hot, hot days.

Doctor Chin began to draw them. She drew picture after picture of this ancient glory, and she drew the most handsome face of the murderous husband. Eventually, an idea came to her. She shared the pictures with her online followers, all four million of them, and they told her: that looks like Ancient Egypt. The Second Renaissance was a great time for finding well-educated, helpful people in every subject.

Research led to Amenhotep III and the west bank of the Nile. The Princess inside Doctor Chin recognised these things with a strange delight, but she was most offended to find no mention of her name or her murder in any of the documents. She had been written out of her own history. It came to her that, if she could return to the scene of the crime, she might find some answers. Surely it would be impossible to stand in the very place where such a terrible thing happened and not feel the echo of it down through the centuries?

She began to pour her idea into Doctor Chin's mind. It didn't take long to have the desired effect.

* * *

"What is the purpose of your visit?" asked the border guard with a palpable degree of suspicion.

Doctor Chin did not answer. Princesses did not explain themselves to lowly border guards.

But, after a long period of waiting in the airport security cell block, the Princess decided that exceptions could be made in this strange modern age, and Doctor Chin talked her way into a visa on the understanding that she had lost her voice but was all better now and wanted to check out Egypt in the hope that it would offer inspiration for a new series of scientific endeavours.

A car and a translator were offered and accepted, and Doctor Chin instructed the driver to take them to Malkata, where the ancient palace had once stood.

Eventually, she arrived, and emerged from the car, resplendent in a ball gown (the only dress that had appealed to the Princess from the entirety of the Doctor's wardrobe) and tiara. She walked around the remains for miles, turning this way and that as if in the grip of the strongest currents of the sea, and nothing pleased her eyes. Dirt and noise, that's all there was. A few traces of the great wall paintings remained, and the Princess could almost feel herself returning to life as she stared at them, but it was not enough. Besides, there were the signs of modern industry everywhere – the locals traded and cajoled, while the tourists snapped their cameras and strolled. The past had become a business that she did not understand.

As Doctor Chin walked on, the Princess began to feel a grudging respect for the busy industry of modern humanity. She could not know that, no matter how much she fiddled with the brain, some aspects of the Doctor's personality could not be changed. Character does not simply sit within a mind. It also sinks into the cells, the blood and the bone, and it can never be entirely destroyed. A process of osmosis was underway; the immutable core of Doctor Chin – imagination, interest, innovation – was sinking into the Princess and changing, changing, changing her in return.

It took only a few hours in Malkata for the process to become irreversible. Doctor Chin was the Princess as much as the Princess was Doctor Chin. She wanted love and flowers and fountains, and to see and shape the future of humanity, and to be treated like royalty and to be treated the same as everyone else. She wanted golden clothes, lapis lazuli adornments, and her lab coat. She wanted to be swept away on a grand adventure in which she could take samples, and she very much wanted to go home, wherever that was. Unsurprisingly, she had a headache.

The Princess had a lot of experience in denying her

instincts. She had, after all, been attempting to live a storybook life at one point. She refused to let go of the one thing that might have – with its disappearance – given her peace. No matter what anyone said or did, she had been murdered. The case was not closed. Even though Doctor Chin's pragmatism had infected her to the point where she could see the futility of her quest for revenge, she clung to it.

If the murderer could not be made to pay then somebody must pay in his place. A man. A man must suffer in the name of all men. It occurred to her for the first time, from a fresh scientific perspective, that her father had not saved her. Wasn't his greatness meant to protect her like a curving fan in the heat? What had he been thinking, to betroth her to a murderer? And why had her Nubian bodyslave not been around to help in her moment of dire need? Her life had not been worthy of a storybook after all, but this wasn't her fault. The supporting characters had never been up to the job.

Doctor Chin turned a corner and there it was – the place where a royal bedroom had once contained a princess and her husband on that fateful wedding night. It was nothing more than a crumbling wall. It spoke of nothing. No mark of the crime existed. She would never know why he killed her.

Crouched at the base of the wall was an evocative figure: a beggar. Beggars are universal. They have a timeless quality; desperation always comes with a certain kind of look, and smell.

"Please," said the beggar. "Please." He stretched out his hands. He looked a little like a long-dead murderer and a little like an ex-husband. Doctor Chin and the Princess looked around. It was a spot far from the usual tourist trail, and it was the hottest part of the day. They delicately lifted the hem of the ball dress and kicked him. He tried to move away, but his legs did not appear to work well, and after a few kicks he stopped trying and curled up tight on his side. They aimed for his face and soon it was a mess of red and hardly looked like a man at all. At that point they put their hands around his throat. It was thin and greasy and the veins could be felt under their fingers.

Doctor Chin and the Princess killed the beggar.

Then they wiped their hands and returned to the waiting car.

* * *

The xenophyophore sat in the pressurised chamber, being its spiky self. Doctor Chin had eyes for it alone. She ignored the questions of her assistants until they obeyed her unusually aristocratic request to be left in peace.

She prepared the probe in silence and approached the chamber.

"I promise," she said, to herself. "I promise."

The probe slid into the body of the xenophyophore, and Doctor Chin felt a tearing of her mind as the Princess ripped free and made her way out of the brain, down the arm, through the probe, and back to that black ball from the depths.

Then there were no more thoughts of revenge or romance. There was only the sensation of being Doctor Chin.

She removed the probe and put her face against the chamber. The xenophyophore looked the same but within it a princess slept. She would be returned to the deepest place on Earth and left there forever more, for as the Princess pointed out, she could neither forgive nor forget. She was simply not cut out for modern life. Every man she saw she wanted to either conquer or kill, and there really was nothing else suitable in the wardrobe to wear.

"Goodbye," Doctor Chin whispered.

She looked around the laboratory. She had the feeling something was missing. No excitement permeated her at the thought of her research or her paintings. The Second Renaissance meant nothing to her anymore.

In desperation she pinched open a screen and called her son.

"Where have you been?" he said. "I left messages."

"Sorry. I had a lot to think about."

They talked for a while, and she was horrified to discover she still felt nothing for him. Had the Princess taken too much back with her to the xenophyophore? Or was it the memory of the beggar's last breaths that forced every other emotion from her head?

The call ended. Doctor Chin closed the screen. She stared into the chamber and examined the giant one-celled creature within. Her head was free of the dreams of the long dead, and instead there was – what? A blank slate? The responsibility to be clean of all definitions of revenge, desire, and storybook fate overwhelmed her.

"Who am I?" she asked it. "Who am I now?"

REFLECTION, REFRACTION, DISPERSION

The players have stopped playing.

Fear spreads through the stadium but it does not touch her, not directly. Eliza feels it as a presence that rains down upon the adults that surround her. They are momentarily frozen by it as it soaks into them. Then they unglue, melt, crouch, lie flat. Her father pulls her down to a space between seats, and jostles her into a gap before curving his body over hers.

Nobody runs. This is not panic.

"Don't look up," he says. "Don't look up don't look up." She wonders if he is talking to her. He's heavy. She squirms to the sound of so many others breathing, sobbing. He shifts his weight, and she turns her body, craning her neck.

She looks up.

* * *

My meal has been sitting before me, the lone object on my corner table, for five minutes and it's still too hot to eat.

It does smell good though, cheesy and cheerful, and I'm happy with that. Nothing terrifying could ever happen with a reheated lasagne in the room, could it? I am a mess of ridiculous beliefs that I have scraped up from the shreds of my normality. Why should I be falling apart, a little more every day, at the age of twenty-seven? Seeing the Effect that day did not bother me for years. But it bothers me now.

The chain pub is a popular spot, filing up quickly around me. Families mostly, but a group arrives and they squeeze around the table next to mine. "Can I take this chair?" says a voice, and I tell him yes vaguely, taking in his shape only in my peripheral vision. He moves the chair around to face his group and they begin their conversation.

"Shall we get started by going around the table?" says a woman, and she tells them that her name is Suzanne, and her daughter was diagnosed three years ago and it's an ongoing battle. Next, Matt tells everyone about his mother's relapse. Then Nicola says that there's not much time left for her husband and she's coping, really, she is coping but she thinks a lot about what happens when the time comes. Will he become one of the Rainbow Effect?

"It's not usually cancer," a man reassures Nicola. "It's violent deaths. I read that online."

"You can't believe everything you read," says an older woman, with sharp disapproval. "Or see."

"You don't believe the videos?" says Nicola. "You don't believe anything you haven't seen for yourself? What about the Atlanta sighting, or the—"

"This group is about support, not conjecture," says Suzanne. Something in her voice – the annoyance and the good manners vying for supremacy – makes me laugh, out loud, and then I try to turn that into a cough, but it's too late. I'm the focus of their attention for a brief moment. I get up, leave the meal, and squeeze past their chairs to get myself free of them, free of their dying relatives and their fear of what might happen next.

Why is it always about fear?

* * *

People collect. I don't mean that they gather objects; I'm saying that they are, themselves, gathered. They flock together as an act of identification: humanity, standing or sitting, sharing a mutual presence, creating their own signature scent. Nothing smells quite like a room full of people. The worst are occasions that come with the expectation of happiness. Weddings and christenings. I spend the entire service with my eyes turned up to the ceiling in case the worst happens, trying not to breathe through my nose.

Once, for my cousin's birthday bash in the year after the Cardiff Effect, my father arrived wearing a neck brace and told everyone he'd been in a car accident and was suffering from whiplash. He couldn't have moved his neck to look upwards at the ceiling if he'd wanted to.

He didn't fool me for a moment.

Now he's given up attending those sorts of events. He says the open air suits him better and spends his time between talking engagements walking for miles, sitting on benches outside tea rooms in national parks, even in the dead of winter. The sky has never betrayed him.

I picture him outside. I lie in bed in my room in the Holiday Inn and look up at the plain white ceiling, and I imagine him stomping around Snowdonia. We can see many things in blank spaces.

The hotel is far from silent. People come and go along the corridor. Next door, someone is watching television. It sounds like a news channel, and I will myself not to pay attention. I need to sleep. I have a busy day at the convention tomorrow. I'm meeting with three different cyber-security suppliers, trying out their wares, finding a reason to choose one over the other for my company. I said to Maggie that I didn't want to attend, and she sympathised, then phrased my attendance in terms of having a job or not having one.

My father stomps over the dales of the ceiling. No dead people will make an appearance in this short and informative film brought to you by the imagination of Eliza Raley.

* * *

A large-screen television, placed high on the wall, dominates the breakfast area. Other guests troop underneath it as they line up for the silver domes that house the buffet items, their eyes glancing to the screen as the headline loops:

Rainbow Effect reported in Cairo stadium

I pick at the bacon on my plate and watch the shaking image taken by a phone. The sound is turned off and I'm glad.

The colours. I remember them. That splay of lights, as if through a prism, splashed across that huge expanse of ceiling, and then arcing down in the curved bands of a rainbow; the effect ends – or does it start? – in mid-air but then seems to hug to the blankness of the ceiling – no, I'm not able to describe it, not even to myself. Nobody is, and the image doesn't hold steady. It's a scattering of thoughts and vision. The camera tries and fails to capture its beauty. It chooses one small part and zooms in as close as it can to show the faces, mouths open, eyes open, not blinking. Their cheeks press against each other; they are packed in tight. Blues, reds, yellows. Every colour.

Authorities working on identification

The writing on the screen scrolls on.

Then zooming out, the entire surface of the ceiling of the Cairo stadium is revealed again. So many faces. Their mouths, their stares. I know the heads aren't flat, although when they are filmed they appear so. They have texture, dimensions. They are not faded, or misty. The television can't portray it accurately; something is lost in transition.

What do the colours mean? Much discussion has settled

on that, for want of answers. If fifteen heads are yellow and only six are blue then our brains leap into gear and make judgements. Judgements become easier to make with less evidence, and there's really no proof here of anything at all.

In the absence of experts, anyone will do. And that description includes my father, who now appears on-screen, and begins to talk.

Did he become qualified in this subject simply because he was one of the people who saw it first? He hasn't studied it. He has few qualifications, and before this had no experience in dealing with the media, but born of the mystifying en masse splay of the dead was his own self-confidence to handle the world's questions.

Recent poll shows 58% of respondents believe
Rainbow Effect is genuine post-life event.

This scrolls underneath him as he talks. He's in the study, at home, with the bookcase arranged just so behind him. His face shines from the screen. I really think he doesn't understand the dangers inherent in this conversation. Nearly everyone tiptoes around any religious connotation, and those who are mad enough to address the issue are soon ripped to shreds from all sides. What does my father think about this? He manages to never quite say. It's an impressive balancing act, but surely everyone can see what he thinks. It's even more obvious with no sound.

Or maybe nobody can see that but me. It's a question of distance.

How can he transmit such happiness about the Effect when he can't even face a ceiling? We're all complicated beings but he is an unfathomable contradiction, which is why I've been finding reasons not to phone or visit anymore. I would prefer him to be solid, in some way. In any way.

His segment finishes and the picture returns to the captured moment at the Cairo stadium. The Effect is long gone, now. It only ever lasts for a minute at most and there's never been an incident recorded in the same place twice, but still my instinct shouts at me to get up, to leave the hotel, to travel as far as it takes and when the time is right to look up, to look up and see—

I look down. The bacon on my plate has congealed to a pink and white curl. Even that reminds me of the Effect.

* * *

So many famous ceilings are decorated. They are their own magnificent spectacle. The Effect never occurs over the Sistine Chapel, or the Strahov Monastery. Unbroken space is what it craves, like the vast curves of superdomes, and it has now been seen in four of the five largest covered stadiums in the world.

I witnessed the very first. We were at the Principality Stadium in Cardiff. The other stadiums are all in the United States: Arlington, New Orleans, Houston and Atlanta.

Houston is the odd one out on this list; there's been no recorded effect there. There have been many other events in different locations, of course, covering vast undecorated ceilings in Germany, Japan, Brazil and South Korea to name but a few. And there's nothing to say that an Effect will happen at Houston at any time soon, or indeed ever.

I shouldn't have worked this out. I shouldn't be left alone with a laptop and the desire to feel like I've ferreted out an answer from thin air.

"Are you ready?" says Maggie, as she passes my desk on the way to her office and I call after her, "I'll be right there." I follow company policy and lock my screen. The screensaver is a photograph of my mother that I've taken from one of my social media accounts. I scanned this one in a few weeks after she died. I was eleven, but she'd been ill for a long time and my father and I shared a sense of relief, I think, at the end, to think of her pain as finite.

After, I went through a phase of finding every photo I could of her. I wanted to put the sight of her everywhere. I still do. The one on display on my locked screen was taken before I was born; she was about the age I am now, I suspect. She had already met my father, but he's not in this shot. Wait – he is in it, just. The side of his face is just visible on the far left and his thick brown hair is jutting out, refusing to lie flat around his ear. I remember now – I only scanned in the parts of the photos that contained her. I wonder if that hurt his feelings, at the time. He never said anything and it's never occurred to me to ask.

"Eliza!" Maggie calls from the doorway of her office, and I get up and follow her voice.

* * *

After careful evaluation I've decided that we should purchase the five-year plan from a respected security firm, who aren't the cheapest but aren't the most expensive option either. I show Maggie the charts and spreadsheets I've compiled on performance, response times and other factors.

"I'll take all that into account," she says, nodding.

I wonder what that means. "The quotes are only good for the rest of this month," I remind her. "After that we'll have to re-evaluate if we decide to go ahead with them. This is a special rate I negotiated at the convention."

"Yep." She closes the notepad she's been doodling on throughout.

"Any feedback you can give me to pass back to them?" I ask.

"I don't…" She leans forward and her hair, in a neat bob, frames her face. I can see a thin line of white running from her forehead to her crown where her dye is growing out. "Between you and me, I don't have a great feeling about it."

"About what?"

"The deal."

It would be easy to dislike her on the basis of this arbitrary statement, but instead I feel the curious encroachment of pity. Is that what it comes down to, even now, in the age of zeros and ones? A bad feeling undoes all evidence.

"Listen," she says. "On a different subject, can I just say that we've received an incident report regarding your mobiles."

"My mobile?"

"The things over your desk. Someone collided with them and got their hair caught up. The person in question had to ask for scissors to be fetched in order to be cut free." Maggie is watching me closely. I'm meant to be making a certain sort of face. I can feel myself not making it. "Can you possibly take down the mobiles?" she says.

"They've been up there for years," I say. Since before Maggie became my boss, in fact. I pitched it to my previous manager as a way to brighten up the place – *break up that expanse of white tiles overhead* – and he loved the idea. I feel like fighting for that long-spent enthusiasm for one of my ideas. "I'd rather not."

And so the usual conversation begins, where I'm sympathised with until it erodes my objection.

"Do you think you're really getting the best out of being here?" asks Maggie, and I tell her no, no I don't think I am, and my next stop is human resources before I can take back the words that make me a solvable problem.

* * *

She's right. I'm not getting the best out of being there, whatever the best means, but it's not new. Still, the notion of the tangled hair upsets me more than I thought it could. Somebody was standing over my desk when I wasn't there.

Doing what? Looking at the photograph of my mother, maybe. Putting their face close to hers.

It's good that I'm taking a break from that place. It'll give me time to get used to the idea of sitting under that particular ceiling, with nothing above me to break up the space.

A team of scientists from the University of California have confirmed that their recent study shows 'no human interference' in the Rainbow Effect. That's what the news tells me this morning as I sit on the sofa in my pyjamas. It's strange to watch it with the sound on for a change.

"The team studied footage, visited locations, and interviewed over three hundred eyewitnesses—"

I don't recall being asked. I'm sure I could have said some rational things about it in my calm, clear voice.

I realise I'm waiting for my father to turn up on-screen, but the time ticks on and he doesn't make an appearance. Instead, a different witness has been chosen and invited to the studio. She's an older woman, with long earrings and cropped hair, and hard-earned enthusiasm scored through her. She talks in strident terms of 'miraculous events' and 'gifts of understanding'.

"Perhaps these spirits, these passed-over people, want to share a final message with us," she says. "That's what I like to believe. Many people report fear when they see the Effect, but I have to say I found it an uplifting experience. It showed me something real."

"What's that?" asks the interviewer.

"I couldn't put it into words, exactly," says the woman.

"Then let me ask you – why now?"

The woman smiles. "Would we have paid attention before?" she says. "Would we have needed to?"

But the faces did not speak. They looked calm to me, and although they were far above, I felt certain they were not trying to communicate with me. So many of them, close together, floating in colour, but they were not a group. Each one looked alone. As alone as it was possible to be.

I reached up and my father grabbed my arm and pinned it back down, underneath him.

The news keeps on going but there is only the report for them to talk about; there hasn't been an actual event in over a week.

I phone my father for the first time in months. He doesn't answer.

* * *

Her father gets to his feet and pulls her up. She risks a glance skywards, wondering if he'll tell her off, but he says nothing and the faces are gone. The wave of fear is receding. People murmur. The sound is reassuring.

The players are still on the pitch, but there's no sign of the game resuming.

"Was it a projection?" says the man in the row behind. "It scared the shit out of me," and her father says, "I don't know, mate," in a tone that holds a note of disapproval. The man says, "Sorry, mate, just a bit shaken up. You all right, darling?"

Eliza realises the man is addressing her. She nods. She waits for everyone to get their act together and go on as adults should, but it's taking longer and longer and that is when the fear hits her. Perhaps things will never go back to normal, not quite, and there never was a normal. Or this is normal, now that her mother is gone. Is that why everyone is afraid? She starts to tremble.

"You all right?" parrots her father. He puts his arms around her.

"I think it was a magic trick, or a stunt or something," the woman in front is saying. "Optical illusion," says the man next to her. People continue to murmur.

Eventually, the players leave the pitch and the fans file out, and a few days later there's an article in the local paper about the cancelled match. It takes over a month before national news picks it up and traces down the faces via photographs taken, at Cardiff and at the two Effects that have followed.

* * *

I've booked a seat at every event happening at the Houston Astrodome for the next two weeks. That's the length of my holiday. I've always wanted to see Texas, I tell myself. A concert. An American football game or two. And the dome is a magnificent sight, filled and thriving as the game begins.

I wish I could get caught up in the excitement, but instead I find myself wondering how many times the Rainbow Effect has happened without anyone being present to witness it;

could it have already graced the long span of this roof? It's a philosophical question in disguise – the tree that falls in the forest. The vision that appears in blackness without any living face turned up to meet it. No reflection or reaction taking place.

I think it needs an audience. That makes no sense, but I believe it.

Around me, the match is happening to the watchers, for the watchers. The clock ticks down. The man on my right has been chewing on an enormous hot dog, his elbow permanently bent to keep his ketchup and onions in place. The smell of it is incredible, mixed with the sheer noise, the size, the momentum of this game. The enthusiasm finally gets to me. I feel it. There's so little time left. The ball is passed, then thrown; it arcs high and it is caught and carried far and fast to the end zone. Touchdown. The man next to me flings out his arms, losing his hot dog as it flies up, separating into roll, sausage, onions, sauce – he is cheering so hard he hasn't even noticed and at that moment, at that moment, I have to look up further, past the sound, past the game, to the roof itself because it's happening, it's happening now.

No.

No, there's nothing there. The sound rebounds. The crowd cheers. The game ends. The man next to me is apologising to the boy behind him who got sauce all over his baseball cap, but they're both smiling. Their team won.

* * *

Eliza thinks of how to ask him why they've stopped going to the matches, but every time she starts to phrase it in her mind it becomes about something other than rugby. *Since Mum died* keeps slipping under her defences, and if it can disarm her then it'll do worse to her father, so she stops trying.

It's only when a new Rainbow Effect is reported on the television – the fifth, as far as she knows, if Cardiff was the first – that he starts to talk to her about it. For the first few minutes she is elated, waiting for her turn to speak and wondering what will come out of her mouth first, but then she realises that he's not really talking to her. She just happens to be the audience for the monologue in which he documents his own version of events. He goes back over a list of the faces he saw, describing each one in detail. He says, "Six thousand three hundred and sixteen people die every hour, on average. Six thousand two hundred and five faces appear in the average Rainbow Effect, so far. These people are all from the same hour. Dying in the same hour."

She wants to tell him that an average of five examples is no average at all, but instead she listens, and listens, and eventually her brain switches off until she realises she's thinking about something else entirely. When he draws breath she offers to make him a cup of tea, and leaves the room before he answers.

* * *

"Dad?"

The screen has a moment of blackness, and then his familiar face appears on Skype. "Hello," he says. "Hello!"

"Hi Dad."

"Are you all right?"

"I'm good." The circle of light thrown by the bedside lamp gives a soft intimacy to the hotel room. I am leaning back, propped up on pillows, with the laptop on my knees. He, in contrast, is in bright light, in his study. Exactly where he'd be sitting if this was an interview for a news channel, but at least he is unshaven and his hair is a mess, still sticking out over his ears. He's not polished. "I just wanted to see how things are with you."

"Fine. I'm—well, I'm tired, actually. I've been busy."

"Me too," I tell him. We smile at each other.

"You look well," he says.

"I keep meaning to come see you."

He shrugs. "You're seeing me now. It's a good start. Come for Christmas."

"Yeah, I'll come down around Christmas."

It's the end of my Texas holiday and there's been no Effect anywhere in the world for the past three weeks now. If they've stopped happening, I don't know what that means. None of us do. I want to tell him that I came here thinking I'd see his face. I'd look up and there would be the Rainbow Effect telling me that he was gone from me. That's another thing I'll never understand, but it didn't happen and now I have to accept that it was all in my head and perhaps it's time to grow up, just a little more.

"Actually, Eli, I'm really exhausted. Could we do this tomorrow, maybe?"

"I can't tomorrow, I'll be on a flight all day, but the day after…"

"You're going somewhere?"

"Coming back. I've been on holiday in the States."

He focuses more intently upon me. "Whereabouts?"

"Texas. Houston."

He pauses. Then he says, "You've been at the Astrodrome?"

"Yeah, I mean… yeah, I went there a few times."

His laugh is wonderful. I can't remember the last time I heard it. It's deep and genuine and his face is filled with delight. "Me too. I've literally just got back. I was out there for a month. I went to every bloody game, every event. Seriously? You're seriously in Houston?"

"I'm in my hotel right now. You were here?"

"Were you at the Rams versus the Saints, day before yesterday? I was in the west section."

"I was east!"

"What did you think? Of the game?"

"Not as good as rugby," I tell him, and he laughs even more.

"I bet you spent the entire time looking up," he says. "That's why you were there, right? Same as me. You worked it out too."

"There haven't been any Effects."

"Not for a while, no." He coughs, and the tiredness seeps back into his face. "What were you looking for? In the Effect?"

I think about it for a while. I can't tell him. "I don't know."

"Well," he says. "I think that's what I was looking for too."

We say goodnight and I promise to visit sooner, before Christmas. As soon as I get home. Once he has hung up I take the laptop from my knees and lie down on the bed, in my small circle of light. We were in the same place and didn't know it. I wonder if I would have seen him, across all that space and so many people, if I hadn't been so busy looking up.

FARLEYTON

The Guard

The ticketless people, waiting in their long, long queues, make comments about how far they've travelled and how long it's taken, and then look at me as if that should mean something. Sometimes they try to bribe me, but the official line is that all of us guards are immune to bribery.

Am I immune to bribery? Well. It's true that I don't like cake much and I've never been one for jewellery. Money comes and goes, as do affections and promises. A bag of butterscotch – now, catch me in the right mood and I might consider a bag of butterscotch, but nobody ever does offer me butterscotch or catch me in the right mood. I am a person, under this suit, even if nobody can find me in here.

Butterscotch reminds me of my grandmother. I bet everyone says that. My grandmother told me the story that led to me taking this job, guarding the gates of Farleyton:

At first there was a man who undertook a journey.
To clarify, my darling:

At first there was a man who stood still, and a journey came to him, in the form of a god. The god brought hardship – a cold wind, an empty stomach – and the man said: This must be a test.

So began a long and difficult relationship, where the man moved to please the god, and tried to guess what form that pleasure took. What placates the makers of pains and puzzles? Devotion, perhaps, or sacrifice. After making many guesses the man gave up, and decided to journey forth to find the god and ask directly: What is it you want from me?

He searched until there was nowhere left to look, and then he began to ask himself if there was a test at all. Thinking up that question disturbed him more than the arrival of the answer.

Because an answer did arrive.

Then I would ask her, "So what is the answer?"

She said, "Farleyton, my darling."

* * *

The Travel Agent

Ahem—

After passing through the great gate you may rest at the lion's head fountain, that proud mane in marble, that mouth that pours forth the purest of waters. Once rested, why not step amid the tulip fields? The tulips are the flowers of a most reverent design for the simplicity of the petals and the straight green fuse of the body. There are paths between the fields which are delineated by colour, a parallel to the span of the rainbow overhead, such order, such beauty.

What are you thinking?

Yes, sir, of course it rains in Farleyton sometimes. Forgive me, but how could there be a lion's head fountain and tulip fields if it didn't?

No, there's no need to worry about waterproofs or an umbrella. It won't be raining when you get there, of course. Pack light is our recommendation. Everything you need is there. I can show you our deposit scheme, sir, just as soon as I've seen your bank statements for the past five years and a written letter from your employer. Do you have those handy, at all?

* * *

The Saver

"It's the most visited place in the world," she said. "Which actually makes me not want to go. But also, to go. To see what I'm missing out on. I'm torn."

"You saved up enough, though?" said her friend, at the next desk. Well, acquaintance, really.

She hesitated, not wanting to talk about money, and then said, "Have you been?"

Her friend shrugged, cheerfully. "I can't afford it."

"Not even a day trip?"

"If you can afford a day trip, I'd keep quiet about it. There are all sorts of unscrupulous people out there."

She put her head down and went back to work. That night, she lay in bed next to her husband and thought she heard people outside the door. She spent some of the carefully saved money on a security camera instead.

*   *   *

The Goodbye Note

You are the king of untouchability. Well, not this time. This time you get to feel it, feel it all, and you'll have to sing the bedtime song and do the picking up and putting away and answering of questions, and making the packed lunches while I'm gone. Don't give them cheap ham – it has nitrates. And don't listen when they say they don't eat granary bread – they will if there's no option. The documents are in the fireproof box under the bed, and when you inform the authorities you can tell them you are to blame for it all, for letting it all slide off you for so many years. You're slick, the problems just don't stick to you, do they? They never have.

This one will. The problem of telling everyone what happened. Of getting along day by day while knowing I've used the money to get into Farleyton.

And you may think that's the point of my leaving – to make you suffer. But that's not it at all. It's bigger than that. See if you can get this into your head:

A pamphlet came through the door. You probably don't even remember it. The pamphlet said that society was broken, all the way from the top to the bottom, and that is why we suffer. Not in that general way, not the collective suffering picture we get in our heads of some place where babies are starving and some old pop song is playing over black-and-white footage. Why *we* suffer. Why *we* can't be happy. You and me. Because *we* won't admit that everything is broken. How can you mend it if you refuse to see the cracks?

I started to try to talk to you about it, and you said things like, *You don't know how good you've got it*, and, *Maybe you should see the doctor if you're depressed and get some pills, I don't mind making an appointment for you.* Because you didn't want to change. You put that first pamphlet in the bin.

You like it broken. You like me broken.

I don't blame you, but I do hate you for it.

The latest pamphlet talked about starting again in a better place. Farleyton. It had pictures and quoted people who live there, talking about fresh air and greenery and playparks and old-fashioned jobs. I sent off for an advance ticket from the address mentioned on the back, and by the time you read this I will already be on my way. I look forward to the day when I'm set up and the kids can come visit. You won't be able to deny it then, when you see them happy. This thing isn't even about me or you. It's about them.

I've left one of the pamphlets with this letter. No doubt you'll throw it away, too, but at least I can honestly say I tried. It breaks my heart to leave them, but it's to find a better way.

* * *

The Walkers

After a while the soles of our feet hardened to leather and nothing could get through, not even shards of glass from the broken windows in the emptied cities: emptied but for the streams of us, the survivors. We trickle and weave down the alleyways. We search for the sea.

There is a map that gets passed between us, and we have collected enough for a ship, we think. We pooled our treasures and take it in turns to carry them. When we reach the shore and negotiations begin, perhaps our solidarity will melt away and we will become him, and her, and them, with values placed upon each individual. But for now we are all valueless, and priceless. Our only worth is in our undeniable number when the camera crews fly in their helicopters overhead.

This – I think as I walk and I remember the rows of students outside the university building, shouting for change and cheering when it came in the form of the removal of choice – this is the only real community I have ever experienced. For this reason, I am glad I chose to make this journey. Not to reach Farleyton – which I suspect is a myth, because everything that is said, everything I hear, now lacks a feeling of truth – but to have walked with others through this dead land and know we are seeing the same thing.

* * *

The Workers

– They need people to work underneath the machinery. People who can speak their language.

– I swear, it's not good. I have a friend, they went in, they didn't come out.

– But the beds. A place to sleep. Even a little money. No papers needed, I heard. It wouldn't matter about my, you know, my condition. All welcome, as long as you can understand and you work.

– They work you to nothing and then they throw you away.

– How is that worse? Here, I have no work and I am already thrown away. I want to be useful. And I'm smart; I can learn how to do the controls of one of the big machines or maybe even be an entertainer or a guard and wear a suit. I can juggle, did you know that?

– Big dreams, huh?

– Better than no dreams at all.

– You think I don't hate living here? In the shadow of Farleyton? We can't even see the sun, these walls are so high.

– No, that's the pollution. From the machinery. The air filters make it good inside the walls and spit out the bad. That's why we'll be better in.

– If we could get in as visitors, just on a day pass. Then we could find an empty house and I heard there are laws about that. If you hold on to an empty house for three months, it's yours. Population laws. There's a plan – a tunnel—

– What do you think this is, some adventure movie? I'm putting my name down for a job.

– Listen. There's something bad in there. So many go in and don't come out. And so much machinery is never a good thing. Those machines work away all day, all night.

– What are you saying?

– I don't know.

– If you don't know, then shut up.

– Don't leave.

– Shut up.

– I love you, though.

– No, you're just afraid of being left on your own. Who could love anyone in this place, anyway? To love someone you need light, and air, and quiet. Love and fear are not the same thing. Besides, if you loved me you'd come with me.

* * *

The Vetter

He felt that if he didn't believe in something then there would be no point in living, and he had chosen to believe in Farleyton. He didn't need to go there himself. It was enough to know a place like that existed. Its appearance had raised the tone of the whole planet. It gave every single person a goal, an aspiration.

He looked up from his monitor and stretched. The muscles of his back and neck ached, and his spine clicked;

age was upon him. But he wouldn't stop. To have been born with money was such a privilege and he hadn't even realised it until late in his life. Now he meant to make good use of it with the time he had left, before the end.

Every day more applications arrived from the website. Each application represented a request for one person to be awarded a grant for access to Farleyton, from the charity he had set up. People couldn't fill one out on their own behalf; the idea was that they nominated somebody. A person with a good heart and a host of kind works behind them. The application form was fifty-two pages long and in the language of Farleyton, but that didn't seem to stop fraudsters from attempting it. About a quarter of the applications, when investigated, turned out to be fakes. People nominating themselves under false names, mainly. Telling lies. How he hated lies.

He returned to the screen. During that brief pause seventeen more emails had arrived from the people he employed to perform the first application filter process. With numbers like these, only one in ten thousand would be given a grant, but he felt good about that. The truly deserving would get in and find a better way of life. The work of uncovering the best people would continue until he was too old and tired to stare at the screen for a moment longer. The work gave meaning to it all.

* * *

The Girl

Around the low fire, amid the corrugated huts and the panoply of smells from street food to shit, the old woman recalled Farleyton. She spoke low, with her eyes closed, in a state of ecstasy. The others listened.

"She was really there!" said the girl, to her mother.

"Sshhh!"

So, the girl waited until the dream state was broken and the old woman had come to the end of her remembrances of clean streets, spring blossoms, gift shops and pancake houses. Well-spoken young men and zebra crossings and butterfly houses, and recycled dreamcatchers and rainbow parades and pesticide-free fresh fruit that didn't even need washing. And the mornings spent on a park bench, of all things. A park bench. With a coffee and a pastry and passing well-behaved dogs on leads with owners who always picked up.

"Why did you leave?" said the girl, then.

"Sshhh!" said her mother again, embarrassed to death by this rudeness; how would her child ever get to Farleyton with such a big mouth? They'd never let her in the gates.

"I didn't," said the old woman.

"What happened?"

"There was a circus planned. A big tent was put up, red and striped. I went along on a Sunday morning, and I was given candyfloss. Do you know what that is, child? It's a pink cloud of sugar. I sat for the show and ate my candyfloss, and then there was the grinding of machinery and the whole tent – all of us within, hundreds of us – spun around and around. I was so dizzy. People laughed. Nothing bad happens at Farleyton, so they laughed where once they might have screamed. Then the tent was gone, and we were standing in a wilderness with only rocks around us. Everyone was confused. At first people thought it was part of the circus. Many refused to come away, even after we found the bodies of others and, in the dust under the bodies, more bodies. Then skeletons. Those who waited, I suppose. And yet still they would not come away.

"So many stayed. But I started walking. I walked and walked, until I got to a small town and they told me where I was. I was on the other side of the world to Farleyton.

"You know what I think, child? I think maybe Farleyton gets full, and so they…" The old woman raised her hands and splayed her fingers wide. "Paff! They zap people out with their machinery. They teleport them. Yes. That's the word. To make room for more."

"Are you not angry that they zapped you?"

"There's not room for everyone."

"I would be angry," mused the girl.

"Well, I've seen a lot of life. And there is more to see. Why waste time on anger?"

"Like what? What do you want to see now?"

"One day, I'd like to see Farleyton again. It was a sight to behold."

"You want to go back? You're crazy," said the girl, and her mother cuffed her round the head and dragged her back to their corrugated hut, only to find that a drunkard had taken advantage of their absence to climb inside and fall asleep, snoring like a bull.

So they slept out in the street and hoped he would leave in the morning. It was a good thing to hope for, the little girl felt. A solid thing.

INTO GLASS

I lie beside you, twenty-seven years into our marriage and everything placed just so in this house, from our possessions to our thoughts to our long patterned days. This burning feeling inside is messy by comparison. It has grown and grown like a weed in good soil. It pushes its way to the surface and tells me that surely, by now, we are secure enough for me to take something back for myself.

The bedroom is warm even though the window is open. I can hear the swish of the cars on the motorway, a few miles away. Do we ever stop travelling? Is there ever a point where we reach a destination, and stop, and say there, enough?

Twenty-seven years is not quite enough. I need to do this once, just once. Just to learn how it is done.

I lift my pillow and slide out the scalpel. It has a leather cover, made specially for it; the black stitches along the soft material are precise and strong, and the blade has stayed sharp.

I do not think of you as a person, exactly. We've been together long enough that I think of you as a part of me or not at all. This won't hurt you at all – I know the theory.

Still, I only touch the tip lightly to your stomach, on the left side, just above your hip. If it wasn't so sharp you would not have been cut, but in the breathless pause after the action there it is: a bead of blood, as dark and heavy as treacle. You don't move. Your face is untroubled; how do you sleep, live, breathe, with so little care? At first I thought you kept your worries from me deliberately, and so I asked you many questions when we sat together, at the end of the working day in front of an endless series of television vignettes. You answered the questions easily. Then, one day, you said – *It's just the usual. It's just life* – and I realised I was only asking because I wanted you to ask me the same questions in return. So, I simply talked about myself instead, about the deep things inside of me, and you listened and calmed me.

I am calm now, calm in the face of your blood. It trickles, slipping along the valley of your thigh and soaking into the sheet beneath.

Just a touch is all it should take, and I couldn't cut deeper anyway, not for the promise of heaven itself. I put the leather cover back in place and slide the scalpel under my pillow. And all the time the blood flows, as I expected, as family tradition demands. The skin around the tiny cut puckers and rises up into thick ridges, bulging outwards, until cracks form that glow orange and expand to let out a lava, so bright that I think it might wake you. But no, you sleep on, and your skin peels back like leaves crisping in the heat. The lava fountains, bubbling up, and it does not fall back down. It elongates until it forms a pillar, standing free from your body, pulsing in time with your slow, even breaths.

Then it begins to change.

It twists and splits and curls, forming arcs and whorls, circles and swirls. It forms a flower; no, a creature. A creature of the sea, as fine and formless as a jellyfish, with too many tentacles to count. They sway, as if dancing in the deep. The lava turns from orange to red, yellow, white, and then it makes a sound. A song. Quiet harmonies, harp-like, reach out to a sweet clear note, and I know what I must do when that note is reached.

I wait. I listen, and when the moment is upon me I reach out and pluck the creation.

It is smooth and cold to the touch. It is glass.

The room returns to darkness. You have not changed. There is nothing different about you, apart from a small raised mark on your stomach, where the skin is no longer seamless. A scar. You might not even notice it's there. Or that something inside you has gone for good.

* * *

My family's sculptures have been exhibited all over the world. Irreplaceable, they are called. In a culture of manufactured precision, nobody can understand why the secret to the method of their creation cannot be unlocked. Each piece remains unique – a form never seen before, beyond any modern technique. The occasional journalist, a young man who wants to make his name, turns up on the doorstep and says, *Your Grandfather really never passed the secret on? Before he—*

They dress it up with some phrase that they have planned in advance. *Passed* is the word they choose most often, and I correct them. *Killed himself. No. He never did.*

This is not true. He told my mother when she turned thirteen as was the custom, and when I turned thirteen, she told me.

You must find someone who really loves you, she said. *It doesn't work without it. Because what you're taking from them is a part of that love. You take it, extract it, and turn it into glass.*

How come you never did it? I asked her. *Did nobody love you enough?* Children can be so cruel. The memory of myself at that age always interfered with my own desire to have children, until it was too late to try. I have not been the bravest person, looking back.

She didn't answer my question. I filled in her half of the conversation years later, piecing her together from the unspoken clues. She had watched her father take love from her mother a tiny cut at a time, and perhaps one day there was nothing left to take. My grandmother died when my mother was sixteen; she would have known the secret by then. She would have seen what was happening. *Heart problems*, they said. While the world admired the glass woodland animals of my grandfather, so delicate, so perfect in form, my mother watched him take the credit.

No doubt he felt guilt; enough of it to open his veins and bleed out on the bathroom floor. *How selfish to die without passing on his talents*, they dared to say. I agree that he was selfish, but for different reasons. It raises the question – how much love can you take?

* * *

It's the weekend, so you're sleeping late. I sit on the end of the bed and hold my glass creature of the deep. I've looked through the pile of photographs in the spare room and come across one that sits next to me now. It was taken on the morning of my mother's wedding. Nobody stands beside her; there was nobody to give her away.

Maybe she always suspected that my father didn't love her quite enough to have any to spare. Although it occurs to me now that she might have tried it, just once. Imagine opening up your husband and finding nothing inside. No glow, no glass. Empty.

I am suddenly and completely aware of how much I love you.

I stay in the moment, guilty and grateful, until you shift and wake up. You have so many lines on your loose, unguarded face and your hair is sticking up, thick and resistant to the hand you run through it, and I love you, I love you. Do you love me just a little bit less?

"Did you dream?" I ask.

You cough, then say, "Hmm."

"What about?"

You shrug. You choose to never remember your dreams. "How long have you been up?"

"Ages." I show you the sculpture. My jellyfish. "I made this."

I want to know if you will catch me out and recognise this came from you, not me. Can we see the parts of ourselves that we lose along the way?

"But I thought you didn't know how."

I'm prepared for this. "I was playing around with my grandfather's old tools and I, I remembered something he said, taught me, when I was very little. I think it's been buried inside me. For years. What do you think?"

You move down the bed, closer to me, and I can feel your senses sharpening, focusing on the creature. "It's really beautiful. Is it a jellyfish?"

"I think so."

"It's amazing."

Yes, yes it is. It is amazing, because it's you.

* * *

It turns out I need at least five pieces to cause a decent stir. The agent is a young man who gets very excited when he sees the jellyfish. I tell him that's all there is and ever will be, but he shakes his head and says that's not the way the world works anymore. There must be more. And so I agree to try.

There are many ways I justify this, later on:

I have lived such a normal life, in the shadow of my family name, and don't I deserve just a little success of my own?

I have been a good lover, so giving, so true. As if love is a bank, and after so many years of saving I deserve to make a withdrawal.

I am not hurting you. In fact, I am showing off your wonderful heart to the world.

I am the last of my family line. The gift will die with me; it would be a crime not to use it.

I tell myself all these things as I cut you four more times. How many times, before your love will be gone, all poured away into glass? I don't know, but I do it anyway.

The creatures of the deep come forth. An urchin, every spike needle-thin and a swirl of colour at its heart like a shy surprise. A crustacean with rough-textured shell and furred claws; a delight to explore with the fingers. A seahorse with a jaunty angle to its segmented tail, its fins fine and splayed as if caught in a current. And a skeletal network of coral, blushing like a bride in shades of becoming pink, maze-like in its complexity.

Could I claim they are part of you and part of me? Maybe this is as close as I'll get to having children. These creations are endlessly fascinating, and I spend hours alone with them, examining them, hoping I'll work out what part of your love for me has been captured in the glass.

No, they are not children. The more I look at them, the more I realise they do not add something to my life. They take something away. And I feel such guilt; it manifests in dreams, in the form of my grandfather. I see him sitting on the bathroom floor, putting the scalpel to his right wrist and cutting down through the skin and veins, so deliberate, so determined. Then he searches through the spurting blood, pushing his fingers into the cut, but there is no sculpture within him.

I jerk awake, as if I have fallen from a height, and I put my hand out in a panic to check: you're there. I can be calm. I am not my grandfather.

I have given you five scars: your stomach, your thigh, the back of your hand, your shoulder blade, and in the soft, deep place behind your earlobe. I won't scar you again.

* * *

The auction is a success. We attend, incognito. How mysterious and, well, rich that sounds. Only wealthy people do things incognito, and we are certainly that.

When we get home, you are distracted. I see it in the way you talk to me, as if one of us is not quite there. You make a cup of tea and forget to ask me if I want one. We are such an old married couple that surely a bit of forgetfulness can be forgiven. But it terrifies me that this isn't age taking its toll. Maybe I took the part that remembers me right. I don't understand how I could have been so selfish. What have my sculptures proved? What have they changed?

The world is filled with more excitable young men, from many professions, and they all seem to have my phone number. I'm too polite to hang up, on the whole, but not so polite that I let them talk me into anything. So, I'm preparing my no without paying much attention to the latest young man, until I realise that he is talking about the past, not the future. He says my mother's name.

Once his meaning gets through to me, I agree to come to his office.

The young man has the sculptures ready for me, on his desk. There are seven of them. He hovers beside them with a careful intimacy that both irritates and amuses me. He feels personally involved, no doubt.

"The instructions were not to inform you of their existence until you'd made your own sculptures," he says. "Perhaps she didn't want to influence you, do you think? These now belong to you, to do as you see fit, although we wouldn't recommend transporting them without great care, of course, and we could arrange for a valuation to take place here…"

His voice runs on and on, and I let him talk.

They aren't sea creatures. They are birds, and they are so beautiful that I find myself expecting them to sing. Wren, robin, swift, wagtail, bullfinch, kingfisher and hummingbird. So small, that hummingbird; I could crush it with a finger.

My father must have loved her after all. He must have loved her very much, right up until she took it all out of him and made these birds. I wonder if that was why he decided to leave and never look back. All his love is here, on this table, used up.

I make arrangements for the solicitor to take care of them for now, while I decide what to do with them, and I go home.

You seem pleased to see me.

* * *

I watch you sleep.

A thought has come to me and I can't push it away. I understood nothing. I pieced together the puzzle and made something so ugly from it. I must wake you and change everything, but I let you sleep for a moment longer. We are not young anymore, are we? We are not beautiful; at least, not on the outside.

"Wake up," I say. "Wake up."

You come awake in a rush, and say, "What?" as if you were waiting for this, as if you were expecting something to be wrong.

"I need you to check me."

"Check you? For what?"

"For scars."

You don't ask questions. You know me well enough to know I am serious, so you turn on the bedside light and help me to pull up my nightdress and you carefully feel your way over my body, your hands so familiar, so sure against my sagging skin. "They might be tiny," I tell you. "Check everywhere."

"Sshhh. I am."

From my toes to my knees to my hips, you search. Under the low curves of my breasts, over the hard calluses of my soles, along the thick bow of my back. My neck, my chin, behind my ears.

Then in my hair, that was once brown and thick. Now it's lighter, wispier; perhaps that's why you find the scars that I have never noticed.

"Here," you say, and I feel your fingers slide over such

small puckerings. Seven of them, on the crown of my head.

What part of my love did she take out of me? What am I missing? I am not a complete person inside, and yet I feel love for her, I swear I do.

You ask me what the scars mean. I tell you. I describe how my family has perfected this unique talent and what it has meant. How my mother has done it to me, and how I have done it to you. I point out your own scars. I was right. You hadn't noticed them.

"But I don't feel different," you say. You don't seem angry.

"Me neither," I say. How much love is there in one person? Perhaps some kinds of love don't come with limits. Who is to say that it can be used up so easily? I am glad that my mother cut me and scarred me and made something from the way I felt. We created such wonderful birds together. Beyond the words she did not say and the stories she never told me, there is such truth.

I fetch the scalpel, and show it to you, and ask you to help me.

At first you are adamant: this is something you can't do. But I reassure you by describing how we will make the very smallest of cuts. Barely more than a scratch. Besides, you know I'll do this alone if you don't help me.

You turn off the lamp. I think it will be easier that way, in the dark. I lie back and put the scalpel to my stomach. You wrap your hand around mine and hold it as steady as you can. But we both tremble.

We make the cut. It doesn't hurt at all. Then we wait to see what kind of creature will emerge.

COMPEL

Day One

It's a bizarre business, to feel grateful for an alien invasion. But it certainly gives meaning in a way few events can. It is change, change itself, change embodied, and there is a strong possibility it will change me. How exciting. I feel alive for the first time in decades.

I call them the compellers, not because that is their name but because nobody else will give one to them. The rest of humanity is mute on this matter; they are compelled to silence. They cannot speak of the arrival, or, apparently, write about it, if my newspaper and television is any indication of events. It surprises me that I can name them here, but maybe that is because I have been recording my thoughts for fifty-three years within my diaries and it is not the existence of the compellers that I place upon the page but my own construction of them. Possibly it takes fifty-three years of writing to recognise the difference.

It seems that this onanistic navel-gazing of an activity known as being a diarist might be good for something after all.

So, I will record the arrival of the compellers in full and I will name today – Day One. Look at the capitalisation! And the use of exclamation marks! I can't remember the last time I used two exclamation marks in one journal entry. Yesterday's entry reflected upon the nature of my ongoing battle with athlete's foot; the punctuation involved reflected the nature of the complaint. Low, repetitive and tedious.

Compellers are worthy of extreme punctuation; I'm certain of that. The world contained behind the screen of mobile phones (that everyone was forever staring at on public transport; I never stooped to owning one myself) would be bristling with dots and squiggles if the compellers had not removed the ability to express oneself in such a manner. But this morning, as I walked to get my paper, nobody was staring at a phone. No interest whatsoever in the world of funny little faces and snapped moments. I can't say I'm sad. Such a reductive form of expression would hardly be appropriate in the face of actual alien existence. And not just that, but alien existence upon each street corner, simply there, simply – there! How can one explain it? One can't, of course. That's the problem. Even *I* am compelled to silence upon this point.

I must be careful not to overdo the exclamation marks.

Here's what I can record (words work for me – shimmying and squeezing around the block the compellers have somehow placed within my mind – I may be the only person on the planet who has this ability):

I first saw one upon stepping out of the house. It was at the bus stop. People were standing near it, staring, not talking. It wasn't looking back at them. It wasn't doing anything, but it was doing something. I have no idea what it was doing, but it was doing it.

I mustn't give in to repetition.

It wasn't big. It wasn't small. It wasn't clever or stupid by any definition I could apply. It didn't remind me of a giant porcupine with the head of a bluebottle and it didn't resemble a multicoloured gladiolus sprouting from a chrome toaster.

I walked past it. I saw another one, at the entrance to Milton Lane. A crowd had gathered nearby – businesspeople in their suits, many of them holding their bags and briefcases against their chests, arms wrapped tightly, as if they were a form of protection. A last form of protection? The final layer of normality, and their fear at it being stripped away! It was palpable. Unlike the compeller, which looked much the same as the first one, and yet not. It was not fat, this time. Also, it was not really thin. It was not pale and it did not contain a darkness. It could not be likened to the rotting corpse of a whale partially covered with a chequered tablecloth and it in no way brought to mind canvas espadrilles.

I saw three more before I reached the mini-market. I bought my paper from Mr Iannopolous and we had a brief conversation about the weather, while his eyes, his eyes, his eyes, I must stop, his eyes, his eyes.

For some reason I cannot write upon that subject.

Moving on, then.

The newspaper contained no report of the compellers and I found I was not surprised. I read it from cover to cover in the park. Well, I say from cover to cover; I read what had been printed. From page eight onwards there were large white spaces where stories should have been, but nobody had yet written them. It was as if the writers had given up on the whole idea and simply stayed silent instead.

So, I returned home, switched on the television and found the glamorous yet intent presenter of the news channel I favour sitting in her studio staring at the camera, her eyes fixed, her mouth opening and closing like that of a large fish. She swam speechlessly in her own vacillation for hours.

It was a full day but I will skip the rest, I think, in honour of the occasion. I could relate my choice of lunch or dinner, my hours spent flicking through the other channels for any sign of intelligent human discourse on the arrival of the compellers. Advertisements and repeats were all I found – the default setting of human existence. Sell it, repeat it, sell it, repeat it. All our ingenuity and yet we have fallen into a terrible pattern of indifference. How can we ever hope to overcome this obstacle placed before us by the compellers, with such disrespect for our own methods of communication?

I've finished my hot chocolate (*creamy choc goodness* indeed), and now I will sleep. I wonder what tomorrow will bring. Perhaps the first tentative steps of the formation of the rebellion? Shall we take to the streets with signs and slogans, with blank spaces where words should be?

Hah. The fall of a silenced civilization, and I will have a front row seat and a lone voice with which to record it.

Also, I should buy some bottled water and cans of peaches at the mini-market tomorrow.

* * *

Day Two

It's getting quite cold; my handwriting is not at its best.

I woke early. The light was grey, grainy through my thin curtains. I saw a com a com a com a com

In the days when late summer turns to autumn in the suburban offshoot of a medium-sized city there is so much for a diarist to note. The changing colours of the leaves, of course, and the creeping chill in the air, if one wants to be predictable. It is an explosion of input for the creative soul, and yet I do not wish to write of it. Not at the end of a very long day in which I lost everything but my pyjamas, my pen and my diary.

I have no wish to write of anything but the one thing I cannot.

It gets harder to make marks about them. Compellers, I write. Compellers. But they will not compel me here, on the page, no matter how I must obey in the physical realm. Can I record what happened today? I must. I will sneak up on the subject and pretend to myself that I am writing of other thoughts, other feelings. To try again—

I emerged from a long dream in which my dear Miriam (gone from me for eleven years now, and who could believe that?) kept telling me to get up and find my trousers. So, trousers were the thought in my head when I awoke, and looked around my room by the half-light of an autumnal early morning.

I saw it, and yet could not trust my eyes. I lay still, waiting for my vision to clear, to reveal its presence as a trick of the light.

It was not a dead squirrel stuffed into a jar of formaldehyde and it was not a slave being crucified along the Appian Way. It did not exactly remind me of fear behind a wide smile, teeth showing, and there was not something of the swipe of a clean, fast scalpel through skin about it.

It was in my room. In the corner, between the wall and the wardrobe.

It was not watching me, and it was intent.

I inched back the duvet until I could slide out my feet and place them into my slippers. I stood, picked up my pen and diary from the bedside cabinet, and left the room.

The kitchen was not far enough away from the com com com, no, nor the living room. I locked myself in the bathroom and could still feel it, as if it breathed out, and in, and out, on the other side of the door. Had it moved? Did it breathe? I couldn't bear it; I stood on the cistern and climbed out through the small window to my back garden, slithering through the gap to the dew-dank grass beneath.

I picked myself up as quickly as my old joints would allow and scrambled to the back gate. Beyond it, I negotiated the overgrown alley that runs along the terrace. Picking my way through weeds, nettles, discarded wrappers, I battled to the main street.

No cars awaited me. No sounds of the city going about its business at all.

Only people.

People, standing in front of their own houses, not speaking, not moving, and their eyes, their eyes, their—no no no

Some were dressed and some were, like me, still in nightclothes. I saw a naked man, but he was as still and silent as the rest, his hands curved around his intimate parts, his gaze on the ground. If there was embarrassment, it was buried deep under the inexplicable event.

I watched as my neighbour, Mrs Fletcher, looked up at her bedroom window and frowned at it, as if it was no longer a place she recognised. Her thin white hair was loose and very long, moving idly in the wind, but at least she had a thick blue flannel nightdress on that covered her from neck to ankle. I wished her a good morning, and we spoke about the wind picking up, and the greyness of the day. The family who live across the street came over and we stood as a group. Their two daughters were wearing pyjamas bearing the images of animated princesses, with the words *unique* and *special* upon them, the letters curved like rainbows. We all attempted pleasant conversation. The words were very hard to find.

Time passed in an odd way, with nobody marking it, asking after it, or commenting upon what they should be doing instead of standing in the street. Just as the sun was beginning to find its way through the cracks in the clouds, a thrumming sound, a vibration, resonated through the concrete. We all turned our faces to the end of the street and saw the vast crowd of people marching over the crown of the road, heading in our direction. There were hundreds, I would say. They walked with purpose, carrying their children, their mobile phones, the odd possession or two.

It did not need to be said that they were attempting to outrun the things behind them. It was in the way they glanced over their shoulders, never stopping. As they reached us, we fell into step with them. I held hands with Mrs Fletcher. She seemed to need the support. I kept my diary and pen in the other hand.

Many more joined this exodus. I have no idea who led it. Possibly we were being corralled like cattle. Either way, nobody fought the destination. We turned through the gate halfway up Church Street and ended up in the park.

Was it only yesterday I sat on the bench, just over there, and read the newspaper? Now the bench has upon it three ladies who are expecting. They stroke their stomachs while others sit in every space around them, from the duck pond to the bandstand. It is a sea of silent humanity.

Beyond the gate? I know they are there. The com the com the com communicating is not going to be possible, it's completely impossible now, I'm so tired, we've been here for hours and hours and it is dark. It's dark.

* * *

Day Three

I will stay calm and record until the end. I don't have long. The park is nearly empty, and I will be compelle comp comp come com co closer close clo com

When I was a young man, I was so very precise about the English language. I was, in fact, such a stickler for the proper and correct usage of it that, at first, it amused my wife, but soon began to annoy her. Eventually, it created a distance between us, for who can talk to a man who criticises each phrase with such dogged dispassion?

I drove Miriam away. I fought against admitting this to myself for many years, reason after reason for our divorce coming easily to me, laying the blame at her little feet. But this behaviour sprang from my own guilt. Guilt creates and inhabits many forms; I wrote about this extensively in diary number one hundred and twenty-two, if memory serves me right.

It all started with our wedding vows. At least, that was the first time she registered an annoyance with my commitment to upholding the standards of our magnificent language.

"Love, honour and obey," I said, a week before the ceremony was due to take place. "Will you promise that, Mim?"

She told me that she would, looking deep into my eyes over the Formica tabletop in the seafront cafe we frequented back when our parents lived on the East Sussex coastline. She thought I was attempting a romantic moment.

"Overused," I said. "Trite. You'll promise it and you haven't even deeply considered what it means. Maybe your assumptions about these words, these concepts, will be totally different to mine, did you ever consider that? They have been weakened through chronic overuse. We should, instead, create a new set of words for our contract that holds a special meaning between us, and us alone. Splorg. I promise to splorg you, Miriam."

She assured me that we would not be promising to splorg each other any time soon, and I thought she had not the intellect to appreciate that, in fact, I was being deeply romantic. A new language for what we shared, was that not a wondrous idea?

Apparently not.

She remarried eight years ago (how time moves, so strangely), choosing an estate agent from Lewes who, no doubt, promised all the usual things without even breaking a sweat. I wonder if she's sitting in a field at this moment, somewhere, in silence beside him while the c c c c c c co coms circle.

Last night was such a long one, perhaps the longest I have ever known. Mrs Fletcher occasionally muttered in her sleep, passing comments such as, *fresh frozen, picked straight from the pod,* and, *date rape, that'll end in tears.* But when the dawn chorus began, the birds raining down their cacophony from the branches above us, she was gone.

I stood, with difficulty, and stretched out my legs while I scanned the park. She was not to be seen and I realised that our numbers were substantially thinned. Patches of grass were now visible through our scattered ranks. The three expectant mothers upon the nearest bench had been reduced to two. There was movement as people made their way in their ones and twos to the gate and beyond.

I watched them while I stretched, working the damp and cold from my old muscles. Their pace was sedate, untroubled, their arms swinging in a curiously limp fashion. Even young children, independent of their mothers and fathers, made their way to the gate and left the park behind without a backward glance.

I would say they felt a call, a compunction. They were compe compe compe led away – to what? For what?

I have not felt any desire to follow suit, even though there are few of us left. We have not gathered together, as one might expect people to do in such a situation. Wouldn't literature have us believe that a band of ragged survivors might come together to defy the might of a terrible invading empire? But without the words we need there can be no unity, and all the terms such as *monster, massacre, alien, apocalypse* – these are but tired, trite words with which we cannot agree a meaning.

No, my fellow park inhabitants keep their distance and avert their eyes as I write, as if shocked by the act. But I must write this down. Not for posterity and not to hide within the familiarity of the scrape of the pen upon paper.

I must write because I believe that I know the nature of the thing we are failing to fight.

They are not alien at all. This is not an invasion. This is a mutation of our own making.

The c c c c c c once upon a time see see see? See the disrespect we hold for even the oldest and greatest of phrases? I write it and roll my eyes at myself. But it allows me to write that—

Once upon a time there was a race of pink-skinned, two-legged creatures who took words in marriage. They tied themselves to the protection and care of these words, and the words were once used well and wisely. To love, honour and obey a word is not an easy task, and soon the creatures began to realise the onus they had placed upon themselves. They could not say *black* and mean *white*; they could not say *good* and mean *bad*.

But then they saw how the children of their marriages had a malleability that their wives and husbands lacked. It was easier to shape these young words to their own desires, to say *natural* and mean *artificial*, to say *pure* and mean *corrupt*. The creatures taught these tricks to the words and never saw how they had weakened the fabric of their own existence.

Wheedle words had been created.

And the wheedle words, so bent, so twisted, grew up. They saw and understood what their parents had done to them when they gave them bastardised, brutalised meaning. So they took form and came for their parents. Came forth for a reckoning. They appeared on the streets and in the bedrooms, and they rounded up the stupid creatures and led them out, one by one, to stand in front of their many children and see what they had done.

What happened after that?

I don't know. I could speculate, but I find I have no taste for that now I've found a way to expound upon my theory. Whatever comes, I've no doubt that all the news channels would describe it as a tragedy. *Tragedy* awaits me beyond the gate, with *massacre* or *bloodbath* and all the other words that have managed to escape our enslavement.

Imagine if this small book, filled with my version of this event, is the only version. All the world will have, if it survives of course, is my depiction of the last three days. Such a thought means that I don't feel tragic. I feel important. My life, my work, my diaries: it has all been so much more important than I ever suspected.

I think I'll leave it there. I'll probably just slip this diary under the hedge, and wait.

CHANTRESS

I sing for the sake of singing. They provide me with subjects to sing about, but my desire is only for my own sound. I don't think they understand that.

I am the Chantress. I'm not to be confused with the Enchantress who lives at the top of the mountain and soothes the stars, night after night, with her pleasing, persuasive speeches. I should also not be mistaken for the Disenchantress who lives in the dark pit of the valley below and mutters if you happen to pass within hearing distance. She is a warning – a demonstration of the depths to which a disobedient woman might sink. She is also responsible for occasionally throwing rocks and directing white and black flies to the nearest vegetable plots.

That's just my little joke.

The women from the village on the far side of the mountain come to me, making the trek on the precarious path their ancestors carved, and I'm quite clear with all of them that the songs I'll form do not have a purpose, in the sense that no song has a direct purpose, but this has yet to stop them from asking. They say, "Sing a song that will make my child better."

"The child probably needs a doctor," I say. Every single time. "I'm no doctor. I have the number for the surgery in the town a few miles away, and the opening times for the cable car that will get you down the mountain. Also, a bus timetable. Here."

Sometimes they accept this information, sometimes not. Every time they say, "Sing it, please. Sing it anyway." They are so reluctant to leave the shadow of the mountain.

Child, stay close, and find your comfort
In the strong tall peak above you
Formed by the Giant Hands that cradle
That mould
That shape
That close about you now.

* * *

I find comedy in the strangest things: the crooked legs of the dead insects on my windowsill; the lost goat hanging on the ledge, bleating, amazed to find itself in such a precarious situation; the skittering of loose pebbles on their way to the valley below. I put it down to being alone for so many years. I say so many years – six, to be precise. I moved here from the town, after seeing the job advertised in the local paper.

Do you want to SING for a rapt audience?

I thought, after years on the circuit, doing the working men's clubs and struggling to be heard over the clink of glasses and roar of innuendo, that it had been placed there purely for me. We make such connections, all of us. We assume there is reason to events, and a thread that runs through our souls and tugs us this way, that way, onwards, with the far end of the thread held firmly in Giant Hands. It's much easier to think that. It gives each life a meaning that I'm not sure it deserves. Still, it worked in my favour this time. I attended the audition with the fervour of certainty. It was my chance to shine, as they say.

I discovered, while standing in front of a row of bearded elders who had agreed to reimburse my bus and cable car costs, that I could improvise with tune and lyrics. They liked the sound of my voice and the words I chose. They told me, *Come and guide the women of our village. They need your voice.*

How they auditioned the Enchantress and the Disenchantress, I don't know. I should remember to ask my sisters, during one of our quarterly meetups.

I sit on the roof of my village-sponsored hut, with a glorious view of the heavy mist that shrouds the mountain peaks; the usual drizzle is headed my way. The Enchantress, high above me, will have a clear view of the sky, which is necessary for her role. The village believes stars are little girls – the giggling children of the sun and moon – who must be gently addressed by a soft voice. She does this well and with dedication.

I don't sit here for the view. I get the best Wi-Fi reception up here, on my antique mobile phone, having been out of contract for five years and eleven months.

I scroll through the headlines.

The news is busy consuming itself, as usual. How important it must seem to those who consider themselves part of that cannibalistic mechanism.

Next up: a report on the deadly disease
sweeping the city – news addiction.
Further updates on this breaking story by the hour.

Not really. I made that one up.

There go some pebbles, dislodged from the path, and then I hear the footsteps approaching, and a firm knock upon my door, three times, as per the custom.

I quietly climb down from the roof on the far side of the hut and walk around to my own front door with the dignified air that is expected of me.

"Can I help?" I say to the villager. She's tall and thin, wearing her hair in a series of complicated long plaits. She's too young to be here about her child, so this must be a visit about the second biggest issue that concerns the women of the village.

"Chantress," she says. "Please. I need a song. A song to make a man love me."

I invite her in, and sit her down, and explain very carefully that the song won't work. She nods, and nods, and then says, "So will you sing it?"

A good, strong heart calls to yours
And you dream of better things

But where will you find them?
In the sky?
Look up, and see the work of Giant Hands
About you
Around you
For you.
They weave clouds from tears
So cry for what cannot be:
Feed the clouds
Then find solace in the good, strong heart
that is waiting.

* * *

Why so many ill children and unrequited love stories? I confess, I do not know. It perplexes me. I harbour theories:

• The village is an experiment run by unscrupulous scientists who want to see if it is possible to regress human achievement back to the Stone Age; the mist of the mountains is actually a powerful gas that works by shrinking the frontal cortex.

• The village doesn't exist at all, and this is an elaborate hoax being played upon me as part of a television programme that airs nightly to the amusement of millions of people. All the villagers are actors. Some are better at acting than others.

• The village has always been my home and everything before, including phones and nightclubs and bus services, has been created by my sick and troubled imagination. And I'm obsessed with sick children and unrequited love. In short, I'm mad.

I could pick one of my theories and stick to it but instead I like to roam free, siding with whichever one suits my mood. Right now, I'm mad. I'm enjoying the broadening complexities of the word. Also, there's a lot of room within my job specification to play madness. The villagers seem to like it, too. It suits their image of me – the things I say and the way I am.

*　*　*

"Mine's burning," I tell her.

"That's okay," says the Enchantress. "The outside gets a bit black but the inside is still yummy. I can't believe you never did this before."

"It wasn't that sort of childhood," I say. I remove my stick from the flames and examine the charred, gooey mess of marshmallow. It has ash stuck to it.

"Seriously, it's delicious," she says. "Pop it."

"I'm not popping it. It's too hot to pop."

A stone is flung out from the darkness; it smacks into the bonfire and dislodges the tent of sticks, which send up a plume of smoke and cinders, and a wave of heat. I put my hand to my face and feel my cheeks, awash with it.

"Just chill!" shouts the Enchantress, and from behind a large rock nearby I hear the Disenchantress mutter, and move off. She'll do it again in a minute or two. She really cannot divorce herself from her job anymore. When we first began these meetups she would join in with the normal conversation and even say amusing things, droll things, every now and again. That hasn't happened for at least a year.

I nibble the marshmallow and taste smoky, sweet strangeness. It's not like any other taste. I'm not sure that I like it, but that doesn't matter. "So, how's your mother?"

"It won't be long," says the Enchantress, throwing back her head. "I can't see the stars from down here. What a relief. Even when I was back in town, getting her moved to the hospice, I'd find myself outside at dusk talking to them. My girls. The stars, I mean. It's just habit. It's all become a habit." I glance up too, and see the smoke rolling skywards, making its own mysterious, curling patterns before succumbing to dissipation. "When she really starts deteriorating, they'll call me and I'll try to get back in time to say goodbye. I've said it anyway, though, just to be sure."

"Said what, sorry?"

"Goodbye."

"How did you do that?" I ask her. I can't imagine it – such a huge thing done at the wrong moment, as a failsafe, simply to make sure it had been done. A rehearsal, perhaps, that might have to be the stand-in for the real show. I never said goodbye to my own parents, not in that way. They're still out there, ongoingly doing parental things; I'm sure of it.

The Enchantress shrugs. "It's just a word." What a strange thing for her, the weaver of words who soothes starlight, to say. I watch her pop her own marshmallow, as if the heat does not affect her, and then she skewers a new one on the end of her stick, taken from the plastic packet beside her. "You want another one?"

"Yeah, okay."

She passes me a white one, and I eat it straight away. It's better cold, I think: soft and dense, intact, soothing in my mouth.

"You're not meant to do it like that," she says. She gives me another one, and I spear it on my stick to make her happy.

"Thanks for sharing these," I say. "I keep meaning to take a trip to town. It's been ages."

"What will you bring back? When you go?"

I try to picture what it is I most want.

A stone flies out again, and smashes into the fire. The Enchantress takes a marshmallow from the packet and throws it, with violent energy, into the darkness. There is a pause. Then the muffled voice of the Disenchantress floats forth.

"Thanks," it says. "Tasty."

"Where's your family, anyway?" says the Enchantress, clearly proving her determination to switch the spotlight away from herself, whether I answer or not. But these are not the kind of questions I like.

"Oh, I don't have a lot to do with them," I say. "They don't really understand me."

"You don't speak to them at all?"

"It's fine. They're farming folk, from the other side of town, beyond. They think I should still be there, milking the cows, and that's not me, is it?"

Her attention is fixed on the fire: the slow settling of the embers after the disruption of the stones. "I don't know if that's you," she says. She drops her stick, stands, and lifts her arms to the sky.

I see you, stars, little girls of light, I see you hiding, peeking out from between the fingers of Giant Hands, and you don't know if we want you to adorn our lives with your bright, fair light because we are so busy down here, too busy to look up and tell you so. But you are wanted. You are loved, little dots, tiny twinkles. You are wanted, and you will be much missed if you do not come out tonight. So, find a way to slip through, we beg you. I am the mouthpiece of the village. I stand at the highest peak and wish I could hold you close, closer. You delight me, stars, with your ageless patterns and delicate beams; I would kiss you, if I could, and wrap myself in you. But I can't. And that's for the best, because you're shy. I know it. I see the way you hide in the Hands. Come out, stars, come out. Slide through the giant's grasp and keep us all in your glow tonight.

The Disenchantress mutters, close to my ear; how did she get so close? This time, for the first time, I hear every word.

You work so hard and nobody really appreciates it. Not one of them. What difference does it make? What difference does it all make, anyway? Pointless. Bloody pointless.

"I know," says the Enchantress. "It's just habit." She sits down again, and we finish the marshmallows, and then start the slow climb back up the mountain to the roles we keep on playing.

* * *

"You are the Chantress?" says the frowning young woman. She falls into none of the usual categories. I don't know what she wants, and what's more, she's caught me at a bad time: I'm fresh from washing my hair and am in my dressing gown. I don't look the part and I don't feel it. I shouldn't have answered the door but it didn't follow the usual pattern of three knocks, and I was curious. Perhaps it was someone else. A person from outside the village.

"If you'll just wait, I'll get changed and be with you."

"No, please, I wish to speak with you, that's all," she says, so I have no choice but to open the door wide enough to admit her. She stands in my hut and looks around, as if searching for something other than the simple furnishings. "They've always said, my mother says, you're from the town. Chosen."

How stilted she sounds. Do any of the villagers have a sense of humour? I've yet to find it. "Yes, I was."

"Didn't you bring any of your own possessions with you when you came to us?"

"Not really." What things did I have? I think of the phone, of showing it to her, but I don't like the way she's making me feel. I'm being judged and showing her the phone would be an attempt to prove myself different. "Did you want a song?"

"What good would it do?"

"None."

"Because there's no such thing as the Giant Hands?"

"That's right," I tell her.

"Yes," she muses. "That's what mother told me you would say. You saved my life once, she thinks. It was when you first arrived. I was fifteen. I had a fever that wouldn't break and you sang for me. Over me. But I don't think it made a difference. I think I survived because I'm strong. Stronger than any imaginary hands, high above."

Nothing about this is going the way it should. I haven't moved from the door; it's still open. "Listen, you go out and I'll get dressed, and then when you knock again I'll be ready to do this the proper way, okay?"

She doesn't move. She says, "I'm leaving the village. I cannot be bound up in these old superstitions about stars and songs and stone-throwing. My mother made me come here, to see you, before I go."

"Does she want me to sing a song that will make you change your mind?"

"Maybe."

"Where will you go?"

"The cable car. Then the bus."

"I have timetables," I offer.

"I don't need help." She moves past me and out of the doorway, to stand in the grey morning light. No doubt it will rain later, but the air is clear, that much cannot be denied. Even if there is no sunshine, the air is clear and fresh and free. She will miss that, at some point, even if she doesn't believe it now.

"I'll sing you a song anyway," I tell her. "That's what you really want, isn't it? Everyone does."

She shakes her head. "Don't sing to me. Your songs: they do work. But not in the way that you think."

And she sings instead. She sings to me:

Why must you fight
Your reason for living?
You are the Chantress:
Your voice, your thoughts, your heart,
Your soul, have been poured into this life
By Giant Hands.
Do not look up to the stars:
They are not your domain.
Do not cast stones and threats upon those who need you.
Sing, Chantress, sing.
It is your gift, made for giving.

She has a good voice. It's not as good as mine, but still, there's something haunting to the melody.

"Goodbye," she says, and sets off, on the rough path. I watch her go. I think about following her, catching her up and going to town together, to start afresh. But I'm not like her, not anymore.

I am the Chantress.

There's nothing out there like it, and nothing could be

as important. I wish I could make a joke of it, but I've run out of punchlines. I, and my fellow employees, have work to do here, for those that believe in us. You might say we are sisters. We are in the care of the Giant Hands.

BLESSINGS ERUPT

Part One

She asks me if she should have faith in her ability.

I want to answer her question. I would tell her it has no rules. It works just as well without the prayer and the singing. But there's no point; I'll never be given the opportunity to do it that way and neither will she. The process has become as important as the miracle she can perform.

So, I don't teach. She is free to watch what I do, and she can make of it what she wants. That's the deal I've struck.

"Believe in whatever you want."

She looks doubtful. How beautiful she is, in her firm, unchanged skin. "But surely, if I believe in myself, it will work better."

"What makes you think that?"

"It's all in the mind, isn't it?"

I shouldn't speak to her at all. There are no words to be said that can't be taken by her as instruction. She traps me into these patterns.

The room is cool. My scarf is itchy; it was a present from a grateful patient, knitted from a coarse plant-mix. My name has been embroidered into it. *Hope.* Or perhaps the patient did not even know it is my name. I've received many presents but this one is my favourite because I have a use for it. The rest belong to an age that has passed but I keep them anyway, in a box under my bed.

I am in my living-room hammock, looking out of the window at the new, vine-clad buildings and the adapted eco-cars, parked in a line along the street, brown as soil and fitted with shiny sun-charging roofs. Why are they so uniform in appearance, now? I've seen pictures of cars before the war, in many different colours and sizes. And why, come to think of it, are there always four wheels outside and a wheel inside, and the gauges and buttons and everything the same, when there was a chance we could have made something new, something different?

I know the accepted answer to this – it's so anybody who remembers an old car can get in and drive an eco-car. If you've driven one, you've driven them all. It's the best design for the whole world.

If I could drive, I would have a car made to accommodate my enormous form. It would not fit anyone else. The apex of good design should be how completely an object is made for its owner, not how easily it can be used by just anyone.

Despite my best intentions, I say, "It's not all in the mind."

I see our car pull up. It's the usual design of course, and

the back seat will barely be big enough for the two of us. I hope it's not a long drive.

* * *

Past the living buildings in rich soil, the baby trees and the fecund eruptions, in the slow steady flow of traffic, we travel towards the Central Apartments.

I like the way the driver's eyes flick to me in the mirror. He doesn't stare. He takes a glance and then returns his attention to the road, calmly. He has the radio on the Good News Network which is saying they're trialling another vaccine, and solar power broke records in our region, and there's been more rainfall than expected: yes, this world is being put back together and we're on an upward trajectory, all of us, together. Now here's some light music.

A pop song, all about happy love stuff, comes on. My student hums along.

"How can you stand it?" I ask her. "It's meaningless."

"I prefer it to the way it used to be," says the driver, and I realise he thinks I was speaking to him about the news broadcast. So, he's old enough to remember the bad old days of constant doom and gloom. Funny, he looks younger. I don't have a memory of this myself. I read about it, once, in a Red Gathering history book Stanislav gave to me. He's given me many books over the years, feeding my interest in the past, in the way it used to work. I guzzled up that dysfunctional world greedily. It made sense to me.

Not only does the driver look young, he also looks familiar. "Did I treat you?" I ask him.

He nods. I see the smooth brown skin crease at the back of his neck, just below the line of his hair, and in the mirror his eyes move to mine and hold my gaze, this time. "You did. Thank you."

"Where was the growth?"

"On the left side of my chest. You smoothed it all out. I haven't aged a day since. It was a miracle."

"I'm glad you're well," I tell him. "But it was no miracle. How much did you pay?"

"Twenty years of service."

"Did that seem like a good deal to you?"

His gaze is firmly back on the road as we crawl along it, keeping pace with the endless traffic. "It did," he says. "I'd pay it again."

The student coughs, then says, "Turn it up, please." So we spend the rest of the journey listening to happy songs.

* * *

We arrive at one of the new buildings, tall and straight, fresh from construction. The tenants will have sold years of their lives for one of these apartments. I wonder how they can afford my services as well?

The driver says he's been told to wait for us. I shift myself from the back seat and lumber indoors, with the student following after. The sliding glass plates admit us to a reception area with mosaic flooring, showing a sun with yellow triangular tiles intersecting with crimson squares that bear the mark of the Red Gathering. At the centre of the sun a tree has been planted, and a sign beneath it reads, in seven languages:

Feel free to breathe on me.

The student stops and speaks to the leaves on a nearby branch. I don't hear what she says.

Stanislav is waiting at the lifts for us. He is wearing a hemp weave kaftan and has grown his beard even longer, with more knotted multicoloured shells within it. He bows to me, says, "Hope, my dear."

"Oh piss off," I tell him. It makes me feel better. He is a grand old man, now, and used to my ways. He doesn't react. I think he wishes I would give him a reason to smile at me, like he used to, when I called him my father.

We all get in the lift and ride to a floor; I don't register which one. A woman waits for us. She gasps at the sight of me and, for a moment, I think she might kneel, but Stanislav tells her smoothly to lead the way, and she takes me through to a spacious living room with a view that bemuses me. I look at the city laid out, the ruins commencing regrowth, the plants providing forms for so many projects built on plastic bones; the trees and buildings are fusing.

The woman, small and subservient, busies herself around us. She lowers sets of blinds over that view, one by one, until we are in shadowy semi-darkness. Then she shifts back the two sofas and the coffee table to make a space on the rug, which is woven through with living thread that is growing tiny white flowers. As she shifts the rug to one side, the flowers release a tender, gentle scent into the room.

"How much?" I ask her. "The rug?"

She doesn't reply. Perhaps she doesn't understand me, or perhaps she doesn't want to say. I'm guessing the price was about three months of her life.

The door to another room in darkness is opened, and she steps aside as the patient emerges with a pained shuffle, side-stepping, crabbing into the room. I feel my hunger building as I sense the presence of his disease. His body is bent to one side in an arc that starts with his knees and continues to his neck. All of him is drawn towards the gravity of his tumour, which erupts from his left hip and is not so big, not anywhere near the size of the first ones I did. Perhaps people are more aware of their options nowadays. They don't wait and hope it's something else until it's nearly eaten them alive. Or perhaps the disease is on the wane.

But no, I don't believe that.

The student moves across the room to take the patient's arm, and he recoils at first. But she is persistent and he gives in and starts to lean on her, to let her take his weight as he crosses to the centre of the room, where the rug was, and stands there. He says something in a language I don't speak.

Stanislav replies with, "Right there is fine. Just lie down."

A long groan escapes him as he does as he is told. He can't lie flat anyway; the tumour is gathering up his flesh, pulling his organs around itself. But it can't hide from me. I lower myself to the floor beside him and pull back the woven trousers he's wearing so I can get a look at it.

The student is close by; I can feel her breath on the back of my neck.

"Go away," I murmur, without turning around. She'll know I'm talking to her.

Stanislav says, "She needs to see. I understand your decision, but we agreed she could see, even if you won't teach her."

"Not this close. I can't get started with her this close."

"What about the prayers?" she says, and I reach behind me to flap a hand at her. She steps back smartly.

Stanislav starts his song. He has always been blessed with a fine voice, low and level, and it has developed a rich, cracked timbre with age. It reverberates around the apartment, makes the darkness draw close around us, holds us in its arms. It is a prayer to give thanks for aid and to recognise that all mistakes carry within themselves the seed of forgiveness, and it visibly relaxes the patient. I don't know how it does that, but it works every time.

I don't know how I do what I do, either. All I can say is that the moment comes, in the heart of that prayer, where I am compelled to put my lips upon skin. I kiss the clammy flesh and take it into my mouth, tonguing it, laving it, until it is slick with my saliva. Underneath it, beyond the dermis, deep-embedded between muscles and organs, is the growth. It begins to move towards the pressure of my mouth. It comes reluctantly; I suck harder. The skin grows hot. The patient shifts, and Stanislav is there still singing, putting his hands upon his head to calm him further. The tumour collects and I picture it, complete, ready for me. Then I stretch my thoughts out wide, into every aspect of the body, and I will my strength into the arteries and veins, the heart and the lungs, liver and kidneys, so he will survive what comes next.

Then I eat.

I take small, quick bites and hit the tumour straight away; it is spongy and fibrous, and it is poison. The concentrated plastic-remains of the old life have soaked into the skin, been ingested, collected into an indestructible, indigestible lump. But I can take it. I chew it down. I swallow. I keep eating and eating until I have removed it all from my patient, and then I sit back and wipe my mouth, but of course there is nothing to see. His skin is unbroken. There is nothing on my chin or on my face. It is inexplicable. The lump of poison is inside me now, and he is free of it.

Stanislav's song changes in pitch. The patient attempts to sit up. The student darts forward and helps him, placing one hand on his back and the other on his elbow. "You'll be fine," she says. "Just relax." Even though she doesn't speak his language, he seems to understand.

"I got it all," I say. "It's good."

Stanislav stops singing. The woman comes to me and presses a golden ring into my hand. Perhaps a wedding ring? Then she moves around the room, rolling up the blinds, one at a time, and relief floods into the room with the sunlight. The patient smiles and touches his hip, running his hands over the rolls of loose skin. He takes the fat between his hands and pinches it.

"Sorry," I say. "I don't do liposuctions." But that's a joke and an operation that belongs to the past. He says a word, the same word, over and over again. His eyes are clearer, and he stretches up his arms, straight, to the ceiling. Yes, he can stand up tall once more.

* * *

On the way back, the driver says, "Did you manage to help him?"

"Do you know him? The patient?"

"He's my cousin. I said to him about you. I told him you could help."

His sickness is settling inside me, moving into position on my left hip, jostling against the tumours that I have already ingested. I am a mass of wobbling disease. "I helped him."

The driver's shoulders slump. "Thank you."

"What will he do now? Will he become a driver, like you?"

"He's not paying for your services. His wife has agreed to do that."

"His wife…?" I think of the small woman in the apartment, drawing the blinds, moving the rug, preparing for the operation with such care. She will work hard for the Red Gathering, and she will age faster than the patient I have just treated. I've placed time between them: time, as a crack in their relationship that will widen further every day, until it is a chasm. The driver's eyes meet mine one last time as he pulls up opposite the house.

"Love is a wonderful thing," he says.

* * *

I don't remember love. I barely remember living on Assembly Island; my first memory is being found there, with the others. Nobody knows how we got there – a shipwreck, maybe? Pregnant women and young mothers were being evacuated from the atolls in the days before the first bombs; some ships didn't make it. Survivors may have swum to the giant pile of plastic in the middle of the ocean. Or possibly people had been living there for generations already, unbeknownst to the world. Marine debris had been collecting for a long time before the war.

Whatever happened, there were no adults, they tell me. The oldest children were caring for the youngest, like myself, upon the brand-new island. Plants and fungi had already adapted and found a way to feed on the detritus, and we were eating anything, everything, to stay alive. The fact that eating fused irradiated plastic was not killing us came as a shock to our saviours, and that is my first memory. A thin woman with such big eyes and open sores, a Red Gathering long-term employee, trying to fish a yogurt pot out of my mouth and realising it was gone. I had sucked it and chewed it and incorporated it.

Learning I could do the same trick on the new diseases, caused by the bombs and the bad air, took a while. I was seven years old, trying to adjust to loud city life as renewable rebuilding was just getting started, when one of my first case workers took me up to the roof of our complex and told me he was dying. I could smell it on him, and I was hungry for it. He had wide eyes too. He never spoke to me again, after, although he sent flowers and a card. To say it was all gone. To say thank you, and goodbye.

Later, I heard I wasn't even the first of us to suck out the poison. It had happened in a separate house of Assembly Island survivors – one of the pupils had latched on to a teacher during a lesson. Apparently they hadn't even known they were ill, so it had been recorded as some kind of attack. No wonder the social-care employees of the Gathering treated us strangely, but still they gave us names of such optimism. Blessing. Gift. Prospect. Hope.

When I got allocated to New Foreston, and to Stanislav's care, I was scared. Of myself, mainly. Of what I might do. Stanislav was a true convert to the theo-organic way of life. He believed in it more than I did. The prayer, the preparation. The idea that I, and others like me, were a miracle.

The student would love me to tell her all these things. She asks often enough, in the evenings, when it's just me and her in the house and she's watching the Good News Network, and I'm trying to find a comfortable position on the furniture that was made for normal people. She has tried a thousand ways to lead me to the conversation she wants to have, and I've refused every one of them.

I won't help make her into me.

But this evening is different. Being the first Tuesday in the month, she gets to put in a call to her family, back in Brazil. I pretend I don't listen in, but as she sits in front of the graphene and glass laptop (cost – I'm guessing three years of a life) and waves at the tiny embedded camera, I feel an ache building inside of me and my ears strain to catch every word. It's almost like the hunger I feel for the poison. I could suck up the way she is when she makes that call.

I only know a little Portuguese, but I'm learning more every time. And some things don't need translation. I can tell she loves them, and they love her. They call her Arama. They gather around their own camera, an extended family of generations all shoved up tight on one old orange sofa that would be banned in this country for its toxicity, and they smile at her as if she is their saviour. Which I suppose she is, having been found to be a plastic eater. They are being compensated generously, no doubt, in goods and services. There is a cross on the wall behind them, one of the new growing ones, sprouting and bearing small red fruit in clusters.

She checks they have everything they want, and they tell her yes. She catches up on their lives, and tells them she is fine. She is happy, that's what she says. I know the words for that:

Estou feliz de viver.

When she finishes the call she usually goes straight to bed, but tonight she turns to me and says, chin jutting out, "Did you understand any of that?"

"I don't speak your language," I tell her.

She raises her eyebrows. She is wiry and well-muscled, with her feet planted firmly in my space. She has taken hold here and she is growing. I realise she has shot up; when she first arrived she barely reached my shoulder, and today she is the same height as me. She must be feeling stable, grounded, to take this new belligerent tone.

"How old are you now?" I ask.

"Fourteen. How old are you?"

I ignore the question and start shifting myself from the sofa so I can go and lie down in my room.

"Do you think God created us to do this work?" she asks.

"I thought we were the new gods."

"I don't understand your jokes. I don't think I ever will."

"I don't tell jokes. I thought you would have worked that out by now. Good night."

"We're not gods," she calls after me.

I squeeze into my room and shut the door quietly behind me, so she knows I'm unbothered.

Then I lie on my bed and try to find a comfortable position, knowing I'll squirm until morning, knowing I'll feel every growth that jostles inside me.

* * *

When I can't sleep I always end up back on Assembly Island.

I imagine walking on it once more. This is an impossibility; it has been closed off to all but the chosen few researchers funded by the Gathering who examine the new resistant forms of life that sprang up upon it. I was shown a video by Stanislav, when I asked about the possibility of ever going home, soon after arriving in New Foreston. He said, *This will have to be your home now.*

The video was filmed by a camera fitted to the protective visor of one of the researchers. The picture wobbled and jerked between sights that I would like to have seen in more detail: the hooded yellow suits of the other researchers; the lime green threads of seaweed that had found a foothold amid the plastic remains; the scuttling crabs that dodged from ragged hole to ragged hole in the heap of detritus. But it wasn't detritus. It was the place itself. It was the first place I knew.

When I was taken away, I couldn't believe that a flat floor existed. After I had learned words, I asked, *What it is made of?* They told me it was pressed and woven from plants, and for a long time I thought *plants* was one of those words that had several meanings. The green crawling life threading through Assembly Island could not also be the controlled, shaped substance under my feet.

* * *

When I rise, with difficulty, I find the student has made her own breakfast. She is eating from a bowl, dipping in her spoon to pick up the small assorted chunks that Stanislav brings us regularly. Chopped up remains of the old world. She finishes her mouthful, then says, "We had a call. The car won't be long."

"Another one? Already?"

"Stanislav says it's an emergency. He says maybe I could help out with this one, as it's a big job and you're still tired from yesterday."

"I'm fine."

"You could supervise."

"I'm fine." I manoeuvre myself into my hammock and look out of the window. The car hasn't come yet. I have a few minutes to watch the traffic go by. I have no appetite at all, but I can gorge myself when the need arises.

"Hope," says the student. "Tell me what I can do to make you trust me."

"That's not the issue." I rock gently from side to side. "That's not the issue at all." The cars travel along the long straight road, all facing the same direction, thinking they made the choice to point that way when the road offers no alternative.

*　*　*

It doesn't fail to strike me as ironic, after such thoughts, when the car comes to a sudden stop and progress towards our destination in the Undergrowth side of the city is halted.

Through the windscreen I can see that those on road duties are out in force, wearing their reflective blue vests that reveal which organisation they have sold their time to, waving their hands to filter everyone into one long lane in order to bypass a brand new eruption. It's not big yet; I can still see the top of it, twisting, getting its bearings. It's perhaps three storeys high. The mutated plant growth will soon begin to accelerate, and by this evening it will be climbing ten feet every hour.

"It's a pretty one," says the driver, as we wait to be waved onwards.

The flowers are, indeed, lovely: big and bold, a vibrant

pink. The flowering ones usually bear fruit, too – waxy balls that grow from the hearts of the blooms once the petals drop off. They are inedible to me, but they will be prized by the local people, no doubt. An eruption like this will be seen as a blessing. A gift.

"A bad place for such good luck," the driver adds. "This'll cause delays until the organic tram link is finally ready."

But nobody would suggest cutting it down. Nature is so precious, now, wherever it recovers and revives.

"My parents said four more came up in Durango, all around the cathedral, and the vines all joined together in the sky, above the cross, to form a…" The student clicks her fingers. "A place you can stand on?"

"A platform," I say.

"No, a floor."

"It's the same thing," I tell her, then correct myself. "No, it's not the same thing. Forget I said that. Can you fetch me a flower?"

"What?"

"Hop out. Fetch me a flower. I want to smell it."

"But…"

"Quick! Before we move off."

She opens the door and gets out, then sets off towards the eruption at a jog. I twist in my seat so I can keep my eyes on her through my window, but I talk directly to the driver. "Listen. I need your help. Tomorrow evening. Can you bring the car to the house?"

"Sure, I can clear it through Stanislav and—"

"No, no Stanislav, not anyone. Get there at ten. Can you do that? Not just because of what I did for you. I can make it worth your while." I keep watching as the student slows, then comes to a halt. She stands there, next to the line of cars, her back straight, her posture rigid.

"You didn't have to say that. Sure. Sure, I'll do it. Tomorrow. What time?"

"Ten."

"*I can make it worth your while*," he mutters. "You sound like those old films people used to watch. You sound like the past."

"Don't say anything to her."

He shrugs. The student turns around and strides back to the car. She gets in and closes the door quietly. The people working road duty for the Blue Collective wave us on and we start to creep forward. We draw level with the eruption and I wind down the window to catch its scent; it smells fresh and sweet and juicy. My taste buds respond, and I swallow my own saliva. It's poisonous to me, but my body doesn't really know that. It's only experience that has taught me not to trust what my body tells me.

"I couldn't do it," she says. "To pluck something so precious just to give you a moment of pleasure would have been…"

"I knew you couldn't do it," I tell her, and there is that feeling again, that doubt she places in me as she insists on learning lessons I'm not trying to teach her. "Music, please."

The driver turns on the radio, and the happy songs save us from the silence.

* * *

Stanislav sings.

It reminds me of the first time I heard him sing, and afterwards, when my patient was healed and radiant, Stan hugged me; back when I could bear to hug back. To be touched. He was my father then, and we moved out into the sunlight and held hands for a time that I still can't describe as an increment of anything, as a minute or an hour or an afternoon. It was freed from all structure, and it still stands apart, in my memory.

He has grown thinner over these years. Seventeen, in total. And nine months. He has wasted while I have swelled, but he's good, he's healthy. There's no sickness in him. His clean kaftan and well-worn sandals only add to the vitality he radiates.

The patient's breathing slows and his little, filmy eyes close. I didn't know the song could work on a baby. Or on a person in such pain, newly born, only a few hours old and with every organ crammed with the plastic disease. I would have said – if the mother had not been lying next to him on the matting, the back of her hand trembling against the curve of his forehead – that it was better to let him die.

I will eat. I will eat all of him, every part of him is delicious with disease; there will be nothing left, that's what scares me. But I put my mouth to his chest and lick the smooth, new skin, and suck. The poison moves through him, gathers just below my lips, and the baby is limp, arms and legs flaccid, splayed. The mother whines, once, and then I bite.

I am so delicate. I measure every mouthful. I become aware of the student moving around me to stand behind the mother, willing her strength into the woman. The round, woven room with its thick branches and hanging vines is hazy to me; the meal is too heavy in my stomach, too rich in taste, and I can feel my grip on the moment start to falter. It's too much. The plants are snaking around me, wrapping me up. The vines lower to take me among themselves, and then lift me high into their care, and I see nothing more, but I can still hear. Stanislav is singing. Stanislav sings.

I come back down.

"It's done," says a voice, "stay still. All is well." I recognise the voice and smile at it; it is a voice I care for. Then I realise is it the student speaking, and I push that emotion away and try to sit up. But I am so heavy inside. I sink. I am sinking through the floor, through the roots and stones, into the rich brown darkness where no pain can penetrate.

"Let's get her home," says Stanislav, and my hearing becomes expansive, acute, clear beyond anything I have heard before as I listen to the leaves of the Undergrowth rustling with dedicated menace all around me. The mother is whispering. She is saying *mercy* over and over, or is it *merci*? And the baby cries, a reedy, warbling, healthy sound of annoyance, maybe hunger.

I love how the rooms grow naturally here, the holes and walkways adapted by humanity in the spaces between growth. We fit around the plants now. We fit. I wish I could speak of it, but my mouth won't work.

* * *

Part Two

A makeshift stretcher later, and with the help of a willing team of Undergrowth residents of all colours and organisations clamouring around me with deference before cheerfully putting their hands on me, I am returned to my house. It's practically a long parade through the streets as I can't be squeezed into the eco-car. People take it in turns to hold the stretcher aloft, or just to put a hand upon it. Others come out of their own houses to join in.

It feels like a celebration. Everybody is so keen to turn bad news into good. I hear the people saying, "A baby saved! What a blessing!" to each other, to every new person that joins the party. No matter what the cost, it's a price worth paying for a baby.

Stanislav oversees my return to the house, and the slow business of negotiating me up the stairs and into my hammock. He is all I can bear to look at while this happens, his familiar old features, which is not without irony. I told him, not so long ago, that I never wanted to see his face again.

Once the party has moved back to the street I say to him, "It's unbearable how they all want to say this is a better world, no matter what the reality suggests."

He takes my swollen hand and I feel a sudden, deep pain that shoots through my elbow, my shoulder, to my head. "Hope," he says. "You just can't see it, can you?"

"If you're going to tell me yet again that we're saving the world, you know I'll kick you out. I've done it before."

"You used to believe we were. Saving the world."

"Did I?" I can't remember. I know I recall too many good things when I look at him and that makes it difficult to stay angry. It hurts more than the pain in my hand, in my head, when I think of when he became my foster father. I was so willing to please him. When we were allocated to this area this became our house, the two of us, and he was the only driver I needed. We'd go to save people, and afterwards he'd drive me to places, new places, changed landscapes. We watched the world remake itself in flora. When the algae reached up out of the North Sea in vast fingers, glittering, bejewelled with fat clams, he took me to see it. And he took me to the woods when the bluebells had melted into a slick that was as warm as butter in the sun. I took off my shoes – shoes still fit me, back then – and rolled up my trousers, and paddled; my feet soaked up the blue and bore the colour for weeks afterwards. Eventually, it faded. As did my ability to think of such moments without feeling cheated.

Cheated that all I would ever have were disconnected moments, dreamlike, between the duties I had to perform. I began to realise that Stanislav could not help me with the burden I carried. He was not my real father. That had not mattered before, but as I sucked out more and more of the poison I felt less and less like a person myself. And to call him *father* became akin to listening to the Good News Network on the radio. It only made me think of everything that was not good and was no longer being said out loud.

"Tell me some bad news," I say to him. I squeeze his hand in mine.

"You're very ill. You should rest."

"No, tell me real bad news. The stuff out there. The stuff we're no longer allowed to know. War. Oppression. Something real."

"It's not a case of not being allowed to know it," he says, and he takes his hand away. I can tell from his tone that I'm getting under his skin. "I have tried to explain how all this works, if you'd ever wanted to listen."

"So explain. Explain the baby I just saved. How much of his life does the Red Gathering now own? Was it a better deal than the Blue Collective? What's the going rate for a cure?"

"Once the baby grows up, he'll work for the Gathering for at least thirty years, I'd imagine. What does that matter, Hope, when your cure has probably extended his life by at least that amount? Would you rather we still dealt in money? That his mother could never afford such a price, so watched him die? Trading in time means he's rich. He has time. Because of you. And they'll find him the right jobs and give him a good education for those roles. He'll get asked what he wants to do."

"Like you were asked?"

"Yes."

"And you chose to work here, with me? You still choose it?"

"Yes," he says, and then his face contorts, and he walks away from me. I listen to his footsteps. The door slams.

Now we're not arguing, I can hear the singing outside in the street. The crowd are singing the prayer.

"Hello?" I call out. I don't want to be alone.

The student replies; it sounds like she's standing close by but I can't see her over the lip of the hammock. "It's for you," she says. "The people are gathering. The word is that you're dying and they want to sing you to a peaceful rest."

"Bad news," I whisper. "Bad news that they want to turn into good."

She doesn't reply.

* * *

The more I lie here thinking about it, the more I can appreciate that Stanislav is right. I don't understand this world and I haven't made much of an effort to. I didn't vote in the last three elections even though he offered to drive me there. The difference between the organisations and the lives they offer with their trades has never been clear to me. Why is the Red Gathering better than the Blue Collective? They promise variations on a theme of happiness, but the tune remains the same. And the people sing it, because the future has become their religion and politics their church.

At least, I think that's true of the people I get to meet, who have already agreed the trade and signed away their years. There must be others who choose not to work for any organisation at all; they are not swayed by the living space, the work, the healthcare benefits. Living wild somewhere.

Living and dying very fast in the remnants of the old world.

The driver will take me to one of these communities. I want to see it, to see what humans are like underneath the trades and treatments. Is it better than the apartment blocks or Undergrowths? What is life like without this form?

* * *

I dream of Assembly Island.

It's one of those hot, hallucinatory dreams, where everything is vivid and verdant. The plants grow through the plastic upon which I stand, and then through me. Inside the skin on the soles of my feet and then snaking through my veins, up, up, up, to blossom in my lungs and force out flowers through my nostrils. What a sweet smell. The smell of my own sweat, I realise, when I wake; I am creating this wet, pungent aroma.

My scarf is too itchy around my neck to bear. I take it off and drop it over the side of the hammock. The skin around my collarbones has taken on a waxy, crinkling quality. It rustles when I run my hand over it, but at least it is painless.

I try to raise my head, but it is too heavy. I moan. The student comes close to me, leaning over the hammock so I can see her beautiful face.

"What time is it?" I ask.

"It's late morning. You've slept right through the night. We didn't want to try to move you to the bedroom."

"Can you call your family?"

She frowns at me. "I'm not due another call for weeks."

"No, that will be too late. Get Stanislav to give you permission. Is he here? Stanislav!"

"Shush," she says, wearily. "He's not here. And I don't need his permission. They're just not expecting my call right now. They'll be sleeping. It's the night, there."

"Oh. Couldn't you… wake them up?"

"Why?"

What should I say? Can I tell her that I've woken from this dream to the certainty that the crowd are right, and I am dying? Would she even understand that when I watch her with her family I feel included? "It's all right. Never mind."

She blinks, once, twice. She's mustering the courage to speak. Eventually, she says, "Listen. I have an idea of how we can make you more comfortable. Let me take some of your sickness. Your burden. I'll lift it from you. I know how to do it. I've watched you so many times."

"No."

"You're suffering. I can do this. Just a little, if you would like."

"No!"

She lifts up her fists; for a moment I think she's going to hit me. "I swear," she says. "I swear, you are the most stubborn, stupid—"

"Not ever."

"Fine." She drops her hands. "Fine." We stare at each other in the silence.

Silence. The singing has stopped.

"The crowd. I can't hear them."

"They decided not to waste their breath on you anymore."

I try to lean over in my hammock, to see out of the window, but I can't get a view of the street below and I feel my balance tipping; I fall – no, she grabs me – and pulls me back to a stable position. Then she says, "I'll get the laptop. My mother might be awake. She doesn't sleep well."

"Why not?"

She shrugs. "She saw too much, I think. Too much of the war, the plastic plague. When you see things like that, they become part of you, and then they're inside and they never come out. Do you want to say hello to her, is that what you want? If she answers?"

"No. I just want to watch."

So, she fetches the laptop and stands beside me as she calls. Her mother's face fills the screen. How old she looks; she has so little time left to trade. But she bathes in the light of the screen and the sight of her daughter, and then she looks – not younger, just happier. Youth and happiness are not the same thing.

* * *

How much time has passed?

Stanislav is close. I know it. I've spent hours drifting in and out of dreams, and now I find the world outside the window is darkening once more and I can tell that Stanislav is here. I call his name.

"Hi." He comes to me and holds the edge of the hammock, swinging me gently.

"What happened to the singers?"

"I thought you didn't like it?"

"I don't remember saying that."

"No," he muses. "No, you didn't. I suppose I assumed it. I organised a service at the new eruption. It's very fruitful. I set it up as a thanksgiving and a memorial event, for you."

"They think I'm already dead?"

"You very nearly are," he says. "You wanted bad news, so there you go. You've moved from very ill to dying."

"How come you're so sure?"

He keeps rocking the hammock, and the gentle motion is soothing. "Because everyone else who was found along with you on Assembly Island – all of that generation of plastic eaters – went through this. They reached a point where their bodies could no longer process the disease. And they all died. You're the last of that generation."

"I'm the last," I repeat. "Why didn't you tell me earlier?"

"What difference would it have made?"

I really am dying.

I thought so.

I'm dying.

I feel – I don't know what I feel. I should feel something.

"I could tell you that we have found many more, like Arama, to take over your work. Plastic eaters are being discovered all over the world, now. The worse the pollution, the more babies are born with this blessing. Perhaps they're the salvation of our species, what do you think? Or if you prefer it, I could tell you again about the good you've done.

But telling you that is the reason you threw me out in the first place, isn't it?"

"Don't ruin it," I tell him. "Don't turn bad news into good."

"Then how about the worst news? Would you like that?"

"The worst news?" I try to nod but my head is rigid, my neck too stiff to bend.

Stanislav says, his eyes fixed on mine, "You cannot appreciate what you've done for others because you've done it. The more people you saved, the more poison you ate. The more poison you ate, the more it changed you. Not just your body – your mind. You didn't start out angry and disbelieving. You were a trusting child, a happy one, when you were found on that island. You don't remember it, I know. Eating the cancer robbed you of the person that you were."

I wonder if that's true.

I wonder if this is, in fact, a good world. An improving one. One that I've helped to make better.

"You think that's bad news?" I ask him.

"I think it's the worst news I could ever give you. Because it means you're wrong about it all. About everything. Now, shall I get some of the singers to come back?"

I can't shake my head anymore. "You sing."

He always had such a wonderful voice. He puts a hand on the top of my head and sings me into peace. I can feel him willing me to let go of my life. He is wishing me towards a happy death, but I'm not going yet. I will hang on for tonight.

The driver promised me he would come.

* * *

I wake, and the driver is standing over me. For a moment I see his unguarded expression: his disgust at my body, his pity at my fate. Then he realises I'm awake and smiles, and says, "I'm here. Where do you want to go?"

I'm going nowhere. I'm cold, and hard, and so heavy. It's all I can do to say, "Look. My room. Under the bed."

"I'll fetch it," says the student. So, she is close by. Good. I listen to her footsteps, going and returning. She comes to stand beside the driver and she is holding the small wooden box that I have kept under my bed since my arrival in New Foreston.

"Open it," I tell her.

She lifts the lid. Inside is a collection of shiny objects that, once upon a time, would have been worth a lot more than the cost of one drive. Over the years I've been given so many of these things by the people I've saved, because it's hard to let go of the idea that they are worth something. Coins. Jewellery. Silver. Gold.

Now I understand that when you have nothing valuable left to sell, you'll try to sell anything else. Even worthless things.

"Take it," I tell the driver.

He shrugs, and takes the box from the student, flipping the lid shut. "But I already said I'll take you anywhere you want to go."

"Not me. Her." I can't raise my hand to point at her, but I manage to flick my eyes in her direction. "Take her home."

"Home?" says the driver, and the student says, "Brazil?" at

the same time, and then says, "No, no, she's out of her mind, leave her, leave her."

I hear Stanislav, calling to the driver, "Come here, come over here." And the driver walks away from me.

"I don't want to go home," says the student.

"You don't have to do this job. To be like me."

"I want to do it. I want to help people. Haven't you understood that? I wasn't made to come here, to sign up to the Red Gathering. I signed the deal knowing what it was. I want it. I want this life. To stay home and do nothing when so many people need help – that would be so selfish."

"You should be selfish."

"No! If I end up looking like you it will have been a good life. Don't you understand? You've had a good life!"

I'm so tired. I can't argue with her anymore and she is so desperate that I should agree with her on the value of my life, my actions. I lay down my resistance and tell her what she has always wanted to hear from me. "Okay. Yes. I have had a good life. You will too. You will do a good job, Arama."

She breathes out, long and low. How sweet, and young, and ripe she is. Like new fruit. "Finally," she says. "Finally, I have managed to teach you something."

STAR IN THE SPIRE

Sammie snatches up her rucksack in the first moment of wakefulness. She decides whether to stay or run in the breath of instinct. Staying wins out.

She was certain something rustled. But beyond the willowy-tree, nothing moves.

Of course nothing moves.

Perhaps it was only a sound that crossed over from her dream, a particular and deep one in which dead monsters came for her and pushed her down in the dirt with their teeth and claws and faces: grumblers and whiners. Sounds buried within from her past – will they return? They used to call at night. She dreads it and wants it.

She relaxes a little, shakes her head. She runs her fingers through the knots of her hair. Still no sound apart from the thin trickle of water and the wind, so she stands, stretches, and decides against washing in the stream. Instead, she takes her flask from the rucksack and swallows a mouthful of water. She pulls up her skirts and urinates on the ground, close to the trunk. Perhaps it will do the roots some good.

Then she parts the brown, curling curtain of the willowy-tree and steps outside.

It's a hot day. Forever getting hotter, and she can't quite remember cold. For a moment Sammie thinks of staying in the shade, but maybe it's also a finding day. Something is different about the morning. Perhaps the smell in the air is a little fresher. Time to follow her nose.

Her instinct tells her to climb to a vantage point, like that time she was taken to look out over a town just to see it had fallen silent. Sammie asked her uncle where all the people had gone, and he had pointed down into the ground. The tower of the church in the town had seemed like a celebration waiting to happen, of rising, of being reclaimed. It had been so tall and yet far below the majesty of the crown of the hill, where Vikin warriors had once been buried. That was what her uncle had told her. She had asked what Vikins were.

Proud warriors, left standing, her uncle said. *Like you.* Then they had started back down the hill and seen a living crow on the way, black and hunched, feathers dull, its claws curved over a dead branch with propriety. *A very good sign.* But of what he did not say.

Anyway, thinks Sammie. She follows the curve of the land. The remaining trees turn from willowy to stretch-out, brittle leaves dotted on lower branches. Then the trees dwindle and the land is laid bare in the sunshine and the stiff wind. The ground is hard with chunks of flint. A few patches of tough yellow grass. How could anybody rise up from that? Softer soil would be needed. The hill becomes steeper. She puts one foot in front of the other until the air changes and she senses she is near the top. Yes, there are a final few steps and then the ups and downs are laid out below her, and – a surprise – a pile of carefully placed rocks has been left at the very highest point of this hill. It is a reminder of all those who must have walked this way before, and it's also a treasure, a finding, but only a tiny one compared to this view.

The valley ahead is alive.

She stares at the sudden, thick wash of colour. So many shades of green. They coat the slopes down to a slick wide river of dark grey. Nestled in the bend before the river disappears from view is a village, the houses squat and snug, rubbing shoulders, arranged as if a hand placed them down and fixed them firm to their spots.

All the soil is dying, her uncle said when she asked him why they always moved on. *But it might be different somewhere. That's where we're going.*

She has found somewhere.

The ground here must be fertile in a new way. Or perhaps this is a different kind of grass. It looks fatter. Riper. There is a church, too. With a point. She searches for the word. A spire.

Sammie thinks of the time she was taken inside a church. By someone. Not her uncle. Everything was dark wood and heavy carving apart from the long strips of colourful light, and there were thick beams built into a roof. But it did not soar to a point on the inside. She remembered how she expected it to taper into darkness, up so high, to contain, far above, a trapped and twinkling star. It had been a disappointment to find otherwise, and she could recall the feeling easily but also could say to herself – silly, silly baby. Why had she been expecting such a thing? Everything had seemed very large to her back then, and on the brink of transformation.

She sits and drinks it all in.

One night, in the tent, when there had still been a tent – before the moment it split down the middle in a storm and left her crying and her uncle raging and neither of them as loud as the screaming wind – she had asked her uncle when he was on the brink of sleep if she could be the one that talked next time they had a meeting. And he had laughed, and said, *Yes, if you've got something to say.* She had been so excited to talk. When the time came and they were gathered, a scrawny handful but still in good humour, she explained what churches were like and how she had once been inside one, thinking it set her apart from the others and they would want to know. They were forever telling her things, after all. How to boil the water and how to find things that still grow. It was a returning of the favour.

They had laughed. *You've never been inside one*, her uncle had said. *Sammie you Silly Sausage. Where did all that come from?* Nobody had any idea of where she could have picked up such thoughts. It had led to a long discussion. Could ideas or memories rise up from the dead? Could they be sliding their thoughts through the soil and entering her? She hadn't liked the idea of it, had shaken her head violently, and they'd all laughed harder. And then came the storm that took the tent.

Being little had made her an object of comedy for the crowd, but they stopped laughing at her, or at anything, as it became impossible to feed them all. There was shouting. That spring the plants all over had come up twisted and wrong, squelchers and smellers, and then the plants all died anyway, and the shouting got louder and louder until the day she woke and found herself alone.

Even her uncle was gone.

She had laughed and laughed, long, at them, as loud as she could in the hope they would hear.

This is a finding day, and there is a church.

Sammie stands, and unpacks the remains of her dried mushrooms from her rucksack. There are many mushrooms in the darker areas, popping out free from the soil. What makes a building push out if not a trapped star trying to get home to the sky? Things need to grow out, get home. And there's nobody to stop her, hasn't been for an age. The path she takes and the legs that take it are all her own.

She nibbles at a mushroom, then starts down the hill. The grass is so thick that it catches at her toes. A wonderful sensation, to have it push against her, alive and strong.

She looks up, and sees it.

Him. A man.

A man in a lower field, standing tall.

Sammie opens her mouth, tries to make a loud sound that comes out as a croak. She hasn't spoken in so long she's nearly forgotten the knack. She sets off to him at a run, feeling the flint catch at her toes, and she nearly trips, twice, but finds her footing somehow and surges on while the figure waits for her – is he waiting? Has he seen her? There's no movement, no movement, until she gets close enough to realise he will never move. He's not real.

What did her uncle call them? She saw one, tall in a field of dried white weeds, and she was scared and excited by it, its shape, its outstretched arms.

It's only a scar-crow.

She slows, tries to calm her breathing as she draws close enough to see it properly. She feels fear again at the sight. Idiot, she tells herself. But there's something to this particular scar-crow that unnerves her. It's in the way the arms don't reach out. They're not raised in the cross but held forward at a low angle. Could they have fallen into that position? Nothing about the scar-crow looks aged, or forlorn. The arms point strongly, with vigour. They point down to the church.

Sammie must find courage to take the final few steps to stand beside it. The head is a leathery ball. The body is a long grey coat buttoned up tight, and the legs are lumpy trousers. There's a strange smell to the figure. Not straw, not soil. Sammie touches the coat.

It's filled with something soft. She pokes it, and it gives under her finger.

She unbuttons it. Just one button. Her spine is hot, prickly. As if someone else is standing nearby, out of sight, watching her. Nobody, she reminds herself. Inside the coat is thick whitish wool, tangled clumps; the scar-crow is packed tight with it. A full, animal smell is instantly strong in the air and she gags, then controls herself and breathes shallow. This is the smell of a bah-bah. A… sheep. She had almost forgotten the word, but it comes back to her now, and more besides. Her uncle had kept a few thin and ragged sheep for as long as he could, until they went the way of all the other animals. And there had been a bedtime book, for a little while, hadn't there? Not in a tent but in a dark blue room, with a large presence – a woman with a warm chest – reading about a sheep that couldn't sleep.

Sammie undoes another button. The wool starts to spill out. She takes handfuls of it and tugs. Inside it's no longer white, but pink. The more she pulls, the more it deepens its colour, and then there's a sudden shade of red and a new smell to match, and then a cold, slippery coil spills out and pools in her hands.

Alive, she thinks, and stuffs it back into the body where it belongs but no, no, it's cold and dead. But fresh dead. Not rot. Couldn't be more than a few hours of dead.

She looks around again, eyes roaming over the lush fields: down to the village, back up to the skyline. She's so afraid of this living being that is the land around her, with creatures living in it, through it, on it. She wants to call out again but her voice will surely fail now there's fear in her as well.

Her hands are wet and stained.

She thinks about wiping them on her coat but the thought of the smell sticking to her makes her change her mind. And besides, she's not done with it yet. She needs to look again. She reaches in and moves the wool, very gently, until a coil of matter is visible. It looks wet. Will it writhe or squirm? Dead, she tells herself, and touches it again, grasps it, feels her confidence returning. She pulls it out and tugs out more. It starts to loop on the ground, by her feet. There's so much of it. Something catches on the waistband of the trousers and up comes a large brown lump, bigger than her two hands put together. It falls onto the pile of coils, loud and sodden. The sound horrifies her. She skitters back to a safe distance and watches the lump. It does not move.

Around it is a long green tendril that does not break. A healthy plant. The tendril stretches, connecting the lump to the body still.

She shakes her head at it. Is it a finding? No, no, she has done something wrong by taking it from the body, something terrible, but she can't bring herself to try to put it all back. She could push it and force it and still so much matter would not stay in, not now. It can't be undone. The buttons of the coat would no longer hold it. The plant grasps at it; it will not give up its lumps and coils.

Go.

She wipes her hands on the ground, the thick grass, then moves slowly, still facing the scar-crow, feeling the way with her feet. There comes a point where the sense of danger lessens just enough for her to turn, to move faster, to put distance between them.

She sees the next scar-crow.

It's lower in the valley, and it wears a long orange dress. There's hair, yellow hair, down to its shoulders, spilling from the leathery ball of a head. Its arms are pointing downwards to the church.

Sammie has to know. She goes to it, crosses the field and then pushes through the longer grasses that are threaded with such delicate wild flowers that she holds her breath. The dress flaps free at the bottom, revealing a chunky pole – no, a trunk. The scar-crow is formed from a tree. It's a kind she hasn't seen before, short, with regular and smooth branches that end in splayed twigs. There's a thick belt of blue rope around the waist, and whatever has been used as stuffing creates the bulbous effect of large breasts.

Sammie says, "Woman." The word must be forced, and even then, it emerges as little more than a whisper. She reaches for the collar of the dress and pulls it apart. Her fingers touch something so soft that she can't believe anything of its kind could exist. She wants to bury herself in it, and she strokes it for a little while before daring to pull the collar further to see what she's touching.

The collar gives, rips, and something familiar is revealed. Rabbits, she thinks. The word comes to her easily. She is remembering more of the old life. Two rabbits, curled and tied tight to form the breasts. The heads have been tucked between their front paws and their back legs are folded up to their ears. Their tails are bloodied and their mouths are open, their teeth showing. From inside both mouths erupt dark green growth, prickly with long black thorns.

Look, her uncle said. *Look, a rabbit.* Pointing across a different field, on a day's walking to a new place to camp.

This is a good sign, if there are still rabbits. He had her hand in a tight grip; she felt his excitement through his grasp. She was scared but he said, *Rabbits never hurt anyone,* and they tiptoed together to where it waited, and trembled, and it did not run. She was so pleased to meet it until she was close enough to see the bloody mucus on its eyes and nose, and its teeth working, working, as its head weaved from side to side.

She pulls the collar back up, as best as she can, to cover the rabbits and the thorns.

The village is below. She has a good view of it now; the scar-crows have drawn her closer. They are so newly dead, so nearly alive. She wants to reach a scar-crow at speed, quickly enough to find a breathing, beating thing inside. She scans the valley and sees a third figure, this one in a white shirt and blue trousers, wearing a curved hat with a neat brim. It's further down, nearer to the village again.

She sprints there, falling once, picking herself up without thought of the stinging pain in her knees.

Inside the chest: teeth, large and flat, set in a jawbone with the flesh of the gum still pink and shiny, hidden within a nest of wet, pulpy grass.

From there to the fourth scar-crow, set back on a discernible path through tall wild flowers. It's shorter than the others and it wears a hooded, baggy top and jeans, with a thin cap on the head, brim turned back to the neck. The top holds in red fleshy petals, veined. And coarse fur, black and white, with four paws that have been severed from limbs, long and curving claws thick with dirt. A grumbler, she thinks. A grumbler only just dead. Or perhaps, she can dare to hope, that it is not newly dead but almost brought back to life.

The fifth scar-crow, by a bushy hedgerow, has a white coat with a silver tag over the pocket bearing letters. Sammie wishes she could remember any of her reading. She never did have the knack for it, and her uncle gave up trying to teach her. Inside the coat she finds a sack formed of grey fur that is fringed with long black hairs. In the bag, a large lump of matter with rubbery tubes emerging from the marbled surface. Inside the tubes are many fruits, packed tight: little balls of black that smell sweet within the meat.

The sixth scar-crow is in the village itself.

Sammie enters the garden of the first house through a painted gate, aware of the empty gaze of the windows upon her. Plants she's never seen before, could not have dreamed of, have grown so tall, so free. They have sprouted into strange shapes that block the way. The figure is made of two small red trees this time, growing in parallel. The arms are budding, outstretched branches. It has only a blanket thrown over it, draping loosely to the ground. But the balled head is the same, balanced in the crook of one tree. No, not quite the same – the leather has split on one side, just a little, and through the gap Sammie can see— can see—

She takes out her penknife from her rucksack. She widens the split and pulls back the fleshy leather.

Skin.

Skin like her own and the corner of an open mouth, and inside that mouth small white teeth. In the darkness within, the curve of a tongue.

She stumbles out of the garden, feeling the plants catching, grabbing at her skirts. She finds herself on the path that leads to the church.

She walks past houses, past post boxes and slatted benches, past signs fixed to walls and fences. The letters are thick and large and there's nobody left to read them. They never make sense to her, no matter how hard to she tries to remember them, remember how everything was. There had been so many living things and they all left her behind. How could she, alone, hold the old world in her head? But this is not a return to the old, after all. This is something new made of the pieces left behind – the flesh and growth and all that once shrank back and was buried, rising up anew.

The church.

She walks under the shadow of the spire, not daring to look up. She reaches the double doors and tries one of the ringed handles, pulling, pushing. Then turning. Something gives, the door swings back, and she enters.

It is just as she remembers. She must have been here before. An aisle, with the dark wooden lines of benches on either side and beautiful light through long coloured windows. There are so many scar-crows.

They are sitting, wrapped in their branches, in their silence. "Hello," she says. "Hello."

Her voice, clear. Getting stronger.

The stones of the floor have cracked and overturned. Tendrils, veins, crawl out, twisting and thickening to become legs, legs for scar-crows. They fill the benches and their ball-heads are all in place, but now she sees their heads are fruits, fruits ripening, and their arms are growing up up up to the spire.

There has always been so much life beneath her, all this time, under the ground. She was trapped in the tip of a spire. She was the very last star, way up high, on top of the world, and the new people have grown up through the dark to meet her.

"You found me," she says, as loud as she has ever spoken, not a grumble or a whine, not a shout at all, but a voice never heard before. Her grown-up voice. The fruits are ripe and ready as they turn to face her, and the vines gentle as they wrap around her feet.

FROM THE NECK UP

"Decapitated," said Megan.

"Mmm," said her mother. "Did you put your CV on that new site?"

"Didn't you just hear? A helicopter took the head clean off a veteran. Look." She held out her tablet. It showed a black-and-white picture of a young man in uniform, handsome apart from the ears, and below it a photograph of a big pile of wreckage in what seemed to be a residential street not very different from the one in which Megan and her mother lived. "He fought for our country, you know. He deserved better. It's a tragedy."

"Was that nearby?"

"Yorkshire. It crashed right into his house. A malfunction of something, it says."

Her mother returned to looking at Facebook on her phone. Yorkshire was, in her mind, both geographically and figuratively miles away.

"There should be some kind of campaign," said Megan. "To stop helicopters from flying low in built-up areas.

Wasn't there an accident like this just a few years ago?"

Her mother stood up and left the living room.

"Somebody has to say something," said Megan. She signed into her online account as MizMeg60060002 and left a long comment under the article about how rich and powerful people were manipulating flight plans so that they got to their illuminati meetings in time. It made her feel slightly better. Then she went upstairs to her room with the intention of perusing job websites and coming up with good reasons why she couldn't do any of the jobs they advertised.

Life is difficult when you hit that dull grey spot between being useful and being dead. The urge Megan felt every day was not to achieve something, nor to actively stop other people from achieving. Instead, she wanted a person to come along and make a particular effort on her behalf. If only a Hollywood star could have knocked on the door – Ryan Gosling, maybe, or Paul Newman fifty years ago – and said, "I see you, Megan. I see that you're struggling. Come take my hand and we'll climb this mountain together." It didn't even have to be a supporter. Anybody would do, really.

But she knew, as she quietly closed her bedroom door and thanked heaven for the invention of wireless broadband, that nobody would come along unless she climbed that mountain herself. Then every happy idiot would rush up and congratulate her – 'Look at us! The happy people!' – and they would all spring about like mountain goats in fresh, clean alpine air, ignoring the morass of melancholiacs far below them.

She hated being at the bottom of the mountain, but she didn't want to be a smug goat either. So, Megan stood still. She stood still in her bedroom doorway and looked at the head in the centre of her bed.

It was an upside-down severed head with a ragged, wet stump where a neck should have been. A mess of tubes, holes and fibrous strands oozed blood, and a lumpy knob of bone poked upwards.

She made a low sound; no, wait, she wasn't making any sound at all. Underneath that open wound, down past the crooked curve of the chin, the mouth was moving. It was speaking.

She couldn't understand what it was saying. All Megan could concentrate on were the eyes, beneath the mouth, that blinked and then focused upon her. They had that unsettling quality eyes get when they're turned the wrong way around, and looked far too knowing and alien. Megan doubted she'd ever feel comfortable with the concept of eyes ever again.

The eyes blinked, the mouth moved. The neck oozed, and her pink and purple duvet cover sagged in the centre under the weight of that head.

"Garrruuummm babababa fffooom," said the head. "Fwop fwop fwop fwop fwop." The eyes stared and the eyebrows flexed as if something very important was being said.

"I don't…" said Megan. "I don't understand." But even as she said the words, she realised that the sounds were self-explanatory. They were helicopter sounds. "Are you the veteran?" she said. "The one in the… incident?"

"Mmmgam," said the head. It frowned at her. No – she

tilted her head and found it was actually a smile.

"You got decapitated. Your head – how come – it's, um, here?"

It didn't reply. Possibly it was attempting to shrug shoulders that didn't exist.

"I'll call the police. They'll come and get you."

She headed back downstairs. And there began a very difficult set of telephone calls with unhelpful officials, who eventually informed her that the head in question had been located not far from the body in question and was currently residing in the Pathology unit of Pontefract Hospital.

"It's not," said Megan. "It's… escaped."

It was the wrong word to use, apparently. The line went dead.

Her mother was in the kitchen, making cheese on toast, with a miserable expression.

"You heard all that then," Megan said.

"Megan, I'm begging you," said her mother. "Get a job. My pension only goes so far. I can't afford for you to have a nervous breakdown."

"Come upstairs and look for yourself. That old man's head is on my bed."

"I told you. I'm not going in your room. I'm not tidying up your mess or making your bed or washing your clothes anymore. I took you in when they made you redundant and you lost your flat. I took you in. That's what mothers do. But I will not be your slave. Not anymore."

Every conversation they had ended the same way, even the ones about the weather. It seemed to Megan that the only thing enslaving her mother was her own thoughts, which inevitably always led in the same direction.

"Fine," said Megan. "Fine." She took out a bin bag and a couple of tea towels and stomped back up the stairs.

The old man's head wore an apologetic expression. "Goash," it said.

"No, it's not your fault. You didn't turn up here on purpose, did you? I'll just tidy you away, and I'm sure everything will just... return to normal."

"Flaaah?" it said, with something approaching hope.

She shook out the bin bag and moved to the bed.

Who was she kidding? The head of a war veteran, and she was about to put it in a bin bag and take it outside to the street where it would wait for collection day, blinking and making odd sounds and waiting to become landfill.

She couldn't do it.

Up close, it wasn't all that gory, really. The blood had stopped pumping and the ripped edges of skin were curling to create quite a decorative effect, if you took it out of context.

"Well, you can't stay on the bed," she told it. She gathered her courage and clamped her hands over its large ears. The skin was cold and soft, and the curves and creases pressed against her palms. It wasn't heavy. Very slowly, she carried it over to her bookcase and placed it in front of her collection of Stephen King novels.

"Thraaa," said the head, when she stepped back.

"You're welcome. Would you rather be the right way up?"

"Schfoo."

"No. Okay."

It was a very polite head. Easy to get along with. The next few hours were spent in pleasant conversation. She talked, and it gave the appearance of being an extremely good listener.

By the evening Megan felt much better about the head, the world, and herself in general. She microwaved herself a moussaka.

"Have you found a job yet?" her mother called from the living room, over the sound of the television.

"Something better. I found a new friend."

Silence. Well, that was better than an argument.

She tried feeding the head some moussaka, but it made a face and the aubergine dribbled up its nose, so she cleaned it up with one of the tea towels. There was a pink, flushed colour to the cheeks, as if the body was off somewhere exercising rather than lying in a mortuary. And the stump looked different, somehow. It was changing colour, getting darker, and the messy bits looked brown and squelchy. A few specks of green were just visible. It reminded Megan of a science experiment she'd done at school, growing beansprouts, documenting the progress of the tiny shoot up through the soil.

She was looking at the beginning of plant growth.

"Um, I don't know how to say this exactly, but I think something is growing in your stump."

The head said, "Plah." It didn't look upset.

"Okay, well, just so you know. I might hit the hay now. Another long day of job hunting ahead tomorrow." But she couldn't get undressed with the head watching her. In the end she apologised and then spread the other tea towel over it, rather like covering a bird cage at bedtime. It didn't speak, so she took it as a sign that it really didn't mind.

Lying in the dark, feeling very aware of what was on the bookshelf, Megan thought she would never find sleep. But there it was, unexpected and welcome, and her dreams didn't feature heads or helicopters or even looking for employment, which was a nice change. In the morning, the bottom of the head, or the top of the head depending on how you look at it, was visible under the tea towel. She could see the old man's hair, thin and silvery, lying around the lines on his ruddy temple.

"So, you're still here," she said. She got dressed before removing the tea towel, and there he was, with a very self-satisfied smile and a big bush of green leaves stretching up tall from the stump of his neck.

"Blimey," said Megan.

His face was really very red, and the plant leaves had a strong smell that reminded her of the greenhouse in the back garden; at least, in the days when her father, rest his soul, had spent hours out there potting and planting and using his green fingers for a good purpose. The vegetables had been so delicious. Carrot soup, that was his speciality. Home-grown carrots.

The leaves growing from the stump were bushier than carrot leaves. She didn't recognise them.

"That's amazing," she said. The eyes blinked.

In the days that followed, Megan charted the intense growth of the plant-head. It flourished, the green shoots whizzing up and then developing a gentle curve as they grew thicker and heavier to droop down and form a curtain around the old man's head. When she parted the curtain to say hello to him, it took him longer to focus upon her, and it soon gave up talking. It seemed to be quite happy becoming a plant.

She researched it, looking up the growths on gardening websites and comparing leaf shape, but no – it was, as far as she could tell, an absolute original. A brand new genus. And it had come to her for discovery.

She took some cuttings and moved them down to the greenhouse, cleaning the filthy glass panes until they admitted the bright sunlight once more, buying compost and pots and even a fancy watering can with the final few pounds from her redundancy pay. The cuttings took, and grew, and became healthy plants of their own. They began to bear flowers.

The flowers were small, and blue, and very beautiful. They looked a bit like forget-me-nots. They had a most wonderful smell.

The flower deserved a name.

Back in the house, her mother was halfway through a packet of biscuits and a daytime television special about attics.

"Where's my tablet?" she said.

"I don't know. Don't ask me to find your things for you. What have you been doing out there, in the greenhouse? You're meant to be—"

"I'm too busy for all that." She found the tablet behind the cushion on the arm of the sofa. A quick search brought up the details she needed. An article about an old man who had lost his head in a helicopter accident. A man who had deserved better. Well, now he had it. And his name was Sergeant Neville Makepeace.

"Makepeace," she said. "Perfect."

Newly christened, the makepeace flowers continued to do wonderfully well. Megan tended them and they filled the greenhouse. After a while, the idea came to her to make little individual bouquets. She formed them with great care, wrapping little scraps of lace around the stems, and took them to town. On the street corner outside the post office, the scent of the flowers touched the noses and hearts of those passing by, and she sold out in no time at all.

That evening, back in her room, Megan found that the head would no longer open its eyes for her.

"Neville," she said, and gently stroked his cheek. "Neville, wake up."

But no. Neville was quiet and the face looked calm, and happy. It looked done.

Downstairs, her mother was looking through the kitchen window at the newly cleaned greenhouse. "You put a lot of work into that," she said. "What are you growing in there?"

"Flowers."

"What about some veg? Your dad used to do great veg."

"I remember. But I like flowers."

"Megan," said her mother. "Flowers aren't going to feed us."

"They might and they might not. But they'll definitely make me happy." Happiness was no longer a difficult concept for her. It turned out it wasn't a mountain to be climbed at all. You didn't look up at it and wonder how anybody ever reached the summit. You simply ignored that mountain and went wherever your feet wanted to take you. It was so much easier than she had ever expected. "And they can make you happy too."

"Please, can't you just—"

"No, I can't," Megan said firmly. "Now come on." She led her mother down the garden path to the greenhouse and ushered her inside. The little blue flowers were dotted everywhere, like specks of a perfect sky. She felt the scent sink into her and work its magic.

Her mother smiled. It was a miracle.

"How lovely. You've got a little nursery down here, have you? I wonder if you could start selling them."

"I already have. Not for much. It's not really about the money, is it?"

"No," said her mother, surprising them both. "It's not. Well, look at this, Megan. I think you found yourself a job."

"Not a job. A vocation."

Her mother looked into Megan's face, and nodded.

THE TEARS OF A BUILDING
SURVEYOR, AND OTHER STORIES

My name is Violet. I'm married to Tom and I'm old, and I'd like to say that's how I introduce myself to people but it would be a lie. I don't introduce myself to anyone. I'm of no interest, not even to Tom, who has heard all my anecdotes so many times that he corrects me when I get the details wrong. Which I, quite deliberately, do.

I am sitting in the fairly chilly conservatory today in an attempt to start writing my memoirs, and if I ever manage to finish writing them I'm going to walk out of the door of this house, leave Tom behind, and start living. That's the promise I've made to myself. Right now he's in the dining room finishing his boiled egg. He cramps my style with his devotion to the truth; he would look over my shoulder if he knew I was writing my life story and have everything recorded the way *he* remembered it.

Maybe we'd agree on the bare bones: I was born in Bourne End; I got married; I had three children; I raised them; they left; I retired; Tom retired; we sat around and got ready for the end in Bourne End. Yes, we could probably agree on that.

But the truth is also this:

The Taj Mahal was a huge white ship on the azure sea-sky. I swear it rocked and swayed on the waves of adulation that kept it monumental. It had a certain song to it that I still hear sometimes, at night, through the open window.

At a dinner party overlooking Martha's Vineyard (she grew wonderful grapes) I turned once to Peter Ustinov and asked if I should endeavour to tell the truth in all things, and he said something so incredibly witty that I can't record it here in case your head should explode. Three people at the dinner party laughed so hard they had to be given emergency aspirin, including Mother Theresa.

I once ate the eyes of a tortoise at the behest of a Bahraini Sheikh. It wasn't even a delicacy: he just felt like setting a test to see how far he could push me. It was that kind of a relationship. I popped them in my mouth, quick, and he was so entertained by the faces I pulled that he gave me the blinded tortoise as a gift. I took the tortoise back to my apartment in Paris and called it Oedipus. It lived for years, and I felt a stab of guilt every time it weaved its little head from side to side. Isn't that appalling?

From my wicker seat – I never noticed before quite how uncomfortable wicker is – I have a good view of the street by the light of another indistinguishable morning. With my notebook open and ready to receive my thoughts, I find myself watching my neighbours as they come and go, forming a tiny corner of a global pattern, like the tiny squares that make up lino. They have such busy lives and all seem to have a purpose. The young man in thirty-one runs up and down the street in tiny shorts, only warming up, no doubt, before a big sprint through the park to keep his figure. I watch him go past every morning, waiting for him to glance my way. To make me feel visible.

Young sweaty bodies are so pink and wet and agile, like salmon jumping upstream. I can't even jump out of this chair.

There's a crisp packet stuck in my front hedge. I'd better go and fish it out. It'll be a bit of exercise for me. And then there's flower arranging at the garden centre, and a hospital appointment for Tom. The results of the latest tests are in.

* * *

Today I want to write about the time I spent in Austria, because that's where my life really started. I'd been travelling with my chaperone, Señor Velasquez, across Europe since the death of my mother. The Señor was kind, but not an approachable figure to a young girl, and he had his foibles. He carried a white cane everywhere that, with the touch of a secret button, could be transformed into a rainbow-striped umbrella. He performed this trick in settings designed to elicit a gasp from those around him, and Salzburg was no different. We disembarked from the train into a light rain, the taste of Munich beer still on our lips after the joy of the Oktoberfest, and hired a two-horse carriage to the Kapitelplatz. The Señor held his cane over his shoulder, a quirk to his lips, putting a kink in the long black line of his moustache.

As he helped me down from the carriage, we stood at the south side of the cathedral, looking up at the mighty dome. The Señor chose that moment to press his secret button, and lo! The rainbow umbrella brightened the rain-washed platz, and the local children, dressed in thick green lederhosen and floral pinafores, crowded around him in delight. I took advantage of the moment to escape the Señor's watchful eyes and stepped into the cool interior of the cathedral, past the flanking golden candlesticks and into the airy, enlightened space that brought peace to my thoughts.

I sat in the nearest pew and gazed up at the white figure of Christ on the dark wood of the cross. I prayed to him and felt a change rise up in me; I felt goodness in myself that I had never suspected of existence. I had been a difficult child, exacerbating my mother's condition, and I had carried a guilt with me since leaving London on that icy February morning. But now I realised that my shame had run its course and I had grown into a young woman with new choices to make, and new desires I could choose to indulge or deny as I wished.

That was the moment I realised I wanted to become a nun.

The Señor found me in the cathedral and ushered me out with little regard for the hushed atmosphere of worship. We strolled around Salzburg, took *kaffee und Linzertorte*, and he bought some *Mozartkugeln* and some cigars from a street vendor. I remained rapt in my vision of the future, and did not comment. I had to choose the time carefully in order to reveal my plans.

Later, in the drawing room of our modest Gasthof, the Señor pressed me on the issue of my withdrawn state. I found I could not dissemble; even though I had sought the perfect time and place for my revelation I stammered out my intention to him, and his joyous reply shocked me, given his own proclaimed Godlessness.

"Fabelhaft!" he said. "My dear Violet, I am delighted that you have reached the same decision as I. You are far too delectable to belong to any man on Earth, and so we must dedicate you to God. Luckily, I am in the position to help you in your calling. There is a wonderful abbey in the hill surrounding Salzburg itself and the Abbess is a long-standing personal friend of mine. Allow me to introduce you to her."

I didn't ask how he had come by such an acquaintance, although the question did cross my mind. Instead, I thanked him, and before I knew it I was wearing a black robe and sneaking off before matins to sing in the hills, throwing out my arms in my uncontained joy of the glory of life. The Abbess tolerated my behaviour – being the wise, benevolent sort – but eventually she confessed to me that she thought my calling might lie in a different direction after all. That was when she packed me off to look after the seventeen wayward children of a local Air Commodore.

It was all downhill from there.

Being a nun is always better in principle than reality, I think. My time in Salzburg taught me that. Get out there and grab life. But grab it with the right man. Don't fall into the clutches of men like the good-looking shorts-wearing man at thirty-one. He's nice to look at but I'm betting he can't be trusted.

I wish I was young enough to find out.

There he goes again, off to the park. Past my window without once looking around. Without once seeing me.

I really did want to be a nun. I'd read a book about a nun who went to the colonies and helped lepers. I wasn't so keen on the leper bit, but generally helping people and looking serene seemed to be the best thing a girl could do with her life. But not being Catholic put a spanner in the works. I still remember my mum explaining to me that nobody really became nuns anymore, particularly when they were Church of England to start with. Still, I thought that I could be a nun in spirit rather than in body, and I worked hard towards that. I never went near the local boys and scowled at any who came near me. This was back when girls went to school not to learn, but to meet. They were meant to meet their husbands. I didn't, of course, and so I was packed off to secretarial college and, in between typing up to eighty words per minute and studying shorthand, I met Ivan.

He was the son of my teacher. He used to wait for his mother outside the building by the bike shed, and he made a comment about my bike. Nice saddle, he said. I was getting a bit fed up of the nun act. Nobody seemed to notice my shining inner goodness. So I thought I'd find out how the other half lived.

I didn't know it back then – boys like thirty-one and Ivan like to give bicycles a test drive, but they're not interested in making the down payment. By the time I found out he'd got me pregnant he'd already moved on to a newer model.

Right, time for Tom's elevenses. Apparently things will really start to go downhill fast in a few weeks or so, so the doctor said I should get as much rest as possible before then. But between providing round-the-clock care and writing a memoir, I can't see that happening.

* * *

Of course, things turned ugly in Austria.

I don't want to go into the details, but I managed to escape by disguising myself as a ticket inspector and taking the Munich Express out of Salzburg. It was an ill-fated decision; we never did reach Munich. The train was diverted before we'd crossed the German border and it gained speed until it seemed that the mountains, pastures and triangular roofs of the farms were blurring together into brown-green streaks, and all the charm of the Grossglockner Pass was lost.

The other travellers began to get nervous. A few asked me questions, demanding to know what was happening, and I lied as well as I could, describing snowstorms in Munich, but it did not persuade them for long. Then the real ticket inspector came into the compartment and my disguise was blown. I was marched to the baggage cart and locked in, for the authorities to deal with when we reached... where? Some unknown destination. Meanwhile, the train sped on.

When it finally shuddered to a standstill, the voices of the passengers rose, and rose, and then the screaming started. I found all my reserves of courage and tenacity had been exhausted. The largest suitcase in the baggage cart – an enormous maroon portmanteau – was the only refuge I could find. Upon opening it, frothy confections of dancing costumes spewed forth, frills and feathers and lace lining galore; I pushed them back in and made a nest for myself like a mouse in a shoebox. I pulled the lid down, and waited, and waited. Eventually, somehow, I fell asleep.

The jarring of my spine through the layers of tulle and tinsel awoke me – the case was being lifted. There was the sensation of movement; was I being carried? The feathers tickled my face and the sequins scratched my hands. I realised I had grasped fistfuls of the material and was squeezing it, squeezing it tightly, trying to release the agony of fear from my body.

A shock, like a slap in face – the case must have been dropped. I felt pain in my neck and back, and thanked God for the costumes that padded my hiding place. I waited until the ache subsided, listening intently, and the sensation of claustrophobia began to creep up over my brain, crowding out all other fears. What if the lid had been locked? What if I was trapped, forever, in this case? The air was thick in my lungs; I couldn't wait a moment longer. I pushed against the lid and it popped open, offering no resistance. Bright light burned my eyes and I curled up in the case once more as a reflex. After a time, I began to make out shapes rotating above me – a triangle, a circle, a square – all pieces of coloured glass spinning on an elaborate series of wires that covered the ceiling. The tall windows at the end of the grandiose hall let in glorious sunlight, illuminating the glass to provide me with one of the most beautiful sights of my life – the show of colour and movement of those ever-swaying mobiles.

And then I looked around me.

I was surrounded by cases, unopened; the rest of the contents of the train's baggage cart were spread out over the floor of the hall, in random order, and every piece of it was spattered in blood. Blood had soaked into the fabric holdalls and turned the material black. It had dried onto the leather suit-holders in crusted patterns and it had caked the plastic luggage sets in gouts.

The smell hit me. It was the fresh tang of the butcher's block, multiplied a hundredfold, so that I gagged and pulled free one of the petticoats from the portmanteau to cover my face. This was an atrocity that had only just happened, around me, while I slept. Whoever committed such a terrible act, to leave this gory evidence, had to be nearby.

How could I escape? The double doors opposite me and the tall windows were too obvious; who could guess what would await me there? I turned around and spied a small grille that had to lead to an air duct against the back wall. There was a chance that I could squeeze inside.

I climbed to it, over the soaking, stinking cases, feeling the gore form a slick on my hands and ooze through the material of my trousers. Within moments I was sodden and barely able to restrain myself from screaming, but I crawled on. The grille was loose, thank God, and I was able to prise it off the wall. Yes, it would admit me; the blood on my clothes slicked the passage and facilitated my entrance. A long metal duct led away from that room of horror and I started to wriggle as fast as I could, praying that it would not narrow and leave me trapped forever.

I crawled onwards and onwards. Time had no meaning. Nor did my exhaustion. I had to succeed.

I have no idea how much ground I actually covered before I popped out of a small hole in the centre of a giant polished sculpture outside King's Cross Railway Station.

I never did find out who – or what – killed those passengers, or to where they were taken.

There's no way to end this part of the memoir nicely. I'm really disappointed with myself. I didn't want to write about blood, or death, or fear. I'm getting enough of all that at home. But the thing I've found about writing a memoir is that the past is always at the mercy of the present. It can't be viewed objectively. I make Tom's hospital appointments, and I take care of him, and I hate it all. I despise him for his weakness and his inability to defeat his own illness. I am filled with hate for him as he suffers, and I am a bad wife and a bad person. And so out it comes in the memoir, this stupid book that will go on and on until I discover where the end lies. I drag the worst of myself into it, and I permeate every page.

It's getting dark outside. Soon *Coronation Street* will finish and I'll take Tom upstairs for his wash. It'll beat sitting in front of the telly and pretending I was once involved in an unexplained bloodbath.

The closest I ever got to a bloodbath was when I miscarried. That was a lot of blood and matter. I don't want to get into describing it, but there was solid matter there. It would have been a baby. Of course, it's a good thing that it wasn't. I'd been too afraid to tell my parents that I was pregnant, so all I thought when I felt the blood running down my legs at the bus stop was *thank God*. It was only a couple of months later that I started crying and couldn't stop.

Nobody knew what was wrong with me. There was a good doctor in Bourne End back then and he had a clue about it, but he was good enough not to make me tell. He packed me off to a decent clinic in London for women suffering with their nerves. I say it was a decent one because it charged a lot and it looked after you, not like some of the other ones around where there was screaming and being tied to a bed and things like that. Or is that only my imaginative side at work, thinking things like that happened? I asked my mother once, when she came to visit. She said that kind of thing only happened in romantic novels and I had far too much imagination. I don't think I'd want to read a romantic novel that had such things in it. It makes me wonder what kind of books she read.

No, it was restful. It had a garden and a piano, but even so I just kept seeing the blood on my legs. I had been so happy about it at first.

It must have cost my parents a fortune to keep me in that clinic for two years; I still don't know how they managed it. They paid up and we all waited for me to get well again, having no idea what would happen next. But then, who does?

* * *

It was safe to say my faith in humanity was lost. I trusted nobody. I could get no answers to the questions endlessly running through my head and I couldn't face returning to my own parents to face their questions in turn.

Had all those passengers died on that fateful train journey from Salzburg? Or had I imagined the whole horrible sight of the white room, glittering glass overhead, gore soaking through my shoes? I slept rough in London for a time; the expression is misleading because I can't remember sleeping. I stared at brick walls wondering if they would disappear or if blood would pour through the cement cracks. I shivered my way through my insanity, feeling hunger, thirst, cold as mere distractions from my madness. I was unreachable, or so I thought. But then the travelling circus found me.

Or, I suppose one could say I found them. I was stumbling along the South Bank – no doubt drawing looks of disgust from the tourists who mistook me for drunk rather than deranged – when I fell into a display of dancing dogs in leaf-green tutus, accidentally kicking the Rottweiler who barrelled into the tap-dancing Shitzu and knocked the Chihuahua pyramid flying.

The assembled crowd laughed heartily, and so did the dogs' owner, to my relief. She was an enormous-bosomed lady called Etheline, and she sported the most impressive blond beard and handlebar moustache I had ever laid eyes on; it was worthy of a Viking. "You should be a clown," she said to me as she scooped me back onto my feet. "You have a gift for comedy, and yet the scent of tragedy is upon you, like all the greatest circus performers. The most terrible of events feed the urge within us all to find a smile." She must have seen in my wild eyes that I did not believe her. "So, this is a lesson you have yet to learn – you have seen the worst in life and have yet to turn it to your advantage, am I correct? Maybe I can be of assistance. Come back to my caravan and let me help you. My life has hardly been free of strife but I've made the weight of my beard work hard for me. Maybe we can do the same for you. What's your name?"

"Violet," I told her, and she laughed.

"An appropriate moniker for a clown, given that you stink of the gutter. You're a walking contradiction, Violet."

My timing could not have been better if I had rehearsed it; I fainted in my exhaustion, and became not a walking contradiction but a prone one, and could not be roused for all the prancing dogs in London.

When I came to, the first sensation I experienced was a tickling on my chest. The next was an aroma: the smell of soap. The third was the sight, when I managed to open my lids, of Etheline smiling upon me, her beard hanging over me like a curtain. For the first time since returning from Salzburg, I smiled. I smiled back at her, and I felt safe.

Etheline saved me. She was the kindest of people, giving up the one bed in her caravan for me and devoting her time to my recovery, yet never asking for anything in return but an audience for the story of her own life, which in many surprising ways paralleled my own, with the addition of facial hair. She too had been found by circus folk at her lowest ebb, when she was unemployed in Greenland, and she was determined to perform the same good turn for me now. When I was rested and strong in my mind and body once more, Etheline provided morning coffee and ginger nut biscuits for the meeting she set up in her own caravan with the all-powerful head of the Clown Division.

This meeting did not take place without preamble.

"He's called Mikachu," she had said, the night before, as she tucked me into bed with the firm fondness of a mother, "and he's a demanding taskmaster. Expect to work hard, but to gain great rewards under his tutelage, if he'll have you. He's trained all the greats: Yogi Wan, Trubblington Gravy and Poopie-Pants the Purple Passionfruit of Bromwich all started with him." These names meant nothing to me, but I nodded, and promised to make my funniest faces in the morning for his perusal.

"No," she said, "don't do any such thing, Violet. Don't try to entertain him. Only try to show him that you have the potential to learn what entertainment is."

This seemed somewhat cryptic to me, so under his gaze I found I had no idea what to do and fell back on not doing anything at all. He was a tall, thin man with jet black hair and a severe set to his mouth that gave him an intimidating air. There was nothing of the clown that I could see about him, apart from the oily white sheen on his skin that I imagined was a permanent residue from his make-up. Etheline did all of the talking at that first meeting, relating my history and assuring him that I would be a great clown given the opportunity. He looked dubious. I could well understand it. The whole thing seemed so utterly ridiculous that I couldn't help but giggle into my morning coffee mug.

His sharp eyes met mine for the first time. I saw a hint of curiosity in his gaze; it softened that mouth, made it appealing.

"Etheline." He had a rough voice, with a broad accent one might expect to hear from a turnip farmer. "Might you leave us for a moment?"

She fluttered out of the caravan. I think she had rather a crush on Mikachu. As soon as the caravan stopped rocking he began to speak, and it was clear that I was not expected to reply.

"I do not think you have it in you to be a great clown, Violet. I'm sorry to say it. Etheline has always been this way, picking up strays and imagining she sees more in them than what they are. Last time it was Budi, the Indonesian orphan whom she thought would make a world-class plate spinner even though he had never handled crockery in his life. But I would like to humour her, being that she is such an excellent attraction and such a benevolent soul to boot, and so I will take you and train you if you wish it. You must promise to work hard and not run away or steal what I'd prefer to give freely, but my instinct tells me that all the hard labour in the world is not going to lift you to the esteemed heights of comedy. You'll be good for a pie in the face or improbably large boots, I'm sure, but no more than that. Still, you are welcome to try to prove me wrong. What do you say?"

I felt the truth in his words. "Okay," I said. "I'll do my best and I'm pretty certain I won't prove you wrong. There's no joy in my soul and there never will be again, so how could I ever bring joy to others? But you can hit me with as many pies as you like. I don't mind at all."

"No joy," he mused, "none at all. But you're still so young. Are you sure that joy may not find you again when you least expect it?"

I smiled. "I'm certain. But you're welcome to try and prove me wrong too, if you like."

We made a deal, sealed with a handshake, and by the end of the first week of training I already knew he had won. I adored him and he made me happier than I could ever have imagined. Since I have quite an imagination that, in itself, was an impressive accomplishment. Yes, he fell in love with me and I with him. I never made a good clown; I was mediocre at my best, but I made him a better wife. At least, I tried to, although it was another role that didn't come naturally to me. Still, I persevered. And I persevere still, believing in the phrase 'till death do us part', although now that the death part is coming up, for him at least, I have days where I wish I'd stuck with Etheline the bearded lady instead.

But no, I opted to become a wife. Violet, married to Mikachu alias Tom, with no laughter left in either of us now he's suffering from skin cancer – perhaps from that thick white make-up he wore for so many years – leaving him with half a face and no time at all.

Fuck him. Fuck watching death crawl up over his face and laying its eggs under his skin. Fuck him for letting it, for making me be part of this slow degradation and then leaving me alone at the end. What a joke this marriage has turned out to be. The greatest joke of his career.

A fitting end for Mikachu, perhaps. If only Tom had been a clown, a great man, then this death could have had some dramatic irony. But in the alternative version of my life he was a building surveyor, working out in the sun, squinting up at high roofs, filling out reports in his small office with the picture of his family on his desk. And there's no meaning, perverse or otherwise, in this end.

That's not to say there wasn't happiness before we got here. I'd be lying if I didn't admit that Tom made me happy when I met him. I went back to my small bedroom in my parents' house in Bourne End when the clinic pronounced me cured, and I didn't go far. I used to walk down to the café – it's a florist's now, but back then it was a very hip place to be, with a jukebox and black and white lino on the floor – and spend an hour over a cup of tea. Tom would come in with his mates from work and put 'Tears of a Clown' on the jukebox. He loved Smokey Robinson, all that Motown music. He had energy. He'd dance along, and then he started asking me to dance with him right in the middle of the café. I always said no, dreading that he'd make me or that he'd stop asking. But he never did stop asking, until one day he stayed behind deliberately after his break, waited until the café was empty apart from us two, and told me I had to dance, or I'd break his heart.

So, I did.

He said he could see I was sad. He said he'd make me smile again. He wanted to take care of me and he meant it. Being taken care of, that's a wonderful thing, until you realise you can't take care of yourself anymore. And then it's the worst thing you ever signed up for. By the time I'd had his children I was tied to Bourne End, and all my dreams of escape followed that first baby, trickling down my legs into the gutter and crying softly in my ear at night.

* * *

"Violet," said God, on that fateful moment last year after Tom had been diagnosed. "Violet, wake up. Meet me in the park in five minutes. Have a quick wee before you leave the house, but don't worry about your hair."

I did as I was told. You don't argue with God. At least, I don't, not after eight years of Sunday school and a run-in with nunhood.

In the park, in the dark, I trembled. I hugged my dressing gown over my chest as I made my way to the playground, feeling the damp soak through my sheepskin slippers. God was waiting for me on the climbing frame, the red and blue one with the slide suitable for five- to eight-year-olds. He was throwing conkers down it, which was quite an achievement since it was late spring. It's hard to say what he looked like. Old and venerable are the words that come to mind, but that kind of person doesn't sit on the top of climbing frames so there must have been something young and carefree about him too.

"I don't think much of this place," he said. I thought about pointing out that everything, including the playground, was made to his design but he gave me such a stare that I didn't bother. Thinking about it now, I'm sure he read my thoughts so there was no point in saying it anyway. I stood there, waiting for him to tell me what he wanted with me – I never thought to ask. It's harder to have a conversation with God than you might imagine.

He snapped his fingers, and in a blink we were on a desert island, a proper one with soft white sand and a translucent sea, and palm trees curving overhead providing shade from the glorious sunshine.

"Is this heaven?" I asked him.

"It's the Maldives," he said. "It's the closest most people get to heaven, to be honest. There's an excellent hotel on stilts just along the beach." His voice reminded me of Alan Whicker, a little bit. "Violet, it's a rare person whom I choose to give answers to, but it seems to me that you could do with some hands-on guidance and in your case I'm not against providing it."

"Thanks," I said. I could feel sand irritating the bunion in my right sheepskin slipper, and my dressing gown was far too hot but I didn't dare strip off down to my nightie in front of him.

"It's like this." He sat down and pressed his fingers into the sand. "Your life has been a test."

"A test?"

"A series of hoops to jump through, if you like. Once in

a while I take a direct interest in a human's life. I couldn't say for sure how I pick 'em – someone leaps out of the crowd even though they look as ordinary as the next person. It's not about shape or size or even about whether they bother to believe in me or not, but I find myself watching them. And sometimes I send certain events their way just to see what they'll do. How they'll react. You've been one of those people, Violet. Ever since I heard you saying 'The Lord's Prayer' at Sunday School. You made it sound like a little sing-song tune of love; it reminded me of Neil Sedaka's 'Carol' a bit. I've always been fond of that one."

"Me too," I said. I sat down next to him and he started scooping sand over my legs until my slippers disappeared under a growing white mound.

"So, anyway, it's my fault, that whole business in Salzburg. I had everyone on the train killed by crazed robbers, who were then bumped off in turn by the mayor in order to cover up his theft of the passengers' belongings. You awoke in his summer house. Beautiful, wasn't it?"

"Apart from the blood."

"And I put the circus folk on the South Bank, ready for you to happen along. And, just recently, I gave Mikachu cancer. He'll die of it, slowly. There'll be another year of suffering yet, but if I didn't make it agonising it wouldn't really be a test for you, would it?"

"Tom," I said. "His name is Tom. Not Mikachu."

"You know what, Violet? You've really done me proud so far. You've soldiered on, you never gave up and you've really never questioned it either, have you? Good for you! You're exactly the kind of person the Kingdom of Heaven needs. Once you kick the bucket, I highly rate your chances of getting in."

I couldn't see my legs anymore; the entire of my lower body was buried under an enormous mound of sand and I couldn't move an inch. I was sweating profusely in my dressing gown, and even in the shade of the palm trees the sun was beginning to burn my face. "Thank you," I said, trying to keep the discomfort from my voice, "I really appreciate that. Do you think I might be able to go home now?"

"Of course! Anything for my favourite customer. I'll take you back to bed. You hang on in there for another sixteen years and then I'll see you again. I'll have a piña colada lined up at the floating bar for you. As long as you handle this last decade and a half with dignity, of course. But I'm sure I can count on you."

God didn't do anything, as far as I could see – there was no click of the fingers or blink of his eyes. I was simply back in bed again, sitting bolt upright, covered in sweat and sand with Tom lying next to me snoring away as usual.

I know a lot of people take comfort from the idea of God. I can't say he reassured me that night. Although I have always been fond of a piña colada.

*   *   *

So, that's the end of this memoir. I'm done with writing, at least until Tom is gone and I'm alone for the first time in thirty-eight years. Who knows what I'll get up to then with the time that remains to me? Maybe I'll travel to Austria. Or rebel against God. That or take up salsa.

I know, I know – I said that once I finished this memoir, I'd leave Tom. I really would love to leave, but I think we've all known that's not on the cards. I'll see him through his death, like the good wife I am.

So, only one question remains. What shall I do with this memoir?

Does it have to be put to some use? I suppose not. I could put it in a drawer somewhere, or even burn it. But I don't think I will.

I can think of one person who might benefit from it.

Yes. I'm going to leave it on the doorstep of number thirty-one. If he reads it, I think he might finally begin to understand that I'm here. That I exist in this world. He might even look round as he runs past and give me a look that means, *I understand you. Being young is not so different from being old, after all. Telling the truth is not so different from lying when it comes to wanting to be alive. To be interesting. To be meaningful.*

I'm going to sneak out tonight, after I've put Tom to bed, and I'm going to put this book where he can't help but see it. Maybe he'll step over it on his way to the park for his morning run. But maybe, on the way back, he'll pick it up.

First thing tomorrow morning, I'll sit here and watch the street, and wait for him to see me. He might knock on the door and start a conversation.

Who knows? Anything could happen.

TO THE FARM

He holds out his bag to me. It's an antique: real leather with a brass clasp. I think they used to call it a doctor's bag. It's far too big for him – he would be better off with a backpack like normal kids have, but Mr and Mrs Collodi would never let him be seen with anything less than the best, not even for this final journey.

"Thank you," he says.

"You're welcome, sir." I take the bag, and open the back door for him. He climbs into his booster seat and straps himself in.

I put his bag on the passenger seat, sit behind the wheel, and swipe the fob. The engine starts, and the car glides down the gravel path. I programmed in the coordinates last night.

"Gerry?" he says.

"Yes sir?"

"Have you been to this farm before?"

"Yes sir."

"Are there cows and pigs?"

"Oh yes."

The first time I drove this route was with Chloe, her blond

curls shining, a blue bow in her hair. The second time it was Kimmie, with glossy black braids and her serious expression. And now it's Petie's turn.

Petie lasted the longest. Seven years, and for the first five he and Mrs Collodi were inseparable. She once said to me, *There's nothing like a little boy, is there, Gerry?* And I said, *No, Madam. There's nothing like a little boy.*

Petie is nothing like a little boy. There's no dirty nose and crusted sweater sleeves, no grazes on knees. Petie never does these things, and he never will.

"I don't remember seeing a place like this before," he says. We are driving into a less salubrious district; the car is drawing attention. I make sure the doors are locked and adjust the windows to heavy tint. Outside, the stores are tatty: small supermarkets, charity traders, hairdressers offering dyes and dreads. The people walk differently here – faster, shoulders hunched, carrying canvas bags. It's been so long since I've been counted as one of their number that I feel a deep fear of them, as if they could recognise my betrayal and rip me to pieces in punishment.

"Gerry, what happens at the farm?"

"There are fun things to do," I say. "You'll have a great time."

"When will you come and get me?"

The other two asked me that question. This time I have an answer ready. "When your parents tell me to."

The stores give way to estates, the houses crammed together, the numbers on the doors running in consecutive order to form long strings of similarity. The cars, the shrubs, the drapes, all the same.

"They're not the same," Jemima used to say. "Look. Our drapes are purple. Do you see anyone else on our row with purple drapes?"

"It's not the colour. It's the principle of it. They make windows that automatically tint themselves now. Nobody should use drapes anymore."

"Rich people have windows that tint. We have drapes. We will draw drapes every day for the rest of our lives, Gerry. We will carry on drawing the drapes. And it really won't be that bad."

She never felt the need to have more, to be more, not even when she was sitting in the state hospice with her wheelchair angled towards the mall car park and the windows framed with threadbare drapes.

The houses continue, for miles, miles, miles. Petie doesn't speak. Maybe he has turned himself off, I don't know.

I don't really understand how they work. It's a mystery to me why anyone would want one of these synthetic children. There are millions of real ones out there needing adoption. But, of course, they come with real problems and no cachet. Petie is the ultimate toy and the best pet you could ever have. You don't even have to toilet train him.

We're on the payway now. The limo ups itself to one hundred and twenty and hits the fast lane. I lighten the windows and see other grand cars doing the same thing, in synchronicity. Bentleys, Jaguars, even a vintage Rolls-Royce that stays in the slow lane. As we pass it, I see the chauffeur, dressed like me, his hat perfectly in place, staring straight ahead.

I have traded one set of similarities for another.

I switch off the automatic and take over driving myself. The alarm sounds for a moment and in the rear-view mirror I see Petie flinch.

"Don't you like loud noises?" I say.

He shakes his head. His eyes are wet. It's a clever trick.

"Shall I put some music on?"

He brightens. "I like Mozart."

"Of course." I choose the Clarinet Concerto and let it wash over me. It's not to my personal taste but Petie seems to enjoy it.

After a while the junction comes up. I indicate the old-fashioned way and reduce my speed. We make the turn, then take the second exit on the roundabout. The farm is not signposted, but I know the way even without the navigation system. The last miles pass to the sound of Mozart and then we are parking outside the visitors' entrance. A length of tall fence encloses the large house with peeling white paint and dirty windows. The fence runs around the sides and continues on, out of view.

I collect the bag and help Petie down from his seat. He looks at the house, the fence, with interest.

"Where are the animals?" he says.

I usher him inside, to the reception. A middle-aged man sits on a sofa opposite the unoccupied desk, his raincoat over his lap. He's wearing a decent grey suit. Not top quality, but not bad. I wouldn't mind one myself.

I ring the bell on the desk. It's another antique, the kind you hit with the palm of your hand. The man says, "They're just sorting out my order and then they'll be back."

"Okay."

"If you're dropping one off you can just leave it here, I think. They don't wander off." He looks at Petie with an intensity that unsettles me. Petie pulls at my trouser leg, but doesn't speak.

I turn around. I walk out of the reception and Petie follows along after me. I put him in the car and deposit his bag on the passenger seat once more. I select full tint on the windows, put the car in automatic, and let it drive back home.

* * *

On the first evening in my room I told him, "You have to stay in," and I know he will never disobey me. I don't know what he does in the long hours when I'm driving the Collodis to their social engagements. I don't think he can switch himself off. There's a watchfulness to him when he goes still. I get the feeling he's taking it all in, trying to make sense of it all, wondering why he has to keep indoors all day and sleep in the wardrobe all night. And he never did get to see the animals.

He never asks about it. But I often ask myself – what difference does it make? I was happier when I thought they simply dismantled the unwanted ones. My suspicions now are so much worse and I don't understand why. Surely, in fact, it's better this way. No real children are being harmed.

If some people must have these terrible instincts isn't it better that they exercise them on objects, not on others with beating hearts?

I find myself wishing for the impossible – that people didn't have such instincts at all.

"You're a fantasist," Jemima said, when she got out of the hospice. "You're not living in the real world. Things are never going to be perfect and equal. Some of us have to struggle. We get given the tough choices and it makes us better people than those who have it easy. We develop real character. I used to love the fact that you couldn't see how much more boring we would all be if you got your way."

I looked at her suitcase, the clasp broken, held together with one of my belts, and said, "Is that how you feel about being misdiagnosed? That it's made you a better person? Three months of sitting there waiting to die, because you got a bad doctor who misread a scan. What a stroke of luck for you! I bet it's given you a sense of perspective, hasn't it? How lucky you are."

"Luckier than you." I remember she looked so sad, at that moment. Her pity was unbearable. I'd visited her every day in that place – held her hand, stroked her face, kept my own feelings pushed back so I could show her only strength, and in return she had pitied me. I looked out of the window at the rows of houses, and realised she had taken down her purple drapes and packed them.

A month later, I got upgraded at work from public services driver to live-in chauffeur. The Collodis had liked my face on the file. I wanted to tell her but she'd left no address. She wouldn't have been impressed anyway.

* * *

I show Petie a picture of Jemima, the one taken in the park. She's sitting on a swing, the sun in her eyes. She's squinting, her top lip drawn up, and in the background there is the brick wall of the public toilet daubed with graffiti: the tags of the local lads. I can even see my own tag from my youth, back when I sprayed *Jezo* on every unguarded surface and thought of myself as a rebel.

"She's pretty," says Petie, which is a lie. It's not the best photo of her and she never was like one of those women on the adverts anyway, but it didn't matter to me. She was different. Above all that. But I'm thankful to Petie for lying. I tousle his hair and he smiles. "Can I call you Daddy?" he says.

I can't think of a reason why not. "All right."

"Daddy. Daddy and Mummy." He stares at the photo with such adoration on his little face that I tell him he can keep the picture.

Every day he picks up a new phrase, a new expression, working out what pleases me. I teach him to play cards. Blackjack. He's pretty good at it. I take out the encyclopedias from the library, one at a time, heavy old tomes with paper pages that smell, and he reads for hours, days, weeks, months. Years.

"Daddy?" he says one night after I've tucked him up in his bed at the bottom of the wardrobe. "Where's Mummy?"

"Travelling. Seeing the world."

"The whole world?"

"As much of it as she can."

"And then she'll come back?"

These lies hurt nobody. "When she's ready," I tell him.

"Travelling is good for the soul," says Petie gravely, and I picture the two of us, hand in hand, walking towards a perfect sunset. A man and his boy, seeing everything there is to see together.

* * *

Even though the human body slows down, technology continues to renew and refresh, sprinting onwards, leaving all but the very young behind.

Petie was the last of the synthetic children that the Collodis bought. They have been out of fashion for years now. Maybe my employers, now they are older, sit and wonder what happened to those things they so loved once. I hope they never find out the truth.

Chauffeurs went out of fashion, too. But I kept my job for a few years longer, not doing much more than sitting in my room with Petie. I have to be grateful for that.

On the evening of my retirement, Mr Collodi gives me a gold watch and Mrs Collodi presents me with a cake she has baked herself. Then they hold out keys to an apartment in a sealed complex for the elderly. They are good people. I couldn't see it before. Or maybe time has changed them as much as it has changed me.

I give Petie the watch. "Sell it," I tell him. "When you get to a village. It's worth a lot. Don't let anyone take advantage of you." He packs it in his doctor's bag along with the photograph of his mother.

Once the night is thick around us we sneak out to the car and I keep the windows tinted as I drive him through the streets where I used to live, onwards to the payway, past the junction that leads to the farm, to the fields of altered wheat that grows taller than elephants. I park up in a layby, as far from the city as I dare to go.

I help him down from his booster seat and give him his bag.

"Go on," I say. "It's a big world out there."

He looks out over the field. "Travelling," he says.

"It's good for the soul."

"Yes."

"Come back once you've seen it all."

He gives me a hug. I feel the coldness of the metal under his synthetic skin and I hug him tighter, willing him to take the memory of my warmth with him.

And then he begins his journey.

THE SPOILS

Some carried their cuts from the corpse of the Olme home with bare hands, choosing to follow tradition. The smell permeated the skin on their palms and became part of them; their sweat would always bear the sweet, rotting scent of it.

Others used gloves or held out tins or bags to receive their piece, sliced with such expertise. For those people there was no smell at all, even if they kept it in the house after the ceremony. It wasn't the gift alone that created the scent. It was the connection between human and beast. The flesh of the Olme had to be touched to make the smell.

1. First Finder: the unused eye

The butcher made the initial cut across the unopened lid and peeled back the slippery skin to reveal the eye. Then she slid the knife underneath it, pushed down and in at a shallow angle, and the cloudy blue orb came free with a loud, sucking sound that reverberated around the cavern.

The crowd watched as the butcher chose the saw from her low table of instruments and worked its teeth against the thick veins that joined the eye to the body. It took real strength to complete the task.

"Step forward," she said, "Michael Rittle."

Michael roused himself from his spot next to the far pillar. He found he didn't want to look upon the bulk of the Olme. It was too reminiscent of the discovering of it, deeper down in the earth, during one of his frequent trips through the lower caves looking for the mosses and lichens that the medic would pay for. By the light of his own torch the Olme had heaved and groaned – how had it managed to squeeze itself so far through such a narrow passage? It had blocked the route entirely, pinned itself solid in rock, and yet it was still living when he came across it. He had not dared to approach it and yet he could not bear to leave it. So he witnessed its weakening in increments, in the struggles that grew fainter, sighs that faded, until his torch was worn down low and he had to head back home in the last wisps of its light or risk being left in darkness absolute.

By the time he had returned with the killing crew the Olme was dead.

"May you see with endless clarity," the butcher said solemnly to the crowd and held out the eye.

Michael took it. He had brought along a pair of gloves, the ones he wore to protect his fingers while down in the sharp-walled mineral caves that made their own light – as blue as the eye he now held – but at the last moment decided to follow the old ways. He'd bear the stink of it all his life, but, well, that seemed right to him. His grandfather had worn the scent, too; that had been the last time an Olme had been found. Now it was his turn. His skin, his gift. A trade.

The Olme's eye, now Michael's, was thought to serve no purpose. A remnant of a time when Olmes had lived above ground, perhaps? Or maybe never an eye at all but used for something else. Some other form of seeing.

Later that evening, Michael came home to find his house in unusual silence. His talkative pet bird, which had been an expensive purchase from one of the surface traders who would sometimes come to the trapdoor, lay dead at the bottom of the cage that hung from the ceiling. He reached for it and it was so very light in his hands. Its bright colours were still vibrant; they seemed more vivid than ever before. Red and yellow. When he put the eye of the Olme into the cage to take the bird's place, it took on those colours and reflected light around the room at sharp, strange angles. He smelled the scent of it rising up from inside him.

2. Retriever: longest toenail

Clare had used her tractor to pull the Olme to the upper caverns and it was not a difficult job. It quickly came free from the rocks between which it had jammed its bulk, and the body was obedient in its response to the hooks she sank into it, and the chains that demanded it follow.

Moving rocks in subterranean farming was usually difficult, heavy labour; she had been expecting much more of a struggle for this task. But the inexplicability of the Olme's smooth passage did not bother her. It suited the elements of mystery and ritual that permeated her life and had been long associated with pragmatic repetition. *The things we do, over and over, that create our place*; these were the words she had grown up with, spoken so often by her grandmother, and they filled her head as she transported the Olme to a storage cave.

The words, in truth, had never meant a lot to her. She had learned by example, and now she was alone and aged, and one day soon would have to attempt to explain all this to the next generation. These were concerns that bothered her sometimes, but mainly she enjoyed being left in solitude. It suited her.

But a crowd had gathered for the final stage of the retrieval and that did not suit her at all. It was – she reflected during the ceremony – the first time she had ever been watched at work by others. The butcher seemed so at ease with their perusal of her cuts and slices; Clare did not think she could ever have done such a task under scrutiny. She admired the precision of it.

"Step forward, Clare Askett," said the butcher, so she did so, with reluctance. She had thought the community smaller than this. Before the ceremony she had enquired about the possibility of receiving her gift in private and had been told that was not an option. It didn't help that it was her lot to receive such an unpleasant object. A toenail, no less. It had a laughable element to it. Would anyone snigger or make a comment as she approached?

They did not. And the toenail was, once sawed through and snapped from the bed of the largest toe on the last foot, a sleek, polished object in a warm shade of reddish-brown that was scored through with curved cream lines. Separated from the Olme it became a sculpture; a statement divorced from reality.

It also became familiar.

"May you cherish movement," said the butcher, and Clare held out her gloved hands to receive the toenail. It was hard and very light. She wished, for a moment, that she had not opted for the gloves. But did she really want to be marked in such a way? Impregnated, forever, by this one event? Her grandmother had smelled so strongly of it and had talked of dragging the Olme forth in a tone of wonder. All the secrets of their trade forgotten, her granddaughter's name gone from her mind, but the Olme remembered. *A toenail, they gave me,* she had said, over and over. *It's my favourite decoration.* She had kept it by her bed, at the end. The smell from her skin had been so strong.

It had never occurred to Clare before, but she could not remember ever seeing that old toenail since her grandmother's death. Where had it gone? Why was there never anything to show for service but some memories and a bad smell?

She kept the gloves on and tried to think of this as an unremarkable event. She did not want it to become the one thing she remembered, at the end.

The toenail came home with her. She tried her hardest to think of it as a curio, a knick-knack. She moved it from one decorative position to the next and could not find a spot where it felt like a background object. It seemed, to Clare, that it needed to be matched. One of a pair. It was not, after all, unique.

She took to searching through old possessions, dank corners, and found many strange objects she could not fathom: instruments from older forms of farming, perhaps? There was no matching toenail anywhere. She started to scan the caves where she farmed, searching among the pigmentless plants and insects that she cultivated, but the further she walked the less she knew her place. Things were newly inexplicable.

She kept walking between her farming tasks. It became a habit. She did not find another toenail to make her own diminish in meaning.

3. Reader of Rites: tip of the tongue

Adam held out his exposed hands. Putting a barrier between his own tools and any surface was unthinkable. And he already smelled, so what did it matter? The pages of the books he read were made of the skin of the Olme anyway, and the act of curing and preparing the skin released the scent.

"May you learn the gift of sound, Adam Budding," the butcher said, and passed him his cut.

The tip of a tongue had sounded like a small gift, but this – this was a heavy mess of flesh, soft, like a haunch of meat for roasting.

Adam had once read, in Farbington:

To read in the absolute dark one needs to learn how to touch. People think they have this skill simply because they are born with hands but they are wrong. They pick up, they handle, they grasp. They use the tools on the ends of their arms for utilitarian purposes.

You will learn to embrace the art that lives in the tiny folds of each finger and the curve of both palms. You will translate these sensations to speech. These books are filled with raised marks that contain such nuance. Embrace it. Speak it.

Adam had lived among such books since the age of four. At first Farbington had made him sleep in the library, with the stench vivid in the darkness, thick and curling in his nostrils. Eventually, he had learned to stop crying and felt around for the door, which was open. It had always been open.

First lesson. It had taken him months to learn.

Was it a cruelty? Well, life was cruelty; the words had taught him that. Nowhere was that second lesson more evident than when holding the tongue of that rarest of creatures and celebrating its death. It had been in pain, confused. Bewildered as it headed up to unknown tunnels – this much Adam could read in the harsh, dry buds of the tongue.

He lived in a community that made the most of such deaths. He, personally, had been guiltily delighted to have the opportunity to take down the Book of the Ceremony and feel the tender bumps of explanation. Then he had spoken aloud of it to the butcher, outlining step after step. How he loved the butcher. She had a smile made for candlelight.

She was smiling at him now.

"You can step back," she whispered. She had a soft spot for him, he was almost certain of it. If only he could touch her face, then he would have known for sure. Could love leave a gentle pattern upon the skin that could be traced? This was not a lesson that Farbington, long dead, had taught him. It was his own theory that he would pass to an apprentice when he was ready to accept his own cruelty and had found the will to inflict it.

He would put a small child in a library and listen to them cry.

The gift of sound. To hear his own voice clearly or listen to the voices of others?

Years later, he would find himself unexpectedly welcoming the butcher to the library. She enquired after the procedures needed to finish the long-term curing of the skin of the Olme for bookmaking purposes. He found the book in question and repeated passages to her. He was, in that moment, transported back to the time that the Olme first found its way to uniting them.

On an impulse, he reached out and touched her face. He tried to read it and could not tell if she loved him. She was, after all his dreams, unknowable.

Then she sighed.

4. *Storage: the tubing*

A deep slice along the side facing the crowd, and then the boring tool was applied to the precise spot between the fifth and sixth leg, measured by an ancient angular device without a name. When the butcher pulled it free a thick, blue, rubbery tube came with it, speared upon its point, stretching from the incision.

"Step forward, Bill and Mary Clement," said the butcher, and the couple waddled up in their thick matching coats and boots. Bill held a long pole and Mary had her arms filled with a sturdy net that she found slippery to hold. Mary felt hot and uncomfortable under the gaze of the crowd. She glanced at Bill for reassurance. He, with his nervous expression, looked as if he was about to embark upon a trying adventure.

"May you bear the gift of forgiveness."

The butcher transferred the tubing to the pole and Bill began to cautiously loop it as it spilled forth. Once the pole was filled with coils Mary opened the net wide and received them. They slid down the pole with ease as Bill angled it with great care into position, and then the whole business began again. The process was repeated four times until the net was bulging and Mary could barely hold it. She braced her legs and thrust back her chest, turning her face to the side as far from the tubing as possible.

Only a few loops into the fifth coil and the end of the tube popped free to reveal a pink, veined, star-shaped growth that flopped into the net and nestled there.

"Done," said the butcher. Bill nodded, took the net from Mary and slung it over his shoulder. Then the two of them manoeuvred their way back through the crowd, who parted wide for them.

"Yes, but what's it for?" Bill said that evening.

The star sat in their largest cooking bowl, in his lap. It had come free from the tubing once they got it to their closest cave and had rolled to Mary's feet, where it glowed so fetchingly that she had scooped it up in the folds of her dress, taking care not to touch it with her bare skin, and carried it home. It appealed to her deeply, even though she felt it should have belonged to a different kind of woman. A glamorous one, perhaps.

"It must have served some purpose," Mary said. "Bodies don't have bits without purpose."

"In this day and age, we should have worked out the internals of the Olme and why all this ceremonial stuff is claptrap," he grumbled.

Brother and sister, side by side in their armchairs, faced the amethyst geode that formed the centrepiece of the room. Owning the largest number of caves in the upper tunnels kept them well off, but it was wealth inherited from the courage and strength of their ancestors who had dug out so much rock with their primitive tools and fought back others to stake their claims. The past was romanticised and inaccessible from their own understanding, and quite useless to them. But now it had been foisted upon them, first by having to accept the bulk of the Olme in one of their caves, then by having to keep a length of tubing that had no obvious meaning. Would it be with them forever? It was an upsetting thought.

But the star was beautiful, Mary thought. It looked alive in the bowl, like a fascinating creature from another world, waving its arms at her. It didn't look dead at all.

"Are we keeping that in here?" asked Bill.

"For a while," she said. She took the bowl from him and put it on her own lap. She watched it rather than staring into the colours of the geode, which had gradually become less interesting to her over time.

In between the light duties of checking their caves for trespassing, Mary sat with her star and found a curious phenomenon: if she truly concentrated upon it her breathing would fall to a slow, steady whooshing through her barely open mouth, her vision would narrow and a strange calm would spread through her. She had never known anything like it. She craved it. This clear state of being brought her knowledge. She began to understand that she had lived her life so far in a state of permanently suppressed irritation.

Bill.

Bill was annoying.

He possessed a ferocious negativity. It was sharp, pointed, and always on hand to prick her. Doing this appeared to be his only enjoyment.

"What a waste of bloody time," he said, without fail, whenever she stared at her star.

Mary started to wear different clothes to him. She wore Tuesday's outfit on Monday and Friday's outfit on Sunday. He frowned and told her she looked ridiculous, at first. Then he lapsed into a wounded silence.

Their ancestors had been so brave; where had that courage gone? She could not find it, even when her ritual revealed to her that she irritated him in equal measure as he her, and she enjoyed doing that as much as he enjoyed doing it to her.

The contemplation of the star revealed to her that this relationship would not change because they had grown together into symbiotic beings of mutual irritation. It was much too late to ever work out how to pull apart, and if they did they would remain two separated, unhappy halves of a whole until their deaths.

In the wake of this revelation, she said to him, aware she sounded unconvincing, "I could leave you. I could go upside," and he laughed, and said, "Not likely," but she heard the tremble in his voice and discovered how to love him again for believing that she might actually be capable of such an act.

So she plunged her uncovered hands into the bowl and picked up the star. She felt no different to hold it, not at first; then she slowly became aware of the smell she now emitted. It had soaked into her skin. It could never be scrubbed away.

Bill stared at her as she stood up and carried the bowl away. She took it to the closest storage cave and laid it atop the long length of the tubing. Then she returned to Bill's side.

"I'm done with it."

"You smell of it," he told her.

"I know," she said.

When they next changed clothes, she dressed once more in matching materials. After completing her tasks she took her seat in the armchair beside his and looked into the depths of the amethyst geode. The scent emanating from her was barely noticeable, sometimes.

5. Watcher: sliced buttock

"Some jobs are so unpleasant that they come with huge benefits," said Kim's mother. "It's the only way they can get anyone to do it. This is one such job. But here's the thing; you do this once, and then you're free forever more. That's what you want, isn't it? To be free of us all?"

Ah, the edge of bitterness: it had just crept in on the final words. They had almost been having a conversation as equals. Kim fell back on her usual weapons since the ceasefire was over. She rolled her eyes.

"Is that a yes or a no?"

She shrugged.

"Right then. I'll tell them it's a yes, and you can tell them otherwise if you like."

That was how Kim ended up sitting next to the hulking carcass of the Olme before the ceremony, for the allotted length of time as laid out in the old books.

It had not seemed like a long time in theory, yet was close to endless in practice.

She tried to think only of her daydreams. They always involved the sun. Standing in it, lying in it, bathing. Being kissed by it. She had spent so much time learning about it when she should have been choosing a trade, and she had run out of time to find an apprenticeship because nobody valued her knowledge of that radiant ball that hung above ground. Her mother had declared her interest a phase, then an infatuation, then an inappropriate obsession caused by faulty hormones. It did not matter – Kim knew she would always love the sun. To be in its presence would complete her life.

The lifeless body of the Olme made strange sounds beside her in the storage cave. It shifted, squeaked, and muttered in the dark. Kim could picture its organs shifting inside it, filling with gases that were then expelled as long, high whines.

Sun, I'm coming, she said in her head. Similar seismic shifts were happening inside her. Her own organs were moving. She felt sure of it. They were travelling in tiny increments, rubbing against each other, growing, shrinking, changing who she was.

Is this making me better or worse? she thought.

The Olme settled further into death.

When the butcher came to start the task of preparation for the ceremony, she looked hard at Kim and then gave her a kindly hug. "How was it?" she asked.

Kim shrugged. She hated the idea that there had to be words for every experience.

"You deserve a prize for your service, Kim." The butcher whispered a word to her: a password, that would open the only door Kim had ever wanted to travel through.

"Thank you," she said. The butcher nodded.

The next time Kim saw her, the butcher was a tall, formal creature of ceremony, carving and sawing and rewarding. She called Kim forward, then looked down her nose as if they'd never met.

"The gift of time."

It was a long thick strip from the hind flank of the Olme. Kim opened the rucksack she had brought along for the occasion and the butcher slid it inside. Then she left the ceremony behind, keeping her eyes cast down as she walked so as to avoid making eye contact with her mother, and started the journey upwards. She travelled through the caves and tunnels that she knew well at first, and on to those she had only visited before when determined to flout her mother's rules, and finally to those that were lined with wires from which steadily burning bulbs dangled making her eyes water.

Nailed to the wall of Cave One was a long ladder. She climbed it, hand over hand, legs working, muscles tiring with the unfamiliar movements. She did not dare to look down. It took all her courage to reach the trapdoor set in the rock at the top and knock against the wooden planks that separated her from the surface.

There was no reply.

She knocked again, then banged. In the fear of not being answered, she remembered why she had come this far and she called out the password, over and over, until the trap door was lifted and a warm red light flooded her vision. It was not sunlight, surely? She had expected to be blinded by it – had been ready to be given eye protection by the surfacers. This light was gentle and dim.

"Where has the sun gone?" she asked. A hand was held out to her and she took it. Pulled up to stand in an open world, lidless, exposed to an expanse of emptiness, she crouched down and grabbed handfuls of soft green flooring to anchor herself. "Has there been an accident? Is the sun still there?"

"Here," said the man who had helped her up. He clapped a heavy hat on her head just like one he was wearing, and the sensation of being closed and covered diminished Kim's terror just enough so that she could take in a little of the world above. It was an indistinguishable mixture of sights and sounds, straight lines and swooping curves, jutting walls and tangling growths and nothing familiar. The man took her arm, and propelled her forward. "Come on."

"Why is there no sun?" she asked again as he led her away from the trapdoor. Everything was changing colour again, from soft red to darker violet, mixed with a creeping greyness.

"There's a sun!" said the man. He sounded amused. "It's just setting. End of the day. But the councillor will want to see you even if we're after hours. It's not far."

He took her to a tall building of chiselled, even stone walls. The roof was slanted to a sharp point. Inside, bright lamplight blazed. Kim, fighting the pain in her eyes, managed to make out a large hall without furnishings. Very long spears had been arranged in crossed designs around the walls. A woman stood before her at the foot of a staircase. She, too, wore a thick hat. Her bearing made her importance obvious. She was like the butcher during the act of cutting up the Olme: businesslike, and prepared to run the show.

"You're from Downtown," said the woman.

The name meant nothing to her.

"Underground. And you know the password. Nobody has used it in a generation. Longer. Does it mean…"

Kim waited. She gave no words away.

"Does it mean you carry part of an Olme?"

"You know about Olmes?" she asked, surprised out of her silence.

"Let me see what you've brought."

Kim took off her backpack and held it open for the woman to see.

"What's that?"

"A slice from its hind."

"It doesn't smell."

"Olme doesn't. Unless you touch it."

The woman reached out, then curled her fingers into a fist and dropped her hand to her side. "It can't possibly be real," she said. Her voice carried excitement and fear in equal measure.

But tests at the local laboratory proved otherwise.

Kim adjusted quickly to a life in which she was the centre of attention and everything she said was greeted with amazement. At first she told the truth about the Olme, as she understood it, to many rich and influential people who held parties for her in grand houses. She described the butcher, the gifts, and the craftspeople who received them. With every retelling she found the crowd who surrounded her filled with wonder and agitation. The Olme grew bigger and more monstrous with each reimagining. Was it in the way she used her voice? She felt a distance springing up between the way it had been and the way she talked of it. She began to hate the sound of her own voice; it had a strange flat timbre in the high-roofed houses.

The sun might have been enough compensation for that but it would not speak to her in any form but anger. Whenever she tried to look at it, she was blinded. She stood in its brightness and raised her arms to it, and after only a short length of time found that her skin burned and blistered. She wanted to love it, but it did not love her.

It was, she discovered, very hard to go on caring about a thing that did not care for her.

At about that time, Kim realised she missed her mother.

She thought about returning to the dark sometimes, but mainly she thought about the slice of Olme that had been taken from her and experimented upon at the laboratory. Had it been taken or had she given it? She wasn't sure. The feeling that she should have kept it bothered her. She felt duplicitous. False, in some way that she couldn't pin down.

She didn't try to explain it. She kept going to the parties even after the people seemed to calm down and find her of less interest. Often she stood on her own beside the crossed spears that decorated every room. She would drink the free drinks, eat the free food, and watch the people mingle in their strange heavy hats that they never took off. Then she would go back to the pointed house that had been provided for her and sleep all day so that she did not have to spend time with the sun.

At one such party, a woman came to speak to her. The woman had sloping shoulders and a curved back. She looked as if she had spent a lifetime doing manual work; she immediately reminded Kim of home.

"Do you remember me?" she said.

Kim shook her head.

"I greeted you. When you first arrived. I was the councillor."

"No," said Kim. That had been a confident person just like the butcher. She realised that time must have done its work on the butcher, too, and everyone she had known. Nothing would be the same down there. "Really? How long ago was that?"

The woman said a number that didn't mean anything to her. "I gave it up a while back. I'm retired now. It was a hard job, making all those decisions for the benefit of everyone. Can I ask you something? Are you glad you came here?"

"Yes and no."

"I wish I'd seen your Olme. Imagine. A living Olme."

"I didn't see a living one."

"No. Well. Do you know what I think about the most when I look back over my time in the job? I think about you offering me that part of the Olme. I wish I'd picked it up."

"You want to smell terrible for the rest of your life?"

"I want to have proof that it happened," said the woman. "Chances are, that was the very last one of its kind. There have been no eruptions for such a long time."

"Eruptions?"

"Drolmeflies," she said, as if that should mean something to Kim. "You know, the next stage. You don't know this? The Olme are the larvae. Then they pupate, hatch, dig upwards. Take to the skies. The last eruption was hundreds of years ago. Over four hundred people were killed before we could bring it down, stop it from feeding. The fact that such an event hasn't happened in so long made us think they were extinct."

"Then... what lays an Olme?"

The woman considered the question. She said, "Something else. Something we haven't seen. It must be terrible, whatever it is. Or was. But the signs are good, aren't they? Maybe that was the very last one. We've lived in fear for so long, but now we can start to believe that the need to hunt the Olmes is over. All your people could return to the surface. Do you think more of you will come up?"

Kim looked around the room. How many people knew why they wore those hats? How many could have picked up a spear and thrown it, straight and true, at a flying monster? The crowd were mingling, laughing. They had their own old jokes to tell and even if they didn't understand the punchlines anymore, they would laugh.

Would the butcher come up to the surface if she knew, or her mother? Would the masters and the apprentices give up what they loved even if it did not love them? There were still some questions that couldn't be answered. She shrugged and rolled her eyes.

Eventually, the woman left her alone, and she abandoned the party and went for a walk in the night air. How fresh it was, and cold. She loved the icy touch of the wind. After removing her hat, she put her fingers to her hair and shook out the loose band that held it back from her face. The sensation was as close to freedom as she had ever felt.

Her feet took her back to the trapdoor. It was sealed up tight and the same guard sat beside it. When he saw her, he jumped to his feet. "Your hat!" he said. "Quick, put it back on." He plucked it from her fingers and clapped it back upon her head.

"Why?"

"It's not polite," he said. "To be seen without one. It's just one of the rules. What are you up to?"

"I want to go home," she said, although she hadn't known it until the words had left her mouth.

"Really?"

"Why does that seem so surprising?"

"Isn't it all hard work down there? It's up to you, though. Here you go. It's a free choice – be up here or down there. Different things suit different people, right? It's all for the greater good."

Kim didn't reply. She started down the ladder, and with each rung she descended she considered what she would say to the people who remained, who had tasks to fulfil, who had decided whether to be rewarded with gifts that bore a scent so strong that it could mark them forever.

'Brushwork' was first published by *Giganotosaurus* in May 2016.

'Many-Eyed Monsters' was first published by *Black Static* in November 2014.

'Three Love Letters from an Unrepeatable Garden' was first published by *Interzone* in September 2016.

'Corwick Grows' was first published by *The Dark* in March 2018.

'Reflection, Refraction, Dispersion' was first published in *Uncertainties IV* in 2019.

'Into Glass' was first published by *Blue Monday Review* in April 2016.

'Blessings Erupt' was first published by *Interzone* in September 2017.

'Star in the Spire' was first published by Calque Press in *An Invite to Eternity* in 2019.

'From the Neck Up' was first published by Unsung Stories in November 2014.

'The Tears of a Building Surveyor and Other Stories' was first published by *Strange Horizons* in September 2017.

'To the Farm' was first published by *On Spec* in April 2015.

'The Spoils' was first published by *Beneath Ceaseless Skies* in 2020.

'Loves of the Long Dead', 'Farleyton', and 'Compel' were written as part of a Patreon project to create strange short stories during 2017/8. Thanks to all who supported that project.

ACKNOWLEDGEMENTS

Thanks to Gary Budden and Max Edwards for getting the ball rolling on this collection, and to everyone at Titan Books for turning the ball into a book. I'm hugely grateful for the cover design skills of Julia Lloyd, and the editing talents of George Sandison and Natasha Qureshi.

This collection represents years of writing what seemed to be unconnected stories; putting them together showed me that they do all share common and fertile ground. Special thanks to all the editors who backed them first time around, and to all the readers who have come across these stories before and chosen to read on.

ABOUT THE AUTHOR

Aliya Whiteley is the author of the novels *The Beauty*, *The Arrival of Missives*, *Skein Island*, and *The Loosening Skin*. She writes novels, short stories and non-fiction and has been published in places such as *The Guardian*, *Interzone*, *McSweeney's Internet Tendency*, *Black Static*, and *Strange Horizons*, and anthologies such as Unsung Stories' *2084* and Lonely Planet's *Better than Fiction I* and *II*. She has been shortlisted for an Arthur C. Clarke Award, Shirley Jackson Award, British Fantasy and British Science Fiction awards, the John W. Campbell Award, and a James Tiptree Jr. Award. Her stories are unpredictable; they can be terrifying, tender, ferocious and deeply funny. She also writes a regular column for *Interzone* magazine. She blogs at: aliyawhiteley. wordpress.com and tweets most days as @AliyaWhiteley.

SKEIN ISLAND
ALIYA WHITELEY

From the author of *The Loosening Skin* and *The Beauty*, Aliya Whiteley, *Skein Island* is a powerful and disturbing look at the roles we play, and how they form and divide us.

Skein Island is a private refuge twelve miles off the coast of Decon. Few receive the invitation to stay for one week, free of charge. If you are chosen, you must pay for your stay with a story from your past: a Declaration for the Island's vast library. What happens to your Declaration after you leave the island is not your concern. Powerful and disturbing, it is a story over which the characters will fight for control. Until they realise the true enemy is the story itself.

"I FIRMLY BELIEVE THAT ALIYA WHITELEY IS ONE OF THE MOST ORIGINAL, INNOVATIVE AND INTELLIGENT WRITERS OF SPECULATIVE FICTION WORKING IN BRITAIN TODAY."
Nina Allan, author of *The Rift*

"WHITELEY SKILFULLY BLENDS GREEK MYTH WITH THE HORRORS OF THE SECOND WORLD WAR AND SCALPEL-SHARP OBSERVATIONS OF CONTEMPORARY SOCIETY IN A COMPELLING, DISTURBING READ THAT EXAMINES GENDER ROLES AND THE POWER OF INDIVIDUALS TO TAKE CONTROL OF THEIR LIVES."
The Guardian

"EXTRAORDINARILY CLEVER"
SciFiNow best of 2019

TITANBOOKS.COM

THE ARRIVAL OF MISSIVES
ALIYA WHITELEY

In the aftermath of the Great War, Shirley Fearn dreams of challenging the conventions of rural England, where life is as predictable as the changing of the seasons. The scarred veteran Mr. Tiller, left disfigured by an impossible accident on the battlefields of France, brings with him a message: part prophecy, part warning. Will it prevent her mastering her own destiny? As the village prepares for the annual May Day celebrations, where a new queen will be crowned and the future will be reborn again, Shirley must choose: change or renewal?

"STARK, POETIC, FORTHRIGHT AND ALIVE
WITH THE NUMINOUS."
Nina Allan, author of *The Rift*

"BEGUILING, BRILLIANT AND ODD. NOT SINCE ALAN GARNER
HAVE SUCH EXPANSIVE THEMES BEEN SO KEENLY TIED TO
PLACE AND SO EVOCATIVELY EXPLORED."
Benjamin Myers, author of *The Gallows Pole*

"AN INTRIGUING 'WHAT IF?' OF A TALE, ONE THAT
KEEPS US TRANSFIXED AND WONDERING RIGHT UP
TO THE FINAL PAGES AND WITH AN ENDING THAT
WON'T EASILY BE FORGOTTEN."
Starburst

For more fantastic fiction, author events,
exclusive excerpts, competitions, limited editions and more

VISIT OUR WEBSITE
titanbooks.com

LIKE US ON FACEBOOK
facebook.com/titanbooks

FOLLOW US ON TWITTER AND INSTAGRAM
@TitanBooks

EMAIL US
readerfeedback@titanemail.com

12